Dragonfruit

MAKIIA LUCIER

nfruit

CLARION BOOKS
An Imprint of HarperCollins*Publishers*

Library of Congress Control Number: 2023937089
ISBN 978-0-35-827210-6

Typography by Molly Fehr
25 26 27 28 29 LBC 9 8 7 6 5

First Edition

For the island kids.
Hafa Adai.

In the old tales, it is written that the egg of a seadragon, dragonfruit, holds within it the power to undo a person's greatest sorrow. An unwanted marriage, a painful illness, an unpaid debt . . . gone. But as with all things that promise the moon and the stars and offer hope when hope has gone, the tale comes with a warning.

Every wish demands a price.

1

BY THE TIME HANALEI TURNED EIGHTEEN, FIVE hundred dragoners roamed the Nominomi Sea, ships built to hunt the seadragons that called the waters home. Every part of the creatures commanded a high price: their scales for armor; their oil for lamps; their eyes, chopped and stewed, or their tongues, dried and powdered, to preserve youth and beauty. And their eggs, most precious of all, though no one had laid eyes on dragonfruit for years.

Five hundred dragoners to capture and kill. And then there was Hanalei.

"Sixty feet, would you say?" Hanalei crouched beside a wild, bushy fern, careful not to be seen. "The blue one there?"

"Sixty feet, yeah, looks good." Her guide's name was Moa, and his response came after much neck craning as they peered from high above the grotto into the watery cavern below. The trouble with seadragons was that they had to be observed at a distance. Unless one was willing to risk death or dismemberment, which Hanalei was not. And so practical matters: measuring their length from snout to tail, or determining eye color and approximate age, these were all things that had to be done from afar.

Three seadragons frolicked in the waves. One red, one gold, one the milky white of pearls. Two more sunned themselves on a massive stone ledge above the water's surface. The larger one lay flat on its belly, sixty feet long, a deep blue in color. The seadragon sprawled beside it was the green of limes. Smaller by ten feet, Hanalei guessed, with a mane, or frill, that was also green. She watched its mouth open in a tremendous yawn, red tongue lolling, and felt her lips curve. It had been a long time since she had seen a pod of seadragons look so at ease, so utterly without guard.

"They are magnificent," she said.

"They are a menace," Moa replied, far less enchanted.

Hanalei took her eyes off the seadragons. Moa appeared to be her age. Neither short nor tall, and wiry, with skin the color of koa wood, smooth and brown. He wore loose trousers and old, comfortable sandals. The tunic he had started the day with had long been shucked off, rolled into a band and tied around his forehead to keep off the sweat. Hanalei wished she could do the same. The air was heavy and damp, perfectly still in a way that hinted at a storm coming. Even the ferns drooped. She was dressed similarly, though her white tunic remained in place and not on her head. A banana leaf hat kept the sun from her eyes, the green blending seamlessly with the surrounding jungle. She tugged the brim low and asked, "Have they hurt anyone?"

Moa nodded grimly. "Two fishermen. The first day. They were supper."

Hanalei sobered. It was a reminder she needed sometimes, of their danger. These were not only beautiful creatures to admire and study.

She had followed the pod west, sailing past the Strait of Salamasina and along the ancient waterways. For six months, she had tracked their migration. A sighting here, a shipwreck there, the hull cracked and splintered, toothmarks along the mast. Definite signs of seadragon. Today, she found herself on an island just south of Kalama, one too small to warrant a formal name or speck on any map. Everyone just called it Little Kalama. The landscape was hilly, thick with trees that twisted and spread around man-sized ferns. Home to colorful, screeching birds: fruit doves and kingfishers, parrotfinches and lorikeets. A village lay at the southern end. It was there that Hanalei had disembarked the night before, lured by rumors of a pod sighting.

Hanalei said, "I saw twenty dragoners docked at Kalama. One word from you, and they'd be here." With their harpoons tipped with poison and their enormous four-person saws, made especially for slicing through dragon skin. The thought sickened her.

Moa's lips twisted. "They'd come quick, yeah. Twenty dragoners, five seadragons. What's worse?"

Hanalei smiled. She liked this guide. With dragoners, one did not have to worry about being eaten. But the sailors on those ships often brought with them a different sort of catastrophe: an oversea disease, typhoid and the pox, or violence mixed with drink, or an overfondness for island women. *Exotic* was a word Hanalei knew well and despised dearly. It was not uncommon to hear of a stolen daughter or sister or mother. She had even heard of a grandmother of twelve who had vanished and gone, dragged away by sailors. *What's worse?* Moa had asked. "The dragoners," she answered.

"Yeah." A mosquito had taken an interest in Moa's nostrils. With one quick swat, it became a black smear on his palm. Absently wiping his hand on his trousers, he added, "Yesterday, the green one, it eats a whale. All by itself. My cousin saw."

Hanalei's skin prickled. She eyed the green seadragon drowsing on the ledge. That was plenty, just for one. Why did it eat so much? Grabbing a fistful of fern for balance, she leaned as far over the grotto's edge as she could, until Moa's warning drew her reluctantly back. Watching from here was no longer enough. She needed a closer look. She rose to a half crouch, taking care to stay hidden behind the ferns and trees.

"Hey." Moa hissed. "Where are you going?"

Hanalei pointed to the steps behind him. They had been carved into the grotto walls and led directly to the water. "Down."

Moa stared at her. "Why? From here is good. Don't be crazy."

"I'll hide behind those rocks. They'll never see me." A satchel hung by her side, crafted of waxed hibiscus bark to protect her belongings from rain and seawater. She rummaged around inside, and as she did, what looked to be a whistle hanging from a cord around her neck swung free. It was made of bamboo, four inches long. A pair of intertwined seadragons had been carved along the wood.

The sight of it distracted Moa from his warnings. He goggled. "Is that a soundcatcher? A Tamarindi soundcatcher? I've only seen drawings." He rose, casting a furtive glance at her hands and the scars that covered them. "I thought you were from Rakakala."

"I never said I was." He had seen her scars and drawn his own conclusions. She had let him. Hanalei tucked the soundcatcher away beneath her tunic, pressed against her heart.

Moa heard the change in her tone. Less friendly. She could see it on his face. It did not stop him from asking the question that was always asked, eventually. "Then who are your people?"

She had none. She was her father's daughter, an exile. And her father was gone. Hanalei pulled a silver squid from her satchel and held it out. "Thank you for bringing me here. I'll find my way back."

Moa looked at the coin she offered. He looked at her closed expression. And finally took the hint. Waving away the silver, he said with a sigh, "Nothing for you, sister. Be careful."

At his words, the longing for home came sharp and sudden, for this was the way of the islands. They had not met before yesterday. But Moa was an islander and she was an islander and likely, thousands of years ago, their forefathers had been cousins. So she got a bargain.

Her fingers closed around the silver squid, and her quiet "thank you, Moa" came only after swallowing past the lump in her throat. He pretended not to notice. She returned the squid to her satchel and left him there with a quick wave. The steps were steep and crumbling. Her descent was a slow one, hard on the nerves. She flailed when a parrotfinch flew past her nose, shrieking and flapping and knocking her hat askew. *Curse you, finch.* She tugged the brim back into place and waited for her heart to settle before continuing on. Two thirds of the way down, she stopped at a flat bit of stone, one large enough for her to sit on and observe through a crevice in the rocks. If she sneezed, they would hear her. When she breathed, she could smell them. The unmistakable aroma of kelp. It was the closest she had been to seadragons in years. *Free dragons*, she corrected. *Living ones*. The dead she had seen plenty of, all of them up close.

Hanalei studied the green one. An entire whale to itself, Moa had said. She sifted through the possibilities. The dragon might have recently emerged from a deep sleep. She had come across an obscure reference to seadragon hibernation patterns, burrowing in underwater caves for months, sometimes years, at a time. It would have woken ravenous. In which case, bad luck for the whale and any other creature it came across. Or the dragon might be recovering from an illness and was simply making up for a lost appetite. Hibernation and poor health. Two perfectly reasonable conclusions.

Common sense returned, reminding her that if she did not work, she did not eat. There was a school on the island of Rakakala, or Raka, that specialized in all living things beneath the Nominomi. The scholars there would pay generously to see, on parchment at least, what she saw now. From her satchel she retrieved a wooden tablet to draw on, a sheet of parchment, and a stick of charcoal, freshly sharpened. She positioned herself so that she sat cross-legged with the crevice directly before her. Time weighed upon her. There was no telling how long the seadragons would remain, napping and frolicking. She had to work quickly.

Hanalei sketched the blue seadragon first. Its long, whiskery feelers were silver, so too were its tail, frill, and horns. Horns curled like a ram's, not pointed like a devil's. Like the green one, it had a pair of stunted legs in the front, none in the back. How very interesting. She leaned forward, sticking her head into the crevice. Legless seadragons were much more common, but sometimes, when the Nominomi was at its clearest, dragons like these were visible walking along the seafloor. Could they travel on land, she wondered? And if so, how far? How fast? Could they climb walls, like giant geckos? Uneasy, she eyed the surrounding stone and drew a little farther back behind the rocks.

The pearl seadragon shot straight into the air, spinning and spiraling, before falling into the water with a splash. Hanalei shook water droplets from the parchment, smiling. A smile that faded when the red seadragon called out to the others, the sound high and pure. Dragonsong. The sound sent shivers down Hanalei's neck.

A moment's hesitation before she reached for her soundcatcher. A soundcatcher was precisely that. It captured something that could be heard: a child's laughter or the sound of the sea, or music. It had been a gift from Sam when they were children, Hanalei eight and Sam nine, carved during an afternoon spent at the beach. She had watched the seadragons come to life in his hands as he whittled the wood away with his father's knife. "You love them so much," Sam had said, tossing it to her with a quick grin. "Keep it." A casual offering, one he had likely long forgotten. It was her most prized possession. She held it to her lips and breathed in, not out, knowing it would come to nothing. Tamarindi magic, no matter how small, only showed itself on Tamarind—

Hanalei caught herself. Why was she like this today? Nearly weeping when Moa called her sister, thinking too much of home. She knew better. The past was the past, unchangeable. Most days, she kept Tamarind tucked down and buried deep, where hard memories belonged.

Hanalei sketched the green seadragon next. A long, sinuous body covered in scales, along with legs and claws, and as she finished its feathery tail, the seadragon lifted its head. The frill rose, like hair blowing in the wind, though the wind was still, and by the time it resettled upon the scales, it had changed color. From bright green to a deep rose. The precise shade of dragonfruit.

Of a seadragon's egg.

The charcoal slipped from Hanalei's fingers, rolling across the stone and falling into the water. Her skin felt cold, then hot. It burned. Hibernation and illness, yes, but there was a third reason for so large an appetite, one she had not dared consider.

The green seadragon was female. When a dragon carried eggs, her frill changed to an unmistakable shade of rose. Always. And an egg, once laid, was no simple egg.

Every child of the Nominomi knew the story, taught by the elders through song and art and dance: *In the old tales, it is written that the egg of a seadragon, dragonfruit, holds within it the power to undo a person's greatest sorrow. An unwanted marriage, a painful illness, an unpaid debt . . . gone. But as with all things that promise the moon and the stars and offer hope when hope has gone, the tale comes with a warning. Every wish demands a price.*

Hanalei knew all about the prices to be paid.

A shadow above broke through her racing thoughts. She looked up, shocked to see not cloud cover as she had expected, but people, dozens upon dozens, gathered around the top of the grotto. Quietly watching. They wore black, dark against the light of the sun. So many, and she had heard nothing. Worse, someone had flung an enormous net into the air and it came drifting down, silent and sure, toward the unsuspecting dragons.

A dragoner's net.

Hanalei rose from her hiding place, heart in her throat. *The past was the past, unchangeable.* And yet that was not always true. Her eyes darted from net to dragons and dragons to net. And then she put her fingers to her lips and whistled.

It moved fast. The blue seadragon, head whipping around to meet Hanalei's gaze across the water . . . a distance that suddenly felt far too narrow. *From here is good*, Moa had said. *Don't be crazy*. Why had she not listened? She pressed her back against the stone, neither blinking nor breathing. Pure black dragon eyes shifted from her to the falling net. A growl emerged; Hanalei felt the rumble of it in her bones. And then it was gone, biting its green companion on the back of the neck and flinging it, *her*, into the water. As the net came down on the three other seadragons, the pair swam off, keeping close to the grotto walls before disappearing beneath the waves. Safe for now.

Not these dragons. Their fate would be different. Hanalei clamped her hands over her ears as they thrashed in their netting and the grotto echoed with the sound of snarls and screams. No more dragonsong. *I am sorry*, she thought, flinching as a harpoon pierced one through the neck. Instantly, its frill changed color, from red to black. The harpoon was tall as a man and had come not from above but from a ship sailing in through an arch. It was black, with a massive, bulging hull that marked it as a dragoner. A white flag with a red cypress flew high on the mainmast. Painted along the side, in gold, was the *Anemone*. A figure stood at its prow, gripping another harpoon. Hanalei had time enough to think, *Of all ships*, before she realized the weapon was pointed directly at her.

With a yelp, she flung herself to the ground as the stone above her shattered, sending down a rainstorm of rocks and pebbles. She threw her arms up to protect her head. Gritting her teeth through the cuts and stings, she thought, *Of all ships, and of all captains.* The harpoon clattered beside her.

She had been recognized. This she knew because her name was being shouted from the *Anemone*, along with words like *damn that girl!* and far worse. Behind her, more curses erupted as boots tripped along crumbling steps. There would be no escape that way. Dread filled her. She wondered if it would be better to slip into the Nominomi and take her chances there, with the sharks and stingrays, other monsters of the deep, but by the time the thought had fully formed, it was too late.

2

IN THE ROYAL MENAGERIE OF TAMARIND, ONE could see beasts of all kinds: panda and python, kangaroo and goruda, an endless variety of bird, from the ill-tempered cassowary to the far more agreeable fruit dove. The menagerie had been built generations ago by the reigning queen. But it was not until recent times, around the month of Hanalei's birth, that a pair of seadragons was presented to the Tamarindi Queen Maga'lahi, gifts from a neighboring kingdom.

The queen was reluctant to accept such an offering, for it had long been said that dragons of the deep belonged to the gods. But she had no wish to insult the gift giver, a friend. After much prayer, during which the gods remained quiet, she took their silence as approval. And when years later one of the seadragons produced dragonfruit, three perfect, rose-colored eggs, Queen Maga'lahi very deliberately did not pray, or ask the gods for permission. Because by then tragedy had struck her family.

Her daughter, Princess Oliana, was the mother of a young son and widow of a fallen warrior. Heir to her mother's throne. Tamarind was a matriarchal society. There, the women ruled.

The island kingdom of Tamarind was an archipelago, ten islands dotting the Nominomi Sea. If one were to look down on the islands from up high, like a bird or a wind god, one would see them strung about like a smile, with the main island, Tamarind, on the eastern edge and Isle Garapan on the west. The smaller islands were governed by men and women who paid homage to the royal house. It was on a visit to Garapan that Princess Oliana fell ill, poisoned by crushed utu seeds stirred into her evening soup.

It had not taken long to unmask the person responsible. For months, the princess had been courted by a prince from Wakeo, an island in the far southern reaches of the Nominomi. The prince had desired the widowed Oliana, but mostly, he desired the spices that grew with startling abundance across the Tamarindi archipelago. Nutmeg, cinnamon, clove, and mace, symbols of the island's wealth. When Oliana rejected his offer of marriage, the prince had reacted badly, with poison. Not long after, he would be found dead in his own kingdom, along with his entire family. Tamarind's Lord Isko had seen to that.

The poison had not killed Oliana. And it had not

harmed her nine-year-old son, Samahtitamahenele, Sam, who had spent the day with friends by the shore. But for the future queen, and for the little girl who served as her page and who had shared her supper, life had become even more fragile. It had placed them into the deepest of sleeps, and no one knew how to wake them. Not the royal healers, or the wisewomen and wisemen who lived in the villages. Not the doctors and physicians from the oversea kingdoms, paid exorbitant sums to sail to a faraway island and offer counsel. Queen Maga'lahi and her people despaired.

And then startling news had come from the royal menagerie. A seadragon had produced dragonfruit, three rose-colored eggs that could, if the stories were true, heal the princess and her page. A terrible wrong could be undone. Only no one knew how they worked.

Much had been written on the other uses of a seadragon. Its scales were made into coveted suits of armor, their hardness easily deflecting spears and swords, axes and clubs. Recipes for stewed dragon eyes were plentiful if one wished to preserve one's youth or beauty. Straightening a stooped back, for instance, or removing the yellow tint from elderly eyes and teeth. And dragon oil, carefully strained, was the preferred fuel for lamps. Its light burned brightest.

Unlike scales and eyes and oil, dragonfruit was rare, for the simple reason that seadragons did not easily give up their eggs. What the old tales did not share was how to properly administer it. Did one eat the entire egg? Yolk, baby dragon, and all the bits in between? Revolting if so, as well as physically taxing. The eggs were large, three feet tall and two feet wide. Perhaps only a few bites or sips would do? And if so, *when* would be the best time to consume the egg? When it was freshly laid? Or freshly hatched? In the morning? Or at night? Or some time in between? No one knew.

It was decided that the eggs would be served to the princess in different ways, at different times, until she woke. The dragonfruit was taken from the menagerie, to be guarded within the royal pavilion. The mother seadragon's keening could be heard throughout the city.

What followed was the worst sort of luck. Earthquakes were common in the Nominomi. Mild ones, stronger ones. Usually, the islanders simply picked up what had fallen, or rebuilt what had broken, and carried on. But one such earthquake occurred as the dragonfruit were being transported from the menagerie to the queen's pavilion, tremors violent enough to overturn the carriage. Two eggs shattered, yolk seeping into red mud, the small dragons crushed beneath the wheels, their blood mingling with that of the injured driver. The queen would not risk feeding any of it to the princess. And so it was that all hope rested on the last remaining dragonfruit.

But late that very night, the egg disappeared from the

royal pavilion. The guards responsible for its safety were discovered unconscious with painful lumps on the backs of their heads where they had been struck. A note had been placed where the egg once rested. Two words scrawled across parchment: *Forgive me.*

One other person was in desperate need of a wish. She was someone's daughter too.

The little page who had also consumed the poisoned soup—her name was Hanalei. Eight years old, the beloved only child of Lord Arihi, whose wife had gone to the gods years before. Seeing his hopes dwindle with each shattered dragon egg, he stole the last one, took his sleeping daughter from their ancestral home, and vanished.

Where they went, no one knew.

"It pains me to say it, Hanalei. But I'm not pleased to see you."

Hanalei glared at the man looming before her. *Don't show him you're frightened.* That had never worked before. "Are you ever?"

"No." Bragadin was captain of the *Anemone*. A man the same age her father would have been, had her father lived. He was an Esperanzan, though his skin, sun-browned from years spent at sea, led many to believe he was descended from islanders. His hair was black, as were his eyes, and Hanalei knew that if his chest were ever to be cut open and his heart exposed, it would be black too.

She had been tossed onto the deck of the dragoner. Not gently. Bruises had begun to form along her arm. A collection of islanders and overseaers gathered around. Rough-looking men and women, part of the captain's crew. One wore her banana-leaf hat. Another had wrestled away her satchel. A man with a red beard pawed through the contents with filthy hands as Hanalei looked on, her right eye twitching. Those were her things. Her drawings and notes, her coins.

"Give it here." Captain Bragadin snapped his fingers, then held out a hand for the satchel. Reluctantly, the red-bearded sailor did as he was told, his expression sour.

The captain did not look inside the satchel, only dropped it beside his boots, the strap dangling from his hand. Every part of him brimmed with annoyance. "I've been following these dragons for months," he told her. "Six months, Hanalei. I know you have too. And yet here you are, always one irritating step ahead. Why is that?"

"Luck, Captain."

Captain Bragadin's eyes narrowed. "Try again," he suggested softly.

Because she could sense them. Sometimes, not always. A feeling that told her to sail north not south. Or to turn around and retrace the path she had taken. It had always been so, ever since her father had stolen a seadragon egg and fed its contents to her, his dying child. Bits of dragon flesh. Drops of yolk. But these were things she would never tell anyone, let alone this man here.

Hanalei kept her tone respectful. Not her words, though. "You're getting older. Just like Captain Salvega." She looked over his crew, lingering over the youngest dragoners. Two boys, fourteen or fifteen years old, their expressions hard already. "I won't be as quick when I'm your age either."

Someone whistled low, that Hanalei would dare to say such things out loud. Bragadin had spent his early boyhood on the streets of Raka, plucking dragonscale in the notorious orphan workhouses before finding work on a ship, then owned by the infamous dragoner Salvega. When Bragadin had turned fifteen and had grown strong enough—he had always been mean enough—he had murdered his captain, feeding him to the day's catch and taking the *Anemone* for his own. Hanalei knew she should take better care with her words. Outrage had made her reckless. The cries from the water had stopped. Three dead seadragons. She wanted to kick something.

Bragadin's lips had curved in reluctant amusement. "Still a disrespectful brat." He lifted her satchel off the ground, testing its weight. "And still peddling your dragon science, I see." He eyed her clothing and shook his head. "Doesn't look like your fancy school pays well. Honest labor rarely does."

"It pays enough."

"So you say." Captain Bragadin's expression turned thoughtful; he slung the satchel over his shoulder. "What am I to do with you? Hm? I have a crew to feed. All these fine people here. And you have cost me two seadragons."

"More than that." A male voice spoke from the back of the crowd. Hanalei started, for this was a voice she knew. She stared in astonishment as her guide Moa came forward, still shirtless, a white band around his forehead. Nothing of his earlier friendliness showed on his face. He barely spared her a glance before turning to the captain, who explained to Hanalei, "Moa was visiting his old village when you turned up. He sent word. I suppose you could say that I, too, have been lucky." Captain Bragadin's eyes gleamed at whatever it was he saw on her face. Dismay, surely, and a hurt that surprised her. *Nothing for you, sister. Be careful.*

Captain Bragadin said to Moa, "What do you mean 'more than that'?"

"One of the dragons, it turned the color of the heart flower before it swam off. Its hair," Moa added, waving his hands around his head for emphasis. "I saw."

Shock rippled through the dragoners. Not all looked surprised. These would have been the ones watching from atop the grotto, the ones who had flung down the giant net. They had seen what Moa had seen, and knew what Hanalei's warning whistle had cost them.

Captain Bragadin's eyes were fixed on Moa. "You're certain? Its frill turned the color of the heart flower?"

"Yeah."

Beside Moa, the dragoner with the red beard muttered, "What color is the color of the heart flower?"

"Pink, you idiot," Captain Bragadin said. "Who else saw this?"

The ship dipped suddenly and violently, forcing Hanalei and everyone else to plant their feet wide and spread their arms to steady themselves. Even so, a few dragoners went stumbling into barrels and crates. Some grabbed on to the railing. From below came shouted orders, followed by the horrible, unmistakable sound of scales scraping against wood. The seadragons were being loaded into the hull through a side hatch.

"Who else?" Captain Bragadin demanded again when the ship had righted itself. There were a few nods and *yeah*s, and when he turned to face Hanalei, his expression was thunderous. He stepped toward her. "Dragonfruit. That seadragon was carrying eggs, and *you scared it off*?"

Hanalei could not help it; she stepped back. "*You* did that. You would have killed her and realized your mistake later. Don't blame me."

"You should want to see them dead just as much as I." With deliberation, Captain Bragadin looked down at her hands covered in scars, then down at his. The same sort of damaged flesh between them—thin, shallow cuts; dragon-scale was sharp—though his were much more faded. "Why don't you?"

Hanalei fought the urge to hide her hands behind her back. "I don't blame the dragons for these."

"No. You blame me. Thankless as usual." Captain Bragadin turned to a woman who stood by the wheel. An islander about his age, whom Hanalei recognized as his longtime navigator, Vaea. She was taller even than Hanalei, with sculpted arms, and dressed in black. Stylized sunrays tattooed her forehead and nose. "We leave now," the captain told Vaea. "They can't have gone far. Take us . . ." His eyes flickered involuntarily to Hanalei, who offered, "South."

Captain Bragadin glared. "*West*. They've gone west all along. So we follow."

Moa's hands dropped to his sides. "What about the girl?" Moa asked. "You want me to toss her?"

Moa thought he was being mean, but hope bloomed within Hanalei. *Yes. Toss me.*

"She can swim." Vaea dashed Hanalei's hopes as quickly as they had risen. She met Hanalei's look with a faint smile.

"Quite well, unfortunately," Captain Bragadin said. "She'll cause more grief later if we let her go. Easier to be rid of her for good."

Moa paused. "So . . . ?" He drew a finger across his throat, eyebrows raised in question. His meaning clear.

Hanalei opened her mouth. No sound emerged. She had spent an entire day in his company. His family had taken her in when she had arrived on the island. His mother had offered her food to eat and a mat to sleep on and her eldest son as guide.

"I'll do it," one of the younger dragoners offered, the fourteen-year-old with the hard eyes. He appeared neither a full-blooded islander nor a full-blooded Esperanzan, but a mix of both. Straight black hair flopped into his eyes. He was shorter than Hanalei by several inches, but broader, with a face full of spots picked at and ruptured.

Stone-faced, Moa glanced over his shoulder at the boy, whose fierce expression wavered. He ducked out of sight behind two very large dragoners. Moa turned back to the captain.

"Not yet." Captain Bragadin answered Moa's question, but only after a very long pause. "Take her below. She cares so much about those blasted dragons. She can keep their corpses warm." He looked past Hanalei, his expression clearing. "Ha. Look who's here."

Another dragoner had sailed into the grotto. Black ship, bloated hull, also flying under the Esperanzan flag. The RES *Lagoon*. A royal Esperanzan ship. A figure with golden hair stood at the helm, his disappointment apparent as he realized there were no more seadragons to be had.

Captain Bragadin cupped both hands to his mouth and

hollered, "Late again, Augustus! Too bad!"

Hanalei recognized the name, and the hair. Prince Augustus was the Esperanzan king's youngest son. He had three older brothers, all in excellent health. The spare of the spare. Which meant he was allowed to partake in dangerous pastimes, like dragon hunting.

At Captain Bragadin's taunting, Prince Augustus raised a hand in a rude gesture. Captain Bragadin and his crew laughed. Behind the RES *Lagoon* came two other ships. The *Nautilus* and the HMS *Whalebone*. The sight of them cheered Captain Bragadin immensely. He was an ungracious winner, and an even worse loser.

Moa grabbed Hanalei's arm. "Let's go." He led her off, down through the hatch and along a passageway that smelled of unwashed bodies and frying fish. They stopped at the far end. At their feet was another hatch in the floor. He checked to see that no one was around. "Hey. Why do you talk to him like that? You want to be dead?"

Hanalei yanked her arm free. "What do you care? You were going to slit my throat."

"He wouldn't say yes," Moa snapped. "The captain doesn't hurt girls."

"Really? Do you believe in sea fairies too?" Hanalei shoved up her sleeve, showing him the three circular scars on the back of her arm, just above the elbow. "Cigar burns," she explained, seeing his eyes widen and taking no satisfaction in his surprise. "When we didn't work fast enough." She pulled her sleeve down. "Does your family know you hunt other things besides dragons?"

Moa's face hardened. He leaned down and threw open the hatch door. "Get in."

Two dragoners came around the corner, stopping to watch them. Hanalei looked into the opening and was met with darkness, but what she could not see she could smell. Bilgewater mixed with dragon blood. Utter foulness.

Hanalei breathed through her mouth. "Will you give me a torch at least?"

The other dragoners heard her and laughed. Moa said, "So you can burn us down? No."

"I wouldn't—"

"Get in."

Why had she bothered to ask? Hanalei lowered herself into the hole, feeling around for a rung in the ladder. Only when she was five rungs down did she stop and look up. Moa watched from above. She put as much scorn into her words as she could. "I hope he pays well. Brother."

The hatch slammed shut, leaving her in the dark and quiet. She waited until the footsteps faded away before descending farther. Her sandals slapped along the rungs, setting off angry echoes. At the bottom, her foot sunk into something cold and clinging, like the thickest coconut soup. Only it did not smell like coconuts here. She yanked her foot upward, grimacing, and turned carefully on the ladder so her back rested against the rungs. Unless she wished to sit in bilgewater and dragon blood, she would have to stand here until Captain Bragadin decided what to do with her. Which could be soon, or it could be never.

She would not cry, not for herself or for the seadragons, in case Moa came back and saw. She did not know how long she clung to the ladder feeling sorry for herself before she realized she could see them. Her eyes had adjusted to the shadows, enough that their outlines were visible, three hulking shapes spread about the hull, ensuring their weight did not tip the dragoner into the sea.

However badly her day had turned out, she still lived. She lowered one foot into the muck, then the other, and waded toward the closest seadragon. The water came to her knees. It felt less repugnant to think of it as water and nothing else. When she reached the dragon, she felt along the scales, careful not to cut herself, until she found its head. Its chin rested against the floor, partially underwater. Its horns were too far up for her to touch. Gently, she stroked its snout, rough like coral, and pressed her cheek to its feelers, feathery soft. The feelers would have turned black upon its passing but its scales remained unchanged, the color of pearls. It glistened faintly in the dark. Not so far into the future, they would be used to make armor, scales overlapping, impenetrable. A symbol of a soldier's wealth and power, paid for with gold.

Hanalei did not know any prayers for seadragons, so she took a human one and did what she could. Olifat was the father of all sea gods, but Taga was his son. The seadragons belonged to him. Placing her hand on dragonscale, she said quietly into its ear,

> *May Taga find your spirit and guide you home*
> *to the sea beyond.*
> *In clear water*
> *where danger will never catch you.*
> *Among the coral and caves*
> *where the bounty is full.*
> *Alongside your ancestors*
> *and their ancestors*
> *that loneliness never hold you.*
> *His kingdom your own*
> *beloved child of the gods.*

And because a prayer stood a better chance of being heard with an offering, she ran her palm along the sharp edge of dragonscale and pressed her blood into its skin.

She did the same with the second seadragon, wading across the hold, murmuring a prayer and farewell, offering blood. It was not until she placed a hand on the third seadragon that she realized it was still alive, though barely. The scales were warm, not cool to the touch, like the others. Air escaped through its nostrils, shallow and soundless, rustling its feelers so that it brushed against Hanalei's arms, neck, face. Unthreatening. A moment later the feelers drifted away.

To die like this. In darkness and filth. Hanalei brushed away her tears, and said, "May Taga find your spirit and guide you home, to the sea beyond . . ."

Much later, when the dragon was no longer warm and Hanalei had pulled herself up onto shelter, in a crook between its neck and arm, her thoughts drifted back to her last night on Tamarind. Ten years ago, when she had been ill, lingering between this life and the next. Everyone had spoken quietly around her. They thought her asleep, dying. It was a conversation she was not meant to hear between her father and Lady Rona, who served as the queen's companion.

"She will kill you if she finds you, Arihi. You can never come home."

"It doesn't matter," Hanalei's father had answered, his voice weary.

"Liar," Lady Rona chided, tears in her words. "It will break your heart not to see Tamarind again. And mine. What of Hanalei? She will—"

"*Live*, Rona. My child will live."

"As an *exile*. Away from all whom she loves. From

Samahti. It is a different sort of death."

"She'll have me."

"And the princess will die in her place. Do you think Hanalei will thank you for it? Such a burden to place on a child—"

"What would you have me do?" Hanalei's father had spoken sharply. "Nothing? Look at her. She's all I have left of her mother. She is my life." Heavy footsteps followed. Her father pacing. "I've found a ship that will take us from here. Tonight. I need your silence, that is all. Will you promise me?"

A hesitation. "You can marry again, Arihi. Have other children."

A quiet fell, one so heavy Hanalei still remembered the weight of it. Her father spoke at last. "You've said enough, Rona. Goodbye."

Now Papa was gone, and Hanalei was no longer a child to be rescued. She reached for dragonscale, swinging it one way and then the other before plucking it free of skin. She tucked the scale beneath her tunic, in the small of her back, mindful of sharp edges.

3

"WHERE DID YOU FIND IT?" SAM ASKED.

"Near Raka, Prince Samahti." The trader was short and trim, with a mustache that grew wild as trailing ivy, the tips brushing against his collarbone. "We found a nest on the beach on one of the outer islands. There were three eggs, but we only had time to take the one."

"We could see its mother swimming back," the second trader added. They appeared to be close family. Brothers or cousins, not yet thirty. "We barely made off with our skin still on."

They were in the royal menagerie on Tamarind. Catamara stood by the door, dressed in his practical animal-keeper clothing, along with Sam's guards, Liko and Bayani. The menagerie's distinctive odors drifted their way. Seawater and kelp, along with the earthier aroma of land animals.

The traders had brought with them a large crate that, when pried opened, had revealed an egg, at least three feet tall. Its color was a brilliant, blinding pink.

Dragonfruit.

Sam thought they could hear his heart pounding furiously. That the whole island could hear. Word had come to him at the royal spice stores, great warehouses built in the heart of Tamarind City. The harvest was coming in, and he had been tasked with inspecting the latest crop in his grandmother's stead. When Liko had turned up with a message from the menagerie, Sam had forgotten all about pepper and nutmeg and mace. He had ridden his kandayo across the city at punishing speed.

"What do you trade in?" Curious, Sam eyed the men in their fine linen robes and feathered caps. Something profitable, most likely.

"Pottery," the first trader told him. "Plates, bowls, cups, carafes, whatever you need. We had stopped to take on fresh water when we saw the eggs. If we had known there was a dragon nearby, we would have sailed screaming in the other direction."

"It was fortuitous," the second trader said. "We are so pleased to be of service to you, and to your lady mother."

His lady mother. Princess Oliana of Tamarind. Mama.

Soft blankets padded the inside of the crate. Sam placed a hand on the egg, feeling the seadragon move within, bumping lightly against the shell. It was close to hatching. After all these years, searching one end of the Nominomi to the other. Only to have it fall right into his lap. Sam looked over at the traders and permitted himself a smile.

The traders smiled back, the first clapping his hands in delight. "Ah, excellent! Very good! We are happy you are happy." He coughed delicately, into his fist. "We had heard, forgive me for mentioning payment, but everyone knows you have been searching for the dragonfruit. Because of the poor princess. We heard there might be a generous reward?"

"Don't be crass," the second trader said under his breath. He stepped forward with a pleasant smile. "With utmost respect, Prince Samahti, we were hoping to be off before the tide turns. Bringing the dragonfruit to Tamarind has taken us quite out of our way."

Sam's two guards were grinning. Even Liko, serious Liko, who rarely grinned. Catamara remained at the door, his expression unreadable.

"Understood." Sam crouched before the crate, looking for cracks. He turned the dragonfruit gently on its padding. It was as perfect as the eggs he had last seen ten years ago. Before two were crushed beneath the wheels of a carriage. The third stolen away by a man who had been like a father to him. He started to rise, then stopped, studying the bottom of the egg. He touched it with a finger.

"Is something wrong?" the first trader asked.

Sam stood. A sour feeling unfurled in his gut. "Catamara, give me your bottle."

The animal keeper frowned. "What bottle?"

"The one you keep in your boot." Sam held out a hand. "Hand it over."

Grumbling, the old man reached down and retrieved a bottle of spirits from his boot. His bones creaked and popped when he straightened. Catamara was partial to rum. The bottle was half-full of the amber liquid.

The second trader laughed nervously. "Never too early to celebrate. It is a happy day."

Sam pulled the cork free and poured its contents over the egg.

"What are you—?" The first trader stopped, dismay written on his face.

Catamara did not drink weak spirits. As the rum coated the egg, the alcohol stripped the rose coloring from it, revealing a pale brown shell.

Bayani's jaw dropped. "Paint. That's no dragon egg!"

The first trader exclaimed, "I'm as shocked as you are! How can this be?" but his voice trailed off as Liko and Bayani each pulled a machete from their belt.

Sam said quietly, "I would think very hard before you lie to me again."

The first trader clamped his mouth shut.

Catamara came to stand beside Sam, who asked him, "What kind of egg is it?"

"A land snake," Catamara said. "A rattler, from Esperanza. Grows to about fifty feet."

"Poisonous?"

"Oh yes. As soon as it hatches."

Which would not be long now. Sam turned to the traders, who had moved closer together, the second clutching the other man's robes. "I'll ask you again, where did you find it?"

The second trader admitted, "At the market on Masina."

The sourness in Sam's gut crept up his throat. "And the paint?"

"We know a boy. An artist's apprentice. Good at mixing colors."

The first trader held out his hands in a conciliatory gesture, smiled. "Prince Samahti, our apologies. But no harm was done here. It was a good try, eh?" He chuckled. "We all have families to feed, babies to clothe. We'll just be on our way—" His words ended in a squeak. Liko's blade rested against his neck. With a cry, his companion fell to his knees and threw both hands up in surrender.

Sam was furious with himself. How easily fooled he had been. These men were not the first to promise dragonfruit, only the latest. Why did he continue to hope? Sam reached for his dagger. Using the hilt, he gave the egg a single, hard tap. Cracks formed, from top to bottom, and a thick pink liquid seeped through. An angry hiss followed, making the traders jump.

"Let's go," Sam said. Liko, Bayani, and Catamara needed no further urging. They hurried through the doorway.

Before Sam pulled it closed behind him, he said, "You should have kept my mother out of it."

The traders pounded on the wood, yelling frantically to be let out. The hissing from the egg grew louder. Sam listened for a time, before asking, "Is it really poisonous?"

"No," Catamara said. "But the fangs will hurt. Even baby fangs."

"Good." Sam instructed Liko and Bayani, "Let them out, but not too soon. Hand them over to Lord Isko. And find their ship. We could always use some good pottery."

The guards were subdued. "Yes, Prince Samahti."

Sam said to Catamara, "You knew it wasn't a dragon egg from the beginning."

"Mm," the old man said.

"How?"

"The color was off. Too pink. What about you?"

"There were spots on the bottom. Dragonfruit doesn't have spots. It's flawless."

"I'm sorry, young prince." Catamara's words were gruff. "That was a cruel trick they played."

There was no hiding his disappointment from Catamara. The man had known him a long time. Sam would have turned away, but Catamara's question stopped him. "How did you know about the spots?"

Sam rubbed a hand against his heart, where it had begun to hurt. "I knew a girl once who loved seadragons."

NO ONE CAME FOR HER UNTIL MORNING.

The hatch door opened high above, and a lantern appeared. The light stirred Hanalei from an uneasy half slumber. Moa stuck his head in, searching the cavernous hull until he found her lying atop a seadragon. She looked blearily back at him, sensing his surprise, before he made an impatient come-here gesture, calling out, "Let's go." His voice echoed in the vast space.

Moa's lantern had chased away the darkness enough for her to see that she had fallen asleep on the gold dragon. She climbed down, stepping lightly upon tail and leg, pressing her face against lifeless feelers one last time. Through the curve of the hull came the cheerful sounds of a busy harbor—bartering, shouting, laughing. The long, pleasant roll of a ship's horn. Which harbor was it?

She waded through the muck and climbed the ladder, pulling herself across the opening. Today, Moa dressed like any other dragoner. In black. He sniffed the air and made a face, putting more space between them. Hanalei was too heartsick to take offense.

She followed him down the passageway, her sandals leaving a slimy trail in her wake. Behind closed doors came the muffled noises of everyday ship life. Two men arguing. Another coughing. Someone played the ukulele. "Where are we?"

"Big Kalama," Moa said.

They had not gone very far. "Why? I thought the captain was in a hurry to follow the dragons."

"The ones we have are slowing us down. We'll unload them here first." They stopped at a door just beneath the prow. When he opened it, she saw that the cabin was tiny, no more than five paces in any direction. It had no windows, no cot or chair, but there was a mat on the floor and clothes on top of a blanket. Beside them, a pair of sandals appeared to be in good condition. And surprise of surprises, a washtub filled with water took up much of the space. A tub. Clean water. Seeing it was like seeing the sun rise after a month of darkness.

"All this for you." Moa leaned against the door, his expression smug. "Go on. Say it. We're not as bad as you think."

"You're no prince." Hanalei dipped a finger into the water. Cold. It was going to be a bracing bath, but it was better than the alternative, which was no bath at all. "You don't want anyone out there to see me. They brand kidnappers in the Nominomi, Moa." She tapped her cheekbone twice. "Right here."

Moa scowled. He reached into his vest, then tossed something at her. When she caught it, she found a sliver of soap. "Use all of it," he advised, and started to close the door before she called for him to wait. "Do you have food?" she asked as her stomach rumbled. A loud, rude, insistent sound. She had not eaten since the day before, when they had shared breakfast on the way to the grotto. A meal prepared by his mother. From the look on Moa's face, he also remembered. He said brusquely, "You'll eat with the captain. Clean up first." The door shut, and an outer latch fell into place.

There was no inner bolt. That would not do, not on this ship. She dragged the heavy washtub across the cabin, water sloshing onto scarred wood, and placed it firmly against the door. Only then did she undress. She scrubbed as quickly as she could, shivering from the moment she stuck a toe in the water. By the time she was done, the sliver of soap was no more. She used the threadbare blanket to dry herself, then put on the black tunic and trousers and slipped her feet into the sandals. The clothing was a snug fit, the sandals a little loose. She was nearly done braiding her damp hair when she heard it.

The sound of the outer latch lifting.

Hanalei spun around. Whoever it was tried to open the door furtively, but the washtub held firm. There was a surprised huff, then a grunt as her intruder tried again. A stronger shove this time, unsuccessful.

Hanalei knew instinctively it was not Moa. She called out anyway. "Moa?"

There was a pause, before the shoving continued. Hanalei considered screaming, but she did not think anyone would come to her aid, even if they heard her. And she hated to have these dragoners know she was afraid. The dragonscale she had taken the day before curved against her back. She left it where it was, running across the small space and throwing her shoulder against the door.

"*Uff!*" The grunt only told her the intruder was male. There was a terrible back-and-forth, pushing on both sides, made even more horrible because it was done in near silence. And then the door cracked open and the tub tipped slightly, spilling water over the side and onto her sandals. There was a triumphant snicker before a hand reached into the gap, fingers wiggling. It was the wiggling that did it; for Hanalei, fright turned to anger. She threw her entire weight against the door. The shriek that followed was ghastly, so too was the sound of bone and cartilage being crushed. Hanalei eased away enough for her intruder to yank his hand back, then listened as he ran off. The outer latch fell into place on its own.

Her breath was coming fast. She did not know how long she stood there with her forehead pressed against the door. No one appeared. So she went back to the mat and dropped onto it, chin propped on knees, and waited some more. Gradually, her breathing slowed and her heartbeat returned to its normal rhythms.

Hours passed, during which the carcasses were unloaded onto the dock. Hanalei felt the ship rise, no longer weighed down by thousands of pounds of dragon flesh. A great cheer went up from the harbor. By then, her stomach rumbles had shifted to far more unpleasant hunger pangs. All other troubles paled in comparison. At last, they left Kalama's harbor behind, but another hour would go by before there was a rap on the door and a man called out, "Captain wants you."

Apprehensive, Hanalei pulled the washtub away from the door and peered out. It was the red-bearded dragoner. The tightness in her chest eased when she saw that both his hands were uninjured. Frowning, he looked down at his hands, turning them over. "What?" he demanded.

"It's nothing." Hanalei slipped out of the cabin.

They went up through the hatch and across the deck. To the east, Kalama's mountains and seaside villages grew smaller and smaller. Around them, dragoners went about their business. None cradled a hand in pain and misery.

Maybe he was gone. Her intruder could have fled the ship, taken his injuries to a healer. *Good*, she thought. *One less dragoner to worry about.*

Once they climbed the forecastle steps, the red-bearded dragoner left her. The room was circular, the walls lined with wooden shutters, every one of them open, and the wind was as rough as the waters below. Captain Bragadin directed a spyglass to the sea behind them. A table had been bolted down in the center of the room. Vaea worked at one end, polishing a sextant. Moa sat at the opposite end, reading over Hanalei's papers. Her satchel lay open beside him. Standing in the doorway, Hanalei inspected their hands. No injuries.

Captain Bragadin lowered his spyglass long enough to say, "Sit." When she did, Moa held up the page he was reading. "Is this a true story?"

"Yes."

"It's Augustus," Captain Bragadin said, preoccupied with the solitary dragoner that trailed in their wake. It was the ship from yesterday. The RES *Lagoon*, captained by the golden-haired prince Augustus. Like the *Anemone*, it flew an Esperanzan flag. "That lazy lordling, he hunts dragons by following me. *That* is his strategy."

"Come away from there," Vaea suggested. "He only makes you drink more."

Disgruntled, Captain Bragadin snapped the spyglass closed and flung himself into a chair beside Moa. He regarded Hanalei across the table. "Sleep well?"

"Not really."

The answer pleased him. Smiling, Captain Bragadin plucked the sheet from Moa's hands, earning a dark look but no protest. "This is all very instructive," the captain told her, holding up the parchment. "Gruesome, but instructive. I don't think I thanked you for it."

He sounded sincere. And perhaps he was. His moods were like the wind, ever changing. Moa retrieved another page from her satchel and began reading it.

Hanalei said, "You'll let me go, then? I can get off at Masina." If the weather held, they would pass the island of Masina sometime tomorrow. She had funds safely stored at a lending house there. Once she disembarked, she could purchase more parchment and write down as many of her father's notes as she could from memory. The captain would not be returning her papers to her, this she knew.

"Always in a rush," Captain Bragadin said, which was no answer. "Do you know, I remember when you first came to the harbor, looking for work. Do you remember, Vaea?"

"No," Vaea said without looking up from her sextant and polishing rag.

"How old were you then?" Captain Bragadin asked

Hanalei, as though his navigator had not spoken. "Four? Five?"

"I was eight," Hanalei said. Moa's lips tipped up at the corners.

"That old? Really?" Captain Bragadin said. "Most brats who seek me out have some sad tale to tell. Their mother's dead, their father's dead, they're hungry—"

"The usual orphan story," Vaea commented.

"All painfully similar," Captain Bragadin agreed. "But not you, Hanalei. You kept to yourself. A quiet little girl in a dirty, costly dress, and a voice that did not sound like any Rakakalan wharf rat."

"You sold my dress," Hanalei remembered. "I saw it on another girl at the market."

"What use did you have for it? Dragon stink is hard on silk and tapa. And it fetched a good price." Captain Bragadin carelessly folded the parchment into quarters, causing Hanalei's fingers to spasm. "I never cared enough then to wonder where you came from."

There it was. A changing mood. A shift in the wind. "Why should you care now?"

"I think you know the answer to that, Lady Hanaleiarihi of Tamarind." Captain Bragadin used her full name, hers and her father's combined, and a title he had not known of until he had gone through her private papers. His voice turned brisk. "Ten days, your father wrote. A seadragon lays its eggs ten days after its frill turns pink. That is the rule."

"In that one instance," Hanalei said automatically, because facts were important. "It could be an anomaly. Different next time—"

"Let's not go looking for trouble," Captain Bragadin said with an air of tried patience, "and assume it will be the same. So. In ten days, nine days now, that green seadragon needs to be on this ship. Along with those eggs."

There was no dissuading him. His mind was set. "I wish you good luck," Hanalei said. "Will you let me off at Masina?"

"Of course," Captain Bragadin said. "Masina, Wakeo, Esperanza. I'll take you wherever you like. Once we have that dragon."

"Captain—"

"Hanalei." Captain Bragadin pointed at her. "You can sense them. Somehow. Because of what your father did. Don't bother to lie," he added when she opened her mouth to do exactly that. "I knew there was a reason you were always finding them first."

For the first time, Vaea showed an interest. "What did her father do with the egg, exactly?"

Captain Bragadin turned to Hanalei. "Tell her. You know best. No? You tell her, then, Moa."

Unlike Hanalei, who had folded her arms and sunk

low in her chair, Moa was agreeable. "Listen to this, Vaea," he said, looking over the parchment. "Lord Arihi put the dragon egg in a washtub and cracked it open. The sea-dragon was born alive . . . He killed it. Wrung its neck like a chicken. Then he put her, Hanalei, in the tub with it."

Vaea grimaced. "Why?"

Captain Bragadin said, "Because of the yolk. He thought it would seep into her skin." He added, with reluctant admiration, "Your papa was thorough, Hanalei."

"And then he made her eat it," Moa said. "The yolk, the tail, the meat. More and more until she woke up. This is disgusting."

"Then what?" Vaea set the sextant on the table. "He made a wish?"

"It's not a genie's lamp," Hanalei said, unable to stay silent a moment longer. "Dragonfruit is supposed to undo a person's greatest sorrow. That is how the stories phrased it. My father asked the gods to undo my illness, to remove the poison. I woke up twelve hours later." She turned to Captain Bragadin. "You threw a harpoon at my head. Yesterday. And now you want my help?"

Annoyance crept into his tone. "I'm not asking you to do it for free. I pay well."

"No, you don't," Hanalei reminded him.

Bragadin chuckled, conceding her point. "For this I would pay very well," he amended. "In advance even. A good-faith payment." He took the parchment Moa was reading, shoved it into the satchel, and slid it across the table to her.

Afraid he would change his mind, she swept the satchel out of his reach and pulled the strap over her head. Only then did she say, "You're giving me back my own things? As payment?"

Captain Bragadin's eyes narrowed. "As a kindness. Gold," he said curtly, and named an amount that had Vaea and Moa staring at him. Hanalei did not blink. "Paid to you directly or deposited in your name at whatever lending house you choose. That is your payment." He placed both hands on the table and leaned forward, eyes on her. "And one dragon egg."

This time Hanalei could not hide her reaction. Captain Bragadin smiled when he saw it. "The dragon will lay three eggs," he said. "So the stories go. Take one. Think of what you can do with it. Or undo."

Hanalei did not have to. She had dreamt this dream before. She would take the dragonfruit home to Tamarind. Princess Oliana would be healed. But at what cost? *As with all things that promise the moon and the stars and offer hope when hope has gone, the tale comes with a warning. Every wish demands a price.* Whose life would be forfeit this time? Sam's? She shuddered. He was the last person she would risk. And even knowing its dangers, she wanted that dragon egg more than anything.

Hanalei said, with difficulty, "I can't help you," and watched the captain's smile fall away. She tried to set aside her animosity long enough to explain. *"Every wish demands a price,"* she recited. "It is a warning, Captain. One my father ignored, because he loved me. He saved my life and died days later. A terrible death. Dragonfruit isn't meant for us. And when we take it, it takes something back."

"Your father was unlucky," Captain Bragadin dismissed. "I won't be."

"Then I wish you good fortune," Hanalei said. "But I can't help you."

The red-bearded dragoner came in, arms laden with dishes. Plates piled high with food. There was guava and mango and sweet bread, a small mountain of drumsticks. The sight and smell of it all made Hanalei dizzy. Following him was the boy dragoner. The one who had offered to finish her off yesterday. Plates were set before the captain, Vaea, and Moa, but when the red-bearded dragoner would have placed one before Hanalei, the captain stopped him.

"Our guest isn't hungry today. But I am." Captain Bragadin took the plate meant for Hanalei, set it beside his own. He bit into a drumstick, chewing noisily. He smacked his lips. "Delicious."

Moa frowned at his plate but said nothing. Vaea's mouth was full of sweet bread.

Hanalei swallowed . She understood. It was an old game of the captain's. Hunger used as a weapon. "These are my choices, then? Help you or starve?"

"Sadly, yes." Captain Bragadin licked his fingers. Then, suddenly, "Ant. What happened to your hand?"

Hanalei stared at the boy. He had tried to hide it, standing partially behind the red-bearded dragoner, but the captain took his elbow and pulled him close. The boy's right hand was wrapped in great swaths of bandaging. He had only carried in one plate, she realized, while the other dragoner had juggled three.

The boy, Ant, looked at his feet. He muttered, "I fell."

"Off what? A church spire?" Captain Bragadin snapped. "Is it broken?"

Ant squeezed his eyes shut. "Yes, Captain."

Captain Bragadin flung his arm away. "What use have I for a dragoner with a broken hand? A right hand?"

"I can do other things, I swear! I'll earn my keep—"

"No," Captain Bragadin said. "You get off at Masina. Make your own way, boy. Out." He jerked his head toward the door. After a venomous look in Hanalei's direction, a tearful Ant ran off, followed by the red-bearded dragoner.

Hanalei watched Ant go, remembering his wiggling

fingers, his hateful snicker. At least he would be off the ship tomorrow, even if she would not. "I've changed my mind," she said. When no one moved, Hanalei reminded him, "Good faith, Captain."

With one finger, Captain Bragadin pushed a plate across the table. He sat back in his chair, watchful. Hanalei took her time, knowing that if she ate too quickly, she would be sick. She broke the bread into smaller pieces. She ate the mango, the guava, two drumsticks. Moa poured her a cup of coconut water. She drank every drop. And when she was done at last, she stood and reached for the captain's spyglass.

"May I?" she asked.

"By all means," Captain Bragadin said.

Hanalei went to a window and looked out through the spyglass. It was as she thought. She stepped aside and offered the instrument to the captain. "Over there. You see? Two seadragons. They're right behind us."

5

CAPTAIN BRAGADIN SNATCHED THE SPYGLASS from her hand. A string of curses erupted as he peered out the window. Moa and Vaea ran over. More cursing followed.

The seadragons were directly behind the ship, halfway between the *Anemone* and the *Lagoon*. One blue, one green. The latter with a rose frill, the color of the heart flower. Hanalei watched with growing dread as they circled the *Anemone* in a wide arc. The second time they swam around, the arc had grown smaller.

Closer.

"They're hungry," Hanalei and Captain Bragadin said at the same time. They exchanged a look of mutual dislike and grudging respect. However much she despised him, there was no denying the captain knew the Nominomi Sea like the back of his hand. The Nominomi and the creatures within. Especially these creatures.

The arc would grow even smaller, Hanalei knew. And then, if nothing was done to deter them, they would surround the ship and squeeze, and squeeze, until the hull cracked and the forecastle collapsed and the sailors fell one by one into the sea. Open jaws. Wide, waiting mouths. There were calls from the deck directed up at the forecastle, asking for orders. No one sounded panicked. This was a dragoner, after all. Dragon hunting was their livelihood.

Moa headed for the door. "I'll get the harpoons. What about fire?"

There was a catapult on the roof of the forecastle. There would be incendiaries stored beside it in a waterproof box. Firebombs. A foreigner's invention, adapted for life at sea.

"No fire." Captain Bragadin turned in a slow circle, following the seadragons' path through the open shutters. The spyglass fell, forgotten, from his hand. Hanalei caught it before it hit the floor. "I won't risk that dragon."

Moa stopped. "Captain, it's the dragons or us, I think."

Hanalei had been looking through the spyglass. The *Lagoon*'s captain must have also realized the seadragons were preparing to feed. It was sailing away. No help would be coming from that direction. Hanalei could see the *Lagoon*'s crew gathered together, turned their way. The yellow-haired captain, Augustus, stood in the center, his own spyglass trained on them. Another figure appeared by his side. Much smaller, delicate. Wearing a red dress. Augustus gave her the spyglass. Hanalei said, "There's an old woman on that ship. She's wearing a crown."

"What?" Captain Bragadin grabbed the spyglass.

"Who?" Vaea leaned out a window, squinting.

"Augusta," Captain Bragadin said after a very long moment. "His grandmother."

"Grandmother?" Moa asked, at a loss. "Who brings their mai mai on a dragon hunting ship?"

Captain Bragadin did not answer. His spyglass remained on the other ship, which was making good headway, putting more distance between it and the dragons. As for them, the *Anemone* had begun to rock as the sailors below raced from rail to rail, watching the seadragons draw closer. "Hey!" someone shouted. "Why are we just standing here scratching our—"

With a snarl, Captain Bragadin broke the spyglass in two and flung the pieces at the wall. He ran out of the forecastle and from the top of the steps shouted, "All of you, shut your mouths!" Silence fell instantly. "Get below and not a sound out of you! We are mice here, do you understand? Invisible. Now go!"

There was a rush for the hatch. Rattled, Hanalei watched what looked to be a whirlpool forming around the *Anemone*. It would have been fascinating to witness, had she not also been aboard. The hatch slammed shut, and a quiet fell over the ship.

It was a good idea, pretending to be a ghost ship. Sometimes seadragons would swim past a quiet vessel, uninterested. But these dragons were hungry and determined. They circled closer. Silence was not going to work, and by the look on the captain's face, he knew it too.

Captain Bragadin stared straight out the back of the ship, hands clasped behind his back. "Moa."

"Captain."

"Two firebombs," Captain Bragadin ordered.

Hanalei wrapped both arms around herself. *It's the dragons or us*, Moa had said. It did not make her feel any less wretched knowing what had to be done. Moa did not bother to hide his relief. He ran for the door, then froze when the captain added, "Aim for the *Lagoon*."

Three sets of eyes turned to the captain, disbelieving.

"Bragadin," Vaea said, her voice strained. "That is the king's son. The king's mother. Kill the dragons."

Hanalei began, "Captain—"

"Are you still here, Moa?" Captain Bragadin spoke quietly, every word a warning.

A muscle bunched along Moa's jaw. He swung around and left. They stood side by side, the three of them—Hanalei, Vaea, Captain Bragadin—listening as the seadragons hissed and the water churned and foamed. Moa pounded up the outer steps to the forecastle roof. A terrible creaking sound followed, the catapult swinging into position. And finally, a single heavy thump as the first incendiary was dropped into place.

The first bomb sailed across the water. It hit the *Lagoon*'s stern and sent splintered wood and human bodies flying. Even from this distance, Hanalei could see one of them wore a red dress. The second bomb landed directly atop the forecastle, and within minutes, the Esperanzan ship was no more. It was not until Captain Bragadin released a breath that she realized the hissing had stopped and the churning had receded. Both seadragons had abandoned them, swimming toward the more convenient meal. There were people among the debris, arms flailing. The sound of screams carried over open water.

Hanalei made herself watch, made herself remember the details. Though she did not believe, deep down, that she would ever have the chance to bear witness to what she was seeing. And when she heard Vaea's words, and the captain's words, she knew.

"You fool, Bragadin," Vaea said softly. "You think you're invincible, but you go too far this time. We'll hang for this."

Captain Bragadin stiffened at the word *fool*, and Hanalei reached for the dragonscale at her back, braced for more violence. But all he said was "Only if we're caught. Only if someone tells."

6

THEY LOCKED HANALEI IN HER CABIN FOR THE rest of the day and night. Long hours stretched before her. Sometimes she paced, which was unsatisfying in this small box of a room. Sometimes she lay on the mat, staring at the wall and wondering *How am I to get off this ship?* One bright spot: no one had come to remove her washtub. It remained shoved against the door, offering a small measure of comfort and safety.

At times, her pacing was more of a stagger, for they had sailed straight into the unwelcoming arms of a typhoon. The *Anemone* rocked wildly. It dipped and swayed, shuddered and creaked. From the shouting above deck, she suspected one or two dragoners had fallen overboard and been lost. Mercifully, they must have caught the typhoon at her tail end. The waters and winds were violent, but brief, and by the time Hanalei settled into a troubled sleep, the worst of the storm had passed.

Occasionally, however, sleep came with its own storms.

She dreamt of Princess Oliana, and an evening lesson. And poison.

"Kalama," Princess Oliana had prompted from across the table. She wore a long, green dress without sleeves. Tattooed on her arm, from shoulder to elbow, was the image of a sleeping fruit bat.

Kalama was too simple, Hanalei thought. A five-year-old would know the answer. She was eight. "Kalama is a trickster god. The goddess of deception and chaos. There's an island in the east named for her."

"And?"

"And it's said she's the creator of earthquakes, typhoons, great waves, and . . ." Here, Hanalei had to stop and think about it. "Volcanoes?"

It had become their ritual when it was just the two of them. The lessons of the day would continue into supper. Hanalei had served as Princess Oliana's page for three years. A great honor. They sat at a table by an open window on the island of Garapan. Three weeks had gone by since they had begun their journey, visiting the various villages and islands of the Tamarindi archipelago. Tomorrow they would start for home.

"Yes. Volcanoes. Very good. And whom does Kalama favor?" Princess Oliana brought her spoon to her lips. She was, in Hanalei's opinion, the most beautiful person on Tamarind. No, the entire Nominomi. Her face was narrow, with sharp, slashing cheekbones, reminding Hanalei of the great statues that stood on the southern edge of the island. The scar on Princess Olli's right cheek resembled a fishhook. She refused to have it tended to, ignoring the unguents and lotions prepared by royal healers. The scar reminded her of her husband, she would say, and of the battle that had wounded her and cost him his life. She would not erase such a memory. Her hair fell to her knees, waves the color of lava stones, polished and shiny. One day, when Hanalei was eighteen and not eight, she would have hair that long and that shiny.

"Kalama favors those of bad character," Hanalei answered. "Mostly thieves, pirates, spies, and Lady Iosefina."

Princess Oliana lowered her spoon. "Lady Iosefina?"

"For breaking Uncle Isko's heart. And for going away. Sam called her a villain."

"Ah," Princess Oliana said. Samahti was her son. "Sam is very loyal to Isko. But we mustn't blame Lady Iosefina for marrying another."

"Why not?"

"Because it was not done out of spite," Princess Oliana told her. "Or unkindness. We love whom we love, Hanalei. The choice is rarely our own."

"But Uncle Isko is lord protector, and he's not here because he's sad. Who's going to protect us?"

Princess Oliana laughed. "Are we not strong women, able to protect ourselves?" She dabbed the corners of her mouth with a cloth. "Even if we were not, we are surrounded by guards, including Captain Erro, my dear. They have machetes." She returned the cloth to her lap. "Don't worry about Isko. He'll come home when he's ready. Now, I believe you have Kalama well in hand. What about Olifat?"

Hanalei broke off a piece of sweet bread and dipped it into her utu soup, which she had to force herself to eat. She did not like the utu fruit. It tasted bad. But any complaint would bring about a lecture about privilege and the plight of those less fortunate. Still, she could not be imagining it. This soup tasted even worse than usual, bitter and crunchy. Someone had forgotten to remove all the fruit seeds. Across the small table, Princess Oliana watched Hanalei struggle to finish her supper, lips twitching.

"Olifat," Hanalei repeated, after swallowing hard, "is the father of all sea gods. His eldest daughter is Tarisso, the octopus goddess. And his eldest son is Taga, god of sea-dragons."

"Taga is just one of the names used by the seadragon god. What are the others?" Princess Oliana reached for a cup filled with coconut water. Hanalei had climbed the tree herself, just this morning. With Princess Oliana looking on, she had twisted a single coconut free, later peeling away the husk and breaking open the shell with a sharp rock. It had been another lesson, in self-reliance.

"Um." Hanalei poked about the utu with her spoon, thinking hard. "He goes by Taga, Hehu, Satawal, Cat . . . Do I really have to finish my soup? There are seeds in it."

Princess Oliana froze. "Seeds?"

Hanalei bit down on a mouthful of seeds. The crunching sound was unmistakable. "See?"

Princess Oliana slapped Hanalei's bowl off the table. It went sailing into the air, splintering onto the stone floor, cold soup everywhere. Hanalei shot up and cried, "What is—" And stopped, looking on in horror.

Princess Oliana had swayed to her feet, clutching the table for support. In the span of seconds, sweat had beaded her forehead and the whites of her eyes had turned a terrifying shade of red. The bat tattooed on her arm had faded to gray. She clutched her throat with one hand and said, with difficulty, "Hana, find help," before crumpling to the floor, eyes wide open.

Hanalei screamed and screamed, and she ran, but just as she reached the door, her legs stopped all on their own. They felt heavy, like stone statues, and a wave of dizziness overcame her. She stumbled against the door, banging her head on the wood. Using her last bit of strength, she opened the door and fell through it, landing on the wood floor, cold against her cheek. Her eyes drifted shut to the sound of running feet. She heard Captain Erro shouting. Another person yelled her name. It was Sam, her friend, lifting her up, holding her close.

Three sharp knocks woke her. When she dragged the tub away and tested the door, she found that the outer bolt had been lifted. The passageway was empty, so she followed her nose up to the deck where a cooking station had been set up. Pork, rice, and strips of papaya sizzled in pans. Two drag-oners, one male and one female, slapped food into bowls and made sure no one took more than their share. Others gathered in small groups, eating quickly and speaking in low tones, or clearing the deck of storm debris. No one paid any attention to Hanalei, but they fell silent when Moa came through the hatch. Bloodshot eyes, hair uncombed. He looked as if he had spent an even worse night than she had.

Moa spoke to her without stopping. "Stay out of his way."

She knew that already. Hanalei had to look up to find Captain Bragadin. He stood on the forecastle roof, another spyglass in hand. She went to the rail to see what had captured his attention.

The seadragons had not been lost in the typhoon. They were in front of the ship this time, pinpricks in the distance, blue and green. Heading west.

It was a simple thing to steer clear of Captain Bragadin. Over the next few days, they rarely lost sight of the sea-dragons, which meant he had no use for her. He kept to the forecastle or to his cabin. His mood following the sinking of the *Lagoon* was even more mercurial than before. The dragoners summoned to his presence did not come away unscathed. It was not uncommon to hear shouting or furniture breaking against walls. It could not have helped his temper to realize that they were being followed by two more dragon ships. Hanalei stayed out of everyone's way, in her cabin with her father's papers and her notes, or in some forgotten pocket of the ship, or helping when she was told.

"You've done this before." The dragoner's name was Papeete. He was an islander in his middle years, a big man with wild, curly hair. It framed his head like a halo, like a full moon. The tattoo on his arm was of Rakakalan design. Bold sunrays drawn with heavy ink. Like Vaea's.

"I have," Hanalei said. So many times, she could do it in her sleep.

It was afternoon out on the deck. The sun was pleasant, the waters calm. Hanalei held a clay pitcher filled with dragon oil. Before her was a jar made of sea glass, a cloth square pulled tightly across its opening. Papeete held the cloth in place as Hanalei poured the oil onto it slowly, so that it did not flow over the sides. The cloth acted as a sieve, preventing dirt and sand from entering, and catching tiny bits of dragon bone. What settled in the jar was pure dragon oil. From the *Anemone*, it would find its way to harbor markets, sold to make ointments and soap, and to light lamps and torches throughout the Nominomi.

All around them, dragoners engaged in similar work. They had been at it all day. Though Captain Bragadin had unloaded the three seadragons at Kalama in a hurry, he had kept back a portion of their fat, preferring his methods for harvesting the oil. By the mainmast, Moa and a female dragoner fed large strips of blubber into cauldrons, massive pots that had to be stirred using oar-sized spoons. The smell was horrendous. Hanalei was glad to be on this side of the deck, away from the stench and fumes.

Papeete sat on a stool across from Hanalei. When the jar was full, he tossed the cloth into a bucket. "Who are your people, girl? You don't sound like a Rakakalan."

"That's because I'm not." Her satchel hung behind her, cumbersome, but she would not leave it behind in her cabin.

Papeete waited, and, when no further explanation was forthcoming, asked, "So. Where are you from? Salamasina?"

"No."

"Wakeo?"

Hanalei selected another empty jar and set it before her. "I'm from nowhere."

"Huh." Papeete snagged a fresh cloth from a nearby mat. "Like the rest of us, then."

Several feet away, the boy dragoner Ant glared in her direction. As though it was her fault entirely his fingers were crushed and his bandage stained with dragon oil. As if he had done nothing at all to deserve it. Hanalei ignored him. They had not docked at Másina to kick him off the ship, as the captain had originally intended. Like her, he knew too much.

The red-bearded dragoner stomped over and dumped an armful of glass jars onto the mat. They clanked alarmingly. His face was flushed with anger as he said, to no one in particular, "Stay away from Vaea. That mean old cat. What's with her?"

Vaea was steering the wheel. Her eyes were narrowed on the red-bearded dragoner, lip curled as though ready to spit.

"What did you say to her?" someone asked.

"Nothing." The red-bearded dragoner sat on a stool, so low his knees almost reached his chin. "I wanted to know about Prince Augustus. That's all. What I should tell people if they ask us."

Quiet fell. Even Hanalei stopped pouring, marveling at his dimness.

Papeete said, "You're new here, Red Beard, so listen. We don't know anything about that yellow-haired prince, or his granny. Never saw them. I've known the captain a long time. And the rules are we do what we're told. We keep our mouths shut. We live long lives."

"But—"

"Your. Mouth. Shut," Papeete repeated. "Lucky for you Vaea didn't feed you to the dragons." There were murmurs of agreement.

"She won't keep her mouth shut." Ant sneered across the mat at Hanalei. "The captain's gonna feed her to the dragons."

Papeete reached around the red-bearded dragoner and smacked the boy on the back of his head.

"Ow!"

"Everyone knows that, boy. No need to say it out loud." Papeete glanced over at Hanalei, spread his palms. "Apologies for the youth."

Hanalei eyed Papeete with dark humor. "His rudeness. That's what you're apologizing for?" Not her death by the captain's hands, which he would pretend he did not see.

Papeete placed the cloth tight over the pitcher, lips pressed in a prim line. "Good manners are important."

"Accepted," Hanalei said, because she knew it would irritate Ant, which it did. He rubbed his sore head and turned his back on her. What sort of name was *Ant* anyway? Short for Anthony? Or had his parents shown foresight into their son's character, and named him after vermin?

More hours passed. Moa lit the first of the deck lanterns as the sun began its descent. The work would continue well into the night. Hanalei started to pour oil into a fresh jar. She stopped, her breath catching. When she shoved the pitcher at Papeete, he was so surprised he nearly dropped it. Hanalei went to stand by the railing, leaning out as far as she could, inhaling deeply. A full minute passed before Red Beard said, "Hey. What's that smell? Is that cake?"

Nutmeg, Hanalei thought. *Clove, cinnamon, mace.* All growing on the mountains outside Tamarind City. Her birthplace.

"The girl smelled it before anyone," Papeete murmured. "So that's where she's from." Then, "That's the Tamarind Archipelago. We won't see it until early morning, but we know it's there from way out here. They're not called the Spice Islands for nothing."

Hanalei had sailed this route several times over the last four years. Never stopping. There was no reason to. But every pass bruised her heart. Her mother was buried on Tamarind, though Hanalei had no memory of her. Her grandparents were buried there, and their parents. Six hundred years of family. And Princess Oliana, who had taken a motherless girl in hand and shown her kindness, and strength. She was on Tamarind too. Besides her father,

Hanalei had loved her most of all.

It was one thing to pretend she was from nowhere. It was another to understand exactly where she came from and know she could never return.

No one yelled at her to get back to work, so Hanalei stayed where she was, her gaze sweeping from the sea-dragons to the setting sun to the two dragon ships trailing in their wake. It was as she was watching those ships that she spotted a small boat hanging off the very back of the *Anemone.* It swayed gently in the wind and was secured by rope. Her mind raced. Dragoners didn't normally carry rowboats, unlike explorers or trading ships. She had not thought to look for one—

"Don't think about it." Captain Bragadin appeared by her side, making her jump.

He looked terrible. Worse even than Moa. Purple smudges framed his eyes. Heavy stubble covered his face. He had the appearance of someone who slept too little and drank too much. Which was what most people would do if they had just firebombed the Esperanzan king's mother and his youngest son.

The conversation behind them had dropped off considerably. The others were listening.

Hanalei said, "I was thinking about the sunset."

"I don't blame you. It's a beautiful one." Captain Bragadin

leaned his arms on the railing. "We're docking at Tamarind," he said, looking over in time to see her flinch. "The typhoon's put holes in the hull. They need to be repaired or they'll get bigger. It will be a short visit," he emphasized. "That prince isn't overly fond of me. Better if he doesn't know I'm there."

Sam. There was only one prince of Tamarind. It felt strange to hear the captain speak of him. Strange and dangerous. "What did you do to him?"

"You assume it's my fault, not his," Captain Bragadin said drily. "It was a misunderstanding, but the boy holds a grudge." He gave her an appraising glance. "You knew him well, I suppose. Being his mother's page."

"I didn't."

"Really?"

"Pages don't spend much time with princes." Hanalei lied without hesitation. What the captain knew he used against you, eventually. She steered the conversation into safer waters. "What will you do with the dragonfruit? You can't bring Prince Augustus back from the dead—"

A snort. "I'll only have three eggs. Why would I waste one on him? Or the old woman?"

Three. So much for giving her one. How did he think to get out of this? He could not keep what he had done a secret. Someone on this dragoner would talk. Deliberately, for a price. Or accidentally, like that red-bearded dragoner was bound to do. The moment the Esperanzan king learned what had been done to his family, Captain Bragadin would become the hunted. No longer the hunter.

Unless.

This ship. His crew. What was she thinking? He did not need a dragon's egg to solve this particular problem. He only needed to be rid of his ship and those on it. Not such a difficult task. He had done something similar only days ago. It had taken minutes.

"You're too smart for your own good." Captain Bragadin had been watching her. "And your face too expressive sometimes." He turned back to the water. "You'll remain in your cabin while we're docked, under guard. Don't do anything foolish."

"I wasn't going to."

"Good. Because it will not work. First, you would have to get to the rowboat without being seen." He glanced behind him at the dragoners spread about the deck. Dozens of them, all with their eyes down and working diligently. He looked over at Moa, who had finished lighting the lanterns and now watched over everything from the forecastle roof. Moa nodded his head once in acknowledgment. "Which is unlikely," Captain Bragadin continued. "Then you would have to cut the ropes, but you have no dagger, no knife. Even if you managed that, our harpoons carry a long way.

And maybe you've forgotten, but there are monsters in the water."

In the water. Right beside her. Monsters everywhere.

Never let him see you're frightened. Hanalei stared straight ahead. "I haven't forgotten."

"Good," Captain Bragadin said again. He walked off, then turned back and said, for her ears alone, "There's nothing for you on Tamarind, Hanalei. Your family's dead. You're all alone. No one's coming for you."

7

WHO'S THIS, THEN?

Sam strode along the cliff's edge, watching the ship approach. A dragoner by the look of things. There was no mistaking the shape of that hull. It had sailed near enough for him to see the figures crowded onto the deck, turned toward the shore, and him. The sight made his blood quicken. A dragon ship usually meant seadragons; seadragons, for the last ten years, meant hope. Whose ship was it?

The night had a rain-swept feel, earthy and damp after the typhoon. Nutmeg scented the air, along with cinnamon and clove, a hint of mace. Under the light of a full moon, Sam could just make out the flag whipping about the mainmast. A red cypress against a white background. This ship sailed for Esperanza. When the name painted along the side came into view, Sam planted his boots wide and folded his arms, scowling into the night. The *Anemone*. His hopes plummeted as quickly as they had risen. He had no use for this ship, and no love for its captain.

The last time Bragadin had docked at Tamarind Harbor, he had sold two seadragons to Sam. Very costly animals. Both had turned out to be sickly, the memory of which had Sam's temper soaring all over again.

"What do you think, Fetu?" Sam wondered aloud. "Should we let the good captain anchor? Or send him on his way?"

Sam wore the uniform of the royal guard: plain trousers tucked into boots, tunic capped high on his arms, its color the green of the jungle that rose up behind him. What looked like a tattoo of a bat covered his right arm, inked from shoulder to elbow, its wings furled and its head tipped low as if asleep. A tiny pearl cuff rested above his right foot. Hearing Sam's voice, the bat lifted his head. Small eyes opened, blinking sleepily. Fetu's wings unfurled, rising from Sam's skin, ink becoming fur and flesh and bone, as real as the thousands of fruit bats that made their home in the jungles and caves of Tamarind.

Tattoos, or markings, were common in the Nominomi. Men wore them proudly on every part of their body, from scalp to toe, as did many women. The cost of a true tattoo master was dear, accessible only to the wealthy, or to eldest children, whose parents sometimes saved for years. Those with lesser means made do with an apprentice tattooist or, worse, a dabbler. Cheaper markings were often rough, lacking finer detail. Some were just plain ugly, which was unfortunate, because a marking, once placed, could not be displaced.

Though there were exceptions.

Markings like Fetu were not the work of a tattoo master. They appeared on their own, without warning, in the shape of an animal and usually during a Tamarindi's early adulthood, between the ages of fifteen and twenty. Unlike a normal tattoo, these markings did not stay put. They moved along the skin at will, sliding over arms and legs, faces and backs. Sometimes they rose from the flesh, taking the form of living animals. Companions and guardians until death.

Fetu climbed up Sam's arm and perched on his shoulder, like a bird, not a bat. He did not answer Sam's question about Captain Bragadin, because fruit bats did not speak. Instead, Fetu batted his head against Sam's ear.

It was answer enough. Sam said, "Agreed. Let's get rid of him."

"Samahti," a deep voice said by his shoulder.

Sam flailed, so close to the edge his boots sent pebbles scattering over the cliff and into the abyss. He cast a sour look at the man who stood inches away, trying not to look amused. Sam's heart thumped wildly. At least he had not screamed.

"Uncle," Sam offered in greeting. "I didn't see you there."

"Clearly. Otherwise you would not be caught talking to a bat," Uncle Isko said. Not Sam's blood uncle, but his parents' oldest friend, back when his father was living and his mother was sound. He was shorter than Sam—most people were—wide-shouldered, with stern features. He wore an elaborate sand-colored cloak made of tapa. A heavy necklace lay around his neck, eight strands of gleaming white cockleshells. It was a reminder that Sam too should have been dressed in tapa and shells. He should have been at that supper.

Guilt had Sam hunching his shoulders. "Did my grandmother send you?"

"She did not."

Sam's glance was full of skepticism. Tonight, his uncle's marking appeared on the side of his neck. A shark's head looking upward, jaws open and teeth sharp. It looked ready to bite down on his ear.

"The queen did not send me," Uncle Isko said crisply. He continued to watch the approaching ship, but the eyes of his shark shifted, first staring upward at his uncle's ear, next rolling sideways to pin its disapproval on Sam. "I'm merely wondering why, with so many interesting visitors on island, you've chosen to volunteer for the watch. All alone on this mountaintop."

Sam turned away from the shark's eye. Because among the interesting visitors were twenty females of marriageable age, no coincidence. And with them came their mothers, their fathers, their brothers. Sam had come here to get away from the endless introductions and festivities, as well as the feeling that he was being watched everywhere he went. Hunted. He had just turned nineteen, and the last thing he wished to do was marry. "I feel like meat hanging at the market," he admitted.

"Every prince must go to market. Every princess too."

Said the man who had never married. "Thank you, Uncle. I'm cheered and comforted."

Uncle Isko's lips curved. "It's a wedding, Samahtitamah, not a wake. There are twenty young ladies back at the pavilion. Surely one stands apart?"

Sam thought about it. No, not one. There were too many to consider. Lady Anaa and her sister Andresina, who went by Nina. Princess Elei, Princess Huali, Princess Lalago, and more ladies: Cinta, Noelani, Silivia, or was it Silvia? Sam was having trouble matching names to faces, faces to family, family to clan and kingdom. It had been far simpler to toss aside his cockleshells and flee to this mountaintop.

Uncle Isko said, "What of Lady Rosamie? She's a charming girl. Marriage to her would bring the entire Salamasina Archipelago to our side. A boon."

"I suppose."

Uncle Isko frowned. "What's wrong with her?"

"Nothing."

Silence from Uncle Isko. Then, "What's wrong with you?"

"My parents—" Sam scuffed a boot. He was unaccustomed to discussing such things with his uncle. Their conversations tended more toward war and politics and strategy. Never feelings, or softer things.

At the mention of his parents, the shark stopped glaring at him and so did Uncle Isko, who prompted, "What about them?"

"They loved each other, Uncle. It wasn't just duty." Sam had seen it. As a young boy, he had felt it.

"It was not. Is that what you wish for?"

"Maybe." Sam had answered truthfully before. There was nothing wrong with Rosamie. She was intelligent and pretty. Her uncle was the king of Salamasina. His grandmother approved of the match. Anyone would, should, be pleased to marry her. Why wasn't he? Fetu pressed close to his neck, trying to burrow. Offering comfort.

Uncle Isko was quiet. "What your mother and father shared was rare," he acknowledged, twisting the gold ring on his finger. A thick band with the image of a shark carved upon it. "Most will not find a love like theirs, and perhaps . . . it is just as well."

Sam turned his head. "Why?"

Uncle Isko's shark looked away, and the entire marking retreated downward until it was hidden by the cloak. "Watching Oliana and Sam, it was like watching fire sometimes. Fire burns, Samahti. It leaves scars."

For the first time in a long time, Sam remembered Lady Iosefina, Isko's lost love, who had married another. But before he could think too much about it, his uncle returned to their earlier conversation. "Never mind Lady Rosamie. What about Lady Anaa . . . ?" He trailed off at Sam's glum look and tipped his chin to the approaching ship. "They won't go away. The Esperanzans, the Langlanese. Wakeo. They'll keep coming."

"Yes." Sam watched him clasp his hands behind his back, which meant a lesson was sure to follow.

"We're a small kingdom, with vulnerabilities," Uncle Isko said. "What happened to your mother showed us that. If we wish to remain a kingdom, and not some wretched outpost for another, we must strengthen alliances. With our old neighbors and our new."

Bound by marriage, then by blood. Sam knew what was expected of him. And still. "There are other ways to build alliances. I don't have to marry right away—"

"Samahti." Uncle Isko spoke sharply. "Your grandmother did not have to invite these ladies here. She is giving you a choice. It may not always be so. While you still can, while there is time, choose for yourself."

Sam did not have to ask what he meant. His grandmother, Queen Maga'lahi, was not a young woman. And his mother was dying. She had been dying a long time. He could not inherit the throne. Tamarind was ruled, by tradition and by law, by women. The choices that lay before him were few. He could marry a stranger and hope the gods blessed them with daughters. Or he could find a cure for his mother's curse, one that had eluded them all for ten long years. If he failed, the elders would gather and the crown would pass out of his family for the first time in six hundred years.

Sam hung his head. One should not complain about duty, about being the grandson of a queen. "I understand."

They both fell silent, standing side by side and a sea apart. Finally, after regarding the ship drifting ever closer, his uncle asked, "Who's this, then?"

"Bragadin. The Esperanzan."

Uncle Isko's expression showed his distaste. "The one who sold you those useless dragons? That orphan peddler?"

"The same."

That was another thing. Tamarind relied on trade. The island's spices would be worth little without the merchants who purchased them in vast quantities. It did not have the freedom to turn away every ship it wished. But it could turn away some. Bragadin of Esperanza was a celebrated dragoner, a favorite of his king, because he slaughtered the most seadragons and sent a portion of his profits home to fill the royal coffers. But after Sam had been sold the sickly dragons, he had learned more about the captain than he wished. Stories whispered about, of children in filthy workhouses, paid little to prepare seadragons for sale. One could always tell when someone had labored for him; their hands were covered in scars, sliced repeatedly by dragonscale. Much of Bragadin's fortune had been built upon their small shoulders. Sam would keep such a man off his island, forever if he could.

Uncle Isko said, "What is he thinking, coming here?"

"I wondered the same thing."

"A bold pirate. And a foolish one. How welcoming do you wish to be?"

"Not very." Sam nudged the fruit bat with his head. "Fetu, like we practiced."

The bat needed no further urging. He flew off. Moonlight made it possible to see his wings flapping toward the dragoner. He circled the *Anemone* once, twice, three times, before diving straight down into the water. The sailors, already turned toward the island, had been watching the bat's approach. Half came forward, peering curiously into the sea after him. But the other half, one might say the wiser half, backed cautiously away from the railing.

Sam smiled.

A whirlpool formed beside the *Anemone*. Small at first, before growing larger. Rising from its midst was a bat of such great height that when it straightened fully, the water lapping at his wings, the ship appeared no larger than a toy boat in comparison. The span of his wings was massive. The wings themselves were full of holes. His eyes were empty black sockets and his fangs were sharp and gleaming, the bright yellow of a hibiscus moon. And trapped between the fangs was a fully grown stingray.

"There's no faulting your imagination, Samahti." Amusement laced his uncle's words. "I almost feel sorry for them."

From the sailors there was only shouting. The stingray twisted and turned, trying to escape, only to be flung onto the deck of the ship.

The shouting grew higher in pitch. More scream than shout. At the sound, Sam murmured, "Well done, my dear. You can come—" He broke off as his glance fell on the ship, and something odd. While most of the dragoners crowded the prow, as far from danger as they could get, one remained in the back, at the stern. Just off the stern, a rowboat hung suspended by rope. The figure had reached over the railing and was yanking at the rope. The boat plunged before stopping a good ten feet above the water, one end tipped higher than the other. It swayed back and forth in midair, appearing stuck.

"Someone is not afraid of your bat," Uncle Isko remarked. "Or else he really wants off that ship."

Later, Sam would think back to this night and wonder at the ties that bound one person to another. Across distance and time. Across years. He should not have been on the cliff that night. She should not have been anywhere near this island. He said, "Uncle, will you finish my watch?"

"What? Why—where are you going? Samahti!"

Sam barely heard him, because he was running. Down the cliffside path that ribboned its way to shore. A path wide enough for one, forcing him to slow his pace if he did not wish to fall to his death. He kept his right palm on the cliff's rocky surface, and his eyes on the ship. The wind sent his uncle's voice spiraling down to him, full of annoyance, telling him to *stay out of the water, for pity's sake. Stingrays never travel alone.*

A narrow beach appeared at the bottom of the cliff. Lying beside a boulder was an outrigger, polished and sleek, large enough for three. Sam grabbed one of the oars propped against the rock. After pulling off his boots, he dragged the canoe into the warmth of the Nominomi Sea.

There was someone on the mountaintop watching them. Hanalei stood at the railing with Captain Bragadin and the others, unable to look away from the lone figure who paced back and forth with a restless energy, perilously close to the cliff's edge. More guards would be about, she knew, patrolling the shore or concealed by tree cover. But he was the only one she could see. She kept him in her sights, along with a second figure who appeared beside him, and did not look away.

That is, until she saw the bat.

"What's with the bird?" Moa called down from the

forecastle, holding up a lantern. Moonlight followed a small, flapping creature as it flew from the top of the cliff to the *Anemone*, where it circled overhead.

"That's no bird," Captain Bragadin said, neck craned. "That's a bat."

One that dove straight into the sea in front of them, but not before Hanalei spotted a tiny cuff above its foot. A glint of pearl, there and gone. She would have fallen over from the shock of it had she not been crowded in on all sides by dragoners. She knew that cuff. As a page, it had been her job to polish it.

"Fetu," she breathed. How could that be?

Captain Bragadin glanced at her sharply, before turning back to the water, which had begun to bubble and hiss. An enormous bat rose from the froth and spread its wings. It was not alone. An angry stingray writhed between its jaws. When the stingray dropped onto the deck, the dragoners scattered in fright. Hanalei alone stayed where she was. Fetu was Princess Oliana's marking, her companion. Hanalei did not understand how he could be here when the princess was not. She looked back at the figure on the mountaintop.

Sam.

Fetu leaned over the ship and swept a massive wing along the deck. The dragoners went flying. Bodies knocked into poles and barrels. The red-bearded dragoner sailed right by Hanalei and fell down into the open hatch.

A distraction, Hanalei realized. Fetu was a much-needed diversion. She ducked beneath the wing and ran to the stern where a boat hung suspended over the side. She pulled at the rope. The knots could not be undone. They were too tight. She did not have a knife to cut them with, but she did have dragonscale.

Hanalei leaned over the railing, sawing frantically. The rope frayed and the boat dropped, one end hanging lower than the other. She stood on her toes, trying to slice through the last bit of thread.

"I told you not to try it."

Captain Bragadin.

If she had not been so startled, and if he had not grabbed her braid, yanking viciously, Hanalei would not have done it. She stumbled back, her arm, and the dragonscale, coming down in a wide arc. The captain screamed. She watched as he fell to his knees and clutched his face. Moa appeared, looking first at the captain, then at her. Hanalei would have spoken, but he held a finger to his lips. Moa pointed to the Nominomi behind her and mouthed a single word.

Go.

Hanalei shoved the dragonscale into her satchel. Terror drove her to the rail and over the edge, where she could no longer hear Captain Bragadin. His cries were lost among all the others.

Rough waves slowed Sam's progress. Something bumped the outrigger, rocking it wildly and nearly turning it over. He froze, oar just above the surface. His uncle's warning came rushing back, along with the knowledge that there were far scarier creatures than stingrays in the Nominomi. Scarier, bigger, hungrier. But after several minutes passed and nothing rose up to eat him, he cautiously resumed rowing.

Fetu's apparition continued to harass the dragoners. Sam left him to it. As a distraction, he was proving useful. He had nearly reached the *Anemone* and the figure by the stern when he saw a larger person appear behind the first. They vanished from sight. A moment later the smaller figure reappeared, tumbling from the ship and dangling from rope until Sam brought the canoe directly beneath. He caught the briefest glimpse of a delicate profile. A girl. She dropped into the boat, landing in a crouch, head lowered. A long braid had come partially undone, obscuring her face. She was dressed in typical black dragoner garb. A satchel hung by her side.

Sam hunkered down before her, asking in Esperanzan, "Are you hurt?"

"No," she said in clear, if a little breathless, Tamarindi. Lifting her head, she added, "That is Fetu."

Sam rose slowly, staring down at her. It was the last thing he expected to hear. His bat's name on a stranger's lips. She rose too. A beautiful girl whose face he knew and did not know. Shock coursed through him, racing up his arms and through his heart, like fire.

"Who are you?" His foot struck the oar. He would have toppled overboard had she not grabbed his hands with both of hers. Holding fast.

She said very, very quietly, "Don't you know me, Sam?"

8

HE DID KNOW HER. AS THE OUTRIGGER ROSE AND fell among the waves, Sam took in ten years of change. They had been scrawny children, all arms and legs and scraped knees. Her elbows had once been weapons, sharp enough to stab him in the ribs when he teased her, which was often. Long hair flying and bare feet swift as she raced across the sand and up the trees, exploring the beaches and jungles and caves with him by her side. Her hair was still long, but she was scrawny no longer, instead slender and tall, her head reaching his chin. Still, he knew her.

"*Hana?*"

Her hands slipped from his. She nodded, eyes wary, clearly wondering what he would do.

Which was to say, stupidly, "You didn't die."

"I didn't."

Sam sat down hard on the bench. It could be he just fell. They had searched for years and found nothing. He had thought her dead. And had wept, in secret, where no one could see. It turned out he had not needed to. Hanalei was alive and well, which meant the stories behind the dragonfruit were rooted in truth, not myth. Not just fantastical tales for children. His smile flashed, sudden, delighted. "It worked."

An answering smile touched her lips. "Yes."

"*How?*" If the dragonfruit had worked once, it could again. He thought of his mother asleep in the royal pavilion. Ten years of slumber.

"Papa wrote it down." A satchel hung across her chest. She wrapped an arm around it. "I have it all here."

Papa. How could he have forgotten? Sam rose, the canoe rocking as an old anger rolled over him. "Where is your father?"

Her smile faded away. "Gone, Sam."

She meant dead. Sam could see it on her face. For him, the grief was unexpected and sharp. Sam's own father had been killed when he was a boy, struck down in battle. But two men had seen to it that Sam had not lacked a father's guidance. Lord Isko and Lord Arihi, Hanalei's father. And still, remembering the man's many kindnesses, Sam could not bring himself to say he was sorry. The words would not come.

"Your mother . . . ?" Hanalei asked.

"Nothing's different." His words were gruff. In the distance, the *Anemone* continued to flee the giant bat. Sam whistled softly and said, without raising his voice, "That's enough fun for now. Come back."

The conjured bat stopped abruptly. There was a faint splash as it scooped up the poor stingray from the deck and returned it to the sea. It waded in their direction, movements stiff, like a puppet on a string. The *Anemone* sailed on.

Hanalei asked, "If nothing's different, how do you have your mother's marking?"

Sam understood why she asked. The last time Hanalei had seen Fetu would have been the day of the poisoning. Fetu would have been with his mother. Her marking and hers alone. "When she didn't wake, he came to me. He was on her arm one moment, and then flew to mine. I tried to give him back, but he wouldn't go."

For the span of an indrawn breath, Hanalei looked startled. "How old were you?"

"Nine. Not long after you'd gone."

"That's very young for a marking." Hanalei's expression was troubled. "It's never happened before, has it?"

"No." It had been a shock to everyone. Markings did not hop from one owner to another. And they did not attach themselves to young children. "We keep each other safe, Fetu and I. Until we can get her back." Sam pulled the oar up and around. There was something about Hanalei's voice. It was deeper than one expected, for a female. And curious sounding. It no longer carried the distinctive lilt of one Tamarindi born. Hers was a voice of many islands, one that came from anywhere and nowhere. A wanderer's voice. Where had she been all this time? "How are you here, Hanalei?"

She looked past him to where a far-off figure stood on the beach by Sam's discarded boots. A tapa cloak billowed behind him. "I know I'm not welcome—"

"That isn't what I said."

"I'm sorry." Hanalei's words were quiet. "I don't wish to cause trouble. I had nowhere else to go."

Before Sam could answer, the conjured bat drew up beside the outrigger. Sam and Hanalei craned their necks to see its face way up high. It tipped its head to one side and shook it, as though trying to dislodge something. Fetu came tumbling down out of an ear, like a pebble, with no signs of spreading his wings and taking flight. Before he hit the water, Sam reached up and snatched him from the air, cupping the bat in his hands. Fetu shook himself, wings flapping before hopping onto Sam's shoulder. The apparition waded on toward the beach, sinking with each step, until the top of its head disappeared beneath the waves.

"Hello, Fetu." Hanalei came closer, smiling uncertainly. "It's me. Hana."

Fetu turned abruptly on Sam's shoulder, presenting his back to her. The worst sort of rejection. Hanalei flinched at the insult, her eyes stinging with hurt.

"He doesn't mean it." Sam's hand went up instantly to comfort the bat. "Hanalei. It was hard for him when you left. He doesn't mean it." Sam could have been speaking for Fetu, and for himself. To his dismay, Hanalei's lips wobbled. "No. Stop. Don't cry."

Hanalei burst into tears. "I didn't wish to go, you wretched bat! How could you think it?"

Fetu whimpered. He burrowed against Sam's neck, pressing frantically into skin. Fur and bone disappeared, transformed into a tattoo on Sam's neck. The marking opened its wings wide, spreading along Sam's cheek and shoulder, before it furled its wings and disappeared beneath his tunic. Even though he had returned to a marking, Sam could feel him trembling between his shoulder blades. Claws dug into Sam's skin.

Sam hissed. "Fetu, your claws! Hanalei, sit down—" She flopped onto a bench, weeping, both hands pressed over her face. Her shoulders shook.

Helplessly, Sam looked down at the top of her head. There was nothing to be heard beyond the waves and her tears, tears that sounded and felt like they were long overdue. Sam took the other bench, facing her. He knew his uncle was growing impatient. Sam left the oar at his feet. Waiting. Until, eventually, Fetu stopped trembling and Hanalei had cried herself out. She dropped her hands, looking anywhere but at Sam, who asked, "When did your father die?"

"Ten years ago."

Everything in Sam went still. "What?"

"Ten," she repeated, her voice scratchy and exhausted. "Not long after we left here."

Sam had heard her. He just didn't understand. "Where have you been living?"

Hanalei lifted a shoulder. "Many places. Everywhere."

"Who with?"

"Lots of people sometimes. No one now."

Her answers told him nothing. Sam looked past her toward deeper sea. A terrible suspicion began to form. He had been so distracted by her being here, he had not considered *how* she had come to be here. "What were you doing on that ship?"

Hanalei did not respond. Fetu came creeping out from Sam's tunic, a small head peeking over his shoulder.

I had nowhere else to go. Sam's bad feeling grew worse. "That is an Esperanzan dragoner. Bragadin's ship. How do you know him?"

"Does it matter?" Hanalei wiped her tears away with both fists.

Sam's gaze dropped to her hands. With one swift movement, he stepped over the center ridge and crouched before her. He held out both hands. "Let me see."

She shook her head.

"Hanalei. Let me see."

A single tear fell. She placed her hands in his, palm to palm. They were slender, long-fingered, smaller than his. Sam studied them under the light of the moon. He turned them over. White scars crisscrossed both sides. Sliver upon sliver, one cut after another. Fetu hopped onto Sam's forearm for a closer look. A distressed chirping filled the quiet.

Sam lifted his head, his eyes meeting hers. It took everything in him to keep his voice even. "Dragonscale?"

"Yes."

"Were you . . . You were in a workhouse?" At her nod, "Bragadin's?"

A sniffle. "They're all his. On Raka at least."

"For how long?" Sam willed her to say an hour, or a day. A moment in time. But he braced himself for something worse, because these scars, they had not come to be overnight.

"Six years," Hanalei answered. And when Sam said nothing, because he could not speak, she added, "He doesn't keep anyone past fourteen. Our hands get too big. Less efficient."

Sam sat on his heels, reeling. A memory came to him, one he had not thought of in years. His mother had given Hanalei a ring for her eighth birthday. A simple gold band with a seashell carving. From that day forward, Hanalei refused to take it off. Each time he saw her, she held it up to the light, admiring it. "Don't expect me to call you lady now," he had told her, rolling his eyes, "just because you're eight and wearing fancy rings." Hanalei had laughed, "I *do* expect it. A bow also, Samahtitamah." He had laughed too and did as she asked, bowing extravagantly.

Lady Hanalei of Tamarind. Descended from one of the island's founding families, a bloodline six hundred years old. As old as his. And she had worked in a dragon factory for six years, the remainder of her childhood, with no one to protect her. Sam rose, hands falling away from hers. The rage started in his chest and spread from there. Once again, he looked out to deep sea.

Hanalei said, "What are you doing?"

"I'm going to sink that ship. Fetu. The lanterns."

Fetu bared his fangs. He flew off, anger in every beat of his wings. Hanalei stumbled to her feet. "You can't sink an Esperanzan dragoner . . . Stop."

Sam did not reply. Barely visible in the distance were lanterns swinging from poles. One torch went flying onto the deck. A fire appeared. For the second time that night, shouting emerged.

"It's not just Bragadin on that ship—"

"I don't care."

"Sam! The *Anemone* is protected. You can't burn it down without reason—"

"*You* are reason, Hanalei!"

"No." Hanalei grabbed both of his arms. "I'm no one, and if you burn that ship, you put everyone here in danger." She dropped her hand, turned toward the dragoner, and said, "Fetu, come back."

Sam could feel the bat hovering by a second lantern, uncertain. What had his uncle said? *We are a small island, with vulnerabilities.* Esperanza was no friend to Tamarind, but neither was it an enemy. And the line between ally and foe was a line easily crossed. "Fetu," he said, seething and resentful. "Come back."

Fetu returned and landed on Sam's shoulder. Hanalei dashed away the last of her tears and said, "I'm sorry I called you wretched."

Fetu ducked his head and leaned against Sam's neck. But at least he didn't turn his back to her. It was all she was going to get for now.

Sam took up the oar. His words were brusque. "It's not a big fire. They'll live."

Hanalei returned to her bench. Sam slapped the oar into the sea, taking his anger out on wood and water. There was so much he wanted to ask her. Ten years' worth of questions. He rowed to shore, not knowing where to start or what to say, and so he said nothing at all.

9

"WHAT JUST HAPPENED HERE?" LORD ISKO DE-
manded as Sam pulled the outrigger out of the water. He
barely spared a glance in Hanalei's direction as she hopped
from the canoe onto the sand.

She was grateful, for it gave her time to find her bearings.
Seeing Tamarind from afar had left her heart bruised, but
standing at the shore, with sand clinging to her sandals, her
toes, the damp hem of her trousers, it was a different sort
of hurt.

Two guards had joined Lord Isko on the beach. One
male, one female, both young. They came forward to take
the outrigger from Sam and drag it the rest of the way up
the beach.

When Sam did not answer, Lord Isko said, "Samahti—"

"It's a private matter." Sam's response was curt and followed by a glance at the guards, both within earshot. Fetu
perched quietly on his shoulder.

"*Private—*" Lord Isko sputtered. He jabbed a finger at the fleeing ship. "Scaring that Esperanzan is one thing. Setting fire to a foreign ship is no private matter! Have you lost your senses—"

"It's my fault." Hanalei had been standing partway behind Sam. She came around to stand beside him. "I wasn't on the ship by choice. Prince Samahti was upset on my behalf."

That checked Lord Isko's anger. A female islander, a foreign dragoner. It was a familiar story. "I see," he said. Time had hardened him. Deep grooves bracketed his mouth, and heavy lines framed his eyes. There was more gray than black in his hair. He wore a great tapa cloak, which shielded his marking, his shark, for there was no sign of it. "I'm distressed to hear it. Are you in need of a healer?"

"I'm not, Lord Isko. Thank you."

Something flickered in his eyes. "Have we met?"

"Uncle," Sam said. "It's Hanalei."

The clouds passed overhead, and the moonlight was bright again. It was the lord protector's first good look at her.

"*Hanalei?*" The wind blew his cloak behind him. He had worn a similar one on her eighth naming day, when he had presented her with a jade carving of a seadragon. It had been small enough to carry in the palm of her hand. What had happened to it? Her father had brought so little with them. There had been no time.

"Sir." Hanalei lowered her head briefly, a sign of respect. "Lord Isko."

The title tripped on her tongue. He had never been Lord Isko to her. Only Uncle, an honorific used to address any beloved male elder. Once upon a time, this man had loved her. And her father.

Lord Isko did not speak for the longest time. When he did, it was with great underlying emotion. "Where is he?"

His question should not have hurt as much as it did. Not *I am pleased you're alive.* Only *where is your treacherous father?* "Papa is dead."

Lord Isko flinched. "No. I would have felt it. I would have known."

"He was my father. *I* felt it."

The guards remained by the outrigger, eyes wide. Not even pretending they did not listen.

Lord Isko stalked away. He spun around and strode back, kicking up sand with his boots. "How?"

Sam said, "Uncle—"

"*When?*"

"Ten years ago," Hanalei said. "He left our inn on Raka. He was going to the harbor to meet a ship. There was a message he wished to have sent to you, and to the queen." Here, her voice faltered. "He did not come back. They found him the next day. Someone had robbed him and . . . left him in the water."

There was a brief silence.

"Ten years," Lord Isko repeated. "But where have you . . . Your hands," he said suddenly.

Hanalei folded her arms, hiding the scars from view. Not quickly enough. The look on Lord Isko's face told her he recognized the sort of scars they were. His marking came creeping out above the necklace. A shark's head, flat against the skin and far smaller than any living, breathing shark. Still terrifying, though. But it was not looking at her. The shark's eyes were on the *Anemone*.

"It's late." Sam looked up, searching the clifftop. Another guard stood in his place. Sam raised a hand, the guard did the same. "We can speak later. I'll bring Hanalei back to the city. Grandmother will wish to see her."

"Take them with you," Lord Isko said, meaning the guards.

"Fine."

The guards came forward. They wore the same green uniform as Sam and looked of similar age. His introductions were brief. The female guard was named Liko. She was lean and muscled. Straight hair fell to her waist, free from braids or ties. Her fellow guard went by the name Bayani. His features were wide and friendly, and his words made her think of the western part of the archipelago. He had grown up on Isle Garapan, she guessed, or somewhere very close to it.

Sam brought two fingers to his lips and whistled, making Hanalei jump. Behind them, from the depths of a night-black jungle, came the sound of animals galloping. Four kandayos broke through the palms, coming from different directions. They shared an ancestry with the horses found in the oversea kingdoms. They were of similar height and appearance. These animals, however, were not brown or black or white, but the pale green of sea glass. Their coats, hooves, eyes, and hair, all green. Also their manes, which were thick and ropy, like seaweed strewn along the shoreline.

One stopped in front of Hanalei. She grabbed hold of the saddle, pausing when Lord Isko called her name. She turned to face him.

"You said your father wished to send a message. We never received it. What did it say?" Lord Isko's features were drawn and his words subdued. He had just learned of her father's passing, she reminded herself. She had had ten years to mourn.

"He wished to tell you the dragonfruit worked, that I was growing stronger," Hanalei answered. "He promised to find another for Princess Oliana. When he did, he would return home to face his punishment."

"He didn't find another."

I have, Hanalei almost said. But Lord Isko walked off toward the water's edge, and she swallowed her words.

Sam brought his kandayo over. He favored his mother. Hanalei had seen the resemblance right away, on the outrigger. His face was angle and sharpness, like the statues of his ancestors found throughout Tamarind. Tousled black waves covered his head, and his eyes were a deep brown, more serious than she remembered. A strong, handsome face. "He's happy to see you," Sam said to her, meaning Lord Isko.

Hanalei surprised them both by smiling.

Sam's mouth nudged into a smile of his own. "It's true. Or it will be soon. You're a shock, Hanalei, but not an unwelcome one." He glanced at the soundcatcher around her neck. "You kept it."

Hanalei wrapped her fingers around the carving. "Do you want it back?"

"It was a gift. Yours to keep." His head came up, questioning. "It didn't work off island, did it?"

"No."

"Well, it should, now that you're home." Sam patted his kandayo. "Ready?"

Hanalei swung onto her kandayo and followed Sam and the guards into the jungle. She looked back once, but Lord Isko no longer stood on the shore. His cloak lay crumpled in the sand beside a pile of cockleshells. She saw a figure in the water, arms slicing through the waves. And the outline of a shark fin, right beside him.

The road from the shore to the city was paved in coral, crushed underfoot over the years. Hanalei recognized it by sound, not sight, for there was no light to be had in this dense island forest. Not even from the moon. They rode swiftly through the night. Hanalei could hear the kandayos breathing and the surrounding thrum of the jungle creatures—bats hunting and pigs foraging, sand crickets everywhere.

Most island cities were built near the water. Tamarind was no exception. The ride was a dark one, but swift. In no time at all, they left the jungle behind. The city gates rose up before them. A massive structure, carved with images of Tamarind's founding mothers. Sam's ancestor stood proudly in the center, a leafy crown on her head. Hanalei's ancestor was there on the left. Her grandmother many times removed, wearing a long robe and a plumeria lei four strands wide.

Here the torches blazed bright and clear, without odor. Dragon oil. There were guards up high and guards down low, every one of them armed. Hanalei lost count of the number of spears and machetes, daggers and clubs.

"You favor her," Sam remarked, looking at their fore-mothers.

Hanalei's voice wavered. "Really?"

"You don't see it?"

"Is that you, Prince Samahti?" a guard called from a tower platform. An older guard with a bushy beard, who carried a spear. Hanalei knew him. His name was Nasi.

"It's me," Sam called back. "Open up."

The gates swung open. By the time Sam, Hanalei, and the two guards nudged their kandayos through, Nasi had descended the tower stairs and was there to meet them. He pulled Sam aside, speaking quietly. Sam leaned down from his kandayo to hear. The words "just came from the lagoon" drifted her way, along with "stolen" and "cousin."

Sam returned to Hanalei, his expression aggravated. "There's something I have to see to. It can't wait. Liko and Bayani will take you back to the pavilion—"

"My pavilion?" Hanalei had not thought that a possibility.

"No, to mine. For now."

Liko said, "Prince Samahti. What should we tell your auntie?"

Sam could not contain a grimace. "Tell her I'll explain later." To Hanalei: "I wish there was a better homecoming for you than this, Lady Hanaleiarihi. However you left us, however you returned, Tamarind welcomes you home, to the land of your foremothers." He lowered his head so that his chin nearly touched his chest.

The words were spoken for her benefit, and for those around her. Touched, Hanalei lowered her head. A formal greeting required a formal response. "I could not have wished for a better homecoming, Prince Samahtitama-henele. Thank you for your kindness, and your welcome." They straightened and looked at one another, saying nothing. A choking sound came from Nasi the guard, who gaped first at Hanalei and then at the carving of her ancestor. He had recognized her name. Hanalei watched Sam ride off into the night.

There's nothing for you on Tamarind, Hanalei. Your family's dead. You're all alone. No one's coming for you. Captain Bragadin had been wrong. She was not alone.

Someone had come for her.

10

SAM FOUND HIS COUSIN AT THE LAGOON, SITTING miserably on the sand. Jejomar looked over as Sam rode up on his kandayo, then groaned and turned away. A royal guard stood farther down the beach with another man. Sam went to them first. His cousin could wait.

The guard spoke bluntly. "Prince Samahti. Young Jejomar took this man's canoe without asking. Now it's at the bottom of the lagoon. His nets, his hooks, everything's gone."

The fisherman was older, with sparse gray hair and the tattoo of a fish on his chin. He bowed and said his name was Gafao. "The fish are my livelihood, Prince Samahti. It was an old boat, but a good one. I have nothing left."

Why would his cousin do such a thing? Sam looked out over the lagoon, quiet and still, moonlight reflecting on the surface. His words were curt. "Jejomar. Get over here."

They were distant cousins on their fathers' side, which meant Jejomar and his mother were related to the royal family by marriage, not by blood. He was seventeen, two years younger than Sam. Their resemblance to one another was also distant, Jejomar being of average height and skinny, with dark hair, a face full of spots, and a chin beard wispy as bird down.

Jejomar dragged his feet to Sam's side. His clothes were damp. "Hello, cousin."

Sam instantly smelled the aava on his breath. The fumes nearly knocked him over. Sam wanted to shake him. "This man says you stole his boat and sunk it. Is that true?"

"No! It's not true."

Gafao pointed a finger at Jejomar's nose. "A lie!"

"I didn't steal it!" Jejomar protested. "I borrowed it. It was a dare—"

Sam broke in. "By whom?"

"My friends . . ." Jejomar looked helplessly around the lagoon. There was no one about but Sam, the guard, and the outraged fisherman. "I guess they left."

"Your friends are no good," the guard told him.

"How did you sink it?" Sam asked. His cousin could be careless and thoughtless, but he knew how to sail a fishing boat.

"I swear I didn't try. It hit something big. Like a boulder. Over there."

"I know this lagoon," Gafao said. "There is no boulder to hit. He's drunk."

"Do you wish to submit a grievance?" Sam asked. "It's

within your rights. He'll be held until the next judgment day." Sam addressed the guard. "Which is when?"

"The last one was this morning, Prince Samahti. He'll have to wait until next month."

Jejomar had been rubbing his aching head. At the guard's words, he stopped. "Wait. What?"

"One month in jail," Sam told Gafao. "If you file your grievance. Lord Isko will decide what to do with him after that."

Jejomar's eyes widened. "Lord Isko?"

"A month in jail?" Gafao repeated. "I thought he was your cousin?"

Sam wished he could deny it. One could not choose their family. Too bad. "I don't serve my cousin, Fisherman Gafao. I serve the queen, which means tonight I serve you. You are not without rights here."

Sam knew what the man had expected, for Jejomar to be able to walk away because of who he knew. But Gafao did not know Sam's grandmother. She would have thrown Sam in the cell next to his cousin if he tried it.

Gafao studied Jejomar with a stern expression. The fish marking on his chin traveled upward to the center of his forehead. At first glance, it looked like he had a third eye. "How old are you?"

"Seventeen." Jejomar caught Sam's look, adding hastily, "Sir."

"Old enough to know better." Gafao's stern expression softened. "Maybe too young to share a jail with big, mean men." Jejomar fell back a step. Gafao said, "I won't complain if he buys me a new canoe. And supplies. And silver squid for lost wages."

"How much?" Sam asked.

Gafao named a very high price.

"You'll have it," Sam promised, and Jejomar's shoulders sagged.

"And for him to say sorry," Gafao added.

Sam turned to his cousin, disbelieving. "You didn't apologize?"

Even in the dark, Sam could see the top of Jejomar's ears turn red. He turned to the fisherman and said, "I am very sorry, sir. I was not thinking, and I hope you can forgive me."

Mollified, Gafao stayed for a short while longer as details were discussed, then departed. The guard moved off a little ways to give the cousins privacy.

As soon as he did, Jejomar turned on Sam. "Were you really going to leave me in jail? For a *month*?"

"Maybe," Sam said. "And I might still if he's not paid what he asked. First thing tomorrow, Jejomar."

"Me?" Jejomar looked blank. "But . . . I thought you would pay him."

"Why would I?"

"Well . . . you were the one who asked for a price. And you didn't even barter. Canoes are expensive, Sam."

How were they related? "Now you're beginning to understand."

"I'd pay you back."

"No."

Jejomar's expression was clearing. The fog was going away. "It's nothing to you. The price of a boat. Gold squid falls out of your ears, and you don't even notice." His words were full of resentment.

"Go home, Jejomar," Sam said, weary. He had left Hanalei with strangers, on her first night home in ten years. For this.

Jejomar did not move. He said, in a low voice, "Don't tell my mother."

"Don't make me tell your mother."

Another guard had arrived, relieving the first one, who came over. "Come on," the guard said to Jejomar. "I'm heading back anyway. I'll ride with you." He walked off with a sullen Jejomar. The last thing Sam heard him saying was "That aava will rot your brain, son. Believe me." And "Why don't you spend more time with your cousin? A fine young man, our prince. You should be more like him."

"YOU'RE TELLING ME, GRANDSON, THAT ARIHI'S child has been laboring in a workhouse? For that horrible Esperanzan?"

"For six years, Mai Mai," Sam confirmed. "I don't know the rest."

It was early. Queen Maga'lahi wore sleeping robes, crimson silk embroidered with gold thread, complementing her light brown skin. Her hair was a curling white mass that fell halfway down her back and smelled of coconut oil. At six feet, she was only inches shorter than Sam. A lean, strongly built woman. Sam's friends had kindly old grandmothers. Ones who wore flowing, colorful muumuus and taught their grandchildren how to weave baskets and pickle strips of green papaya. Not Sam. He did not have that sort of grandmother.

She was feeding the fish. They were in a garden down the steps from her bedchambers, one bordered by banana trees and dotted with small ponds. Sam stood beside her holding a basket of fish food, little balls of ground leaves and chopped up worm. She scooped a small amount onto her hand, then tossed it into the pond with perhaps more force than was necessary. Frightened by the splash, the fish fled to the opposite end and disappeared from view. Uncle Isko stood nearby, listlessly dropping pebbles into the shallows. He looked as Sam felt, sleep-deprived and surly. Sam had managed an hour's slumber at the bai, the men's house, before receiving his grandmother's summons. His uncle's marking was unthreatening this morning, a small shark tattooed on his wrist. Fetu was also in tattoo form, a sleeping bat hanging upside down on Sam's left arm, below his shoulder.

Another ball splashed into the pond. "I've thought of a hundred ways to punish Arihi," his grandmother said. "Painful ways, for doing what any father would have done. What *I* did myself, placing my child above everyone else. And he died alone, without prayers."

Uncle Isko said, quietly, "You're not the villain here, Your Grace."

"I'm hardly the hero," the queen responded. "Oliana would not be pleased, I think, to know how I've treated this child, the daughter of her heart. Six years in a workhouse. It is sickening." She looked up at Sam. "*Does* she look sickly? Frail?"

"No. She looks . . ." *Like a dream*, Sam thought. *With a*

voice like night music that danced along his arms.

They waited. His grandmother's eyebrows climbed. "Yes?"

Sam cleared his throat. "Normal. Healthy."

"How flattering," Lord Isko commented, "if you're speaking of cattle." His expression told Sam he was fooling no one. "She looks like her mother at that age, Your Grace. The likeness is uncanny."

"Ah. Lovely, then. Where is she now?"

"With Aunt Chesa." The fish food had clumped together at the bottom of the basket. Sam gave it a few shakes, to loosen them. "Hanalei's old nurse lives with her. Penina. I thought she could use a familiar face."

Uncle Isko dropped the rest of the pebbles onto the grass. "She's hiding something."

Sam lowered the basket. "You barely spoke to her."

"It was long enough," Uncle Isko said. "She was carrying a satchel, Samahti. Do you know what it holds?"

Papa wrote it down. I have it all here. "Her father's notes, she said. For the dragonfruit."

"You didn't see these notes?"

"I did not." Sam strove for calm. They were both weary. "What is this about, Uncle?"

"Yes," Queen Maga'lahi said. "What are you saying, Isko?"

"Your Grace. Hanalei has been gone ten years, much of it spent with the Esperanzans. And she shows up on one of their dragoners, out of nowhere. It is concerning."

Sam said, "You saw her trying to escape that dragoner. We both did."

"We saw something." Uncle Isko held up a hand at Sam's expression. "I'm saying we should take care, that is all. We don't know her, Samahti. Not anymore."

The words came before Sam could stop them. "Who is to blame for that?"

"I beg your pardon?"

His grandmother said, "Samahtitamah."

Sam heard the warning and did not care. The unfairness of it. "You're lord protector, for all of Tamarind. Isn't Hanalei a Tamarindi still? Who's been protecting her? Not me. Not you." Sam threw up both hands, sending worm balls flying into the air. "She kept herself safe. And when she finds her way home, after *ten years*, Uncle, this is how you speak of her?"

Uncle Isko had gone very still. It was an unkind thing to say, knowing his uncle blamed himself for his mother's poisoning. He had been away that day, nursing a broken heart, of all things. He had delegated her watch to another and regretted it ever since.

Sam's grandmother turned to him. "Whom do you think

you speak to in such a way?" she asked, very softly. "In that tone, with those words? Surely not an elder?"

"Mai Mai, you didn't see her hands—"

"I did not ask about hands."

On the other side of the pond, a yellow-and-black banana spider appeared between two trees. It was three feet long, legs skittering as it rounded the pond toward them. It raced up to his grandmother, disappearing beneath her robes. A moment later, a marking appeared on her cheek. A small spider now, flat and unmoving, except for its eyes, all eight of them. They were pinned on Sam, blinking at different times.

Sam called her Mai Mai, Grandmother, but she was known by other names. Queen Maga'lahi, Your Grace . . . and *Para Rana*, Spider, the One That Weaves the Web. The last was never said to her face.

Fetu was no longer asleep, but Sam could feel him squeezing his eyes shut, pretending. He turned to his uncle and bowed. "Apologies."

"Accepted," Uncle Isko said without looking away from the pond.

His grandmother eyed them both. "We have guests on the lagoon this morning. Have you both forgotten?"

Sam winced. He had blocked it from memory. "I didn't forget."

Uncle Isko stirred. "I won't be able to attend—"

"I expect both of you there," the queen interrupted. She twirled a finger at Sam's plain guardsman clothing. "Make yourself presentable. This is not enough. And do *not* be late. After, bring Hanalei to me. I wish to see her."

"Yes, Mai Mai."

His grandmother's eyes softened, though her spider's did not. She reached up and touched his cheek. "You children were so close. We hoped . . ." Her voice trailed off. "Don't plan your life so carefully, grandson, or the lives of others. The gods will only share a laugh at your expense."

She left them there and went up to her chambers. Without a word, Uncle Isko strode off in the opposite direction, through the trees. Sam was left alone. He tipped what remained in the basket into the pond, watching as the fish converged on plant and worm, gorging.

Before Sam left the royal pavilion, he went to his mother's quarters. They were located far away from the public chambers, in a quiet, restful corner. Before her illness, they had lived just the two of them in a nearby pavilion. Now she slept on a bed she had been placed on ten years ago. It rested low to the ground, common on Tamarind. Mosquito netting enclosed white bed coverings. The chamber was cool and shadowy. Leafy ferns grew from pots and trailed from high shelves. A set of doors had been thrown open, and through them came the scent of cinnamon and fragrant tuberose.

Sam pulled aside the netting and looked down at his sleeping mother. Uncle Isko had rooted out the man behind her poisoning. A prince from Wakeo. When Isko had sailed off to seek vengeance, he had taken Sam with him. And at the age of nine, Sam had understood for the first time what it meant to be an enemy of Tamarind. And he had understood a little more of what it meant to be lord protector, a role that would be his someday.

His heart twisted, seeing his mother like this, for he was growing older and she was not. Her face remained unlined. Her hair was long and black, curled like the queen's. Someone had braided it and tucked plumeria blossoms here and there. Sam pictured himself years from now, a stooped old man, visiting his mother, who never woke, never aged, who never again said his name.

He leaned down and kissed her forehead. "Mama, I have news."

Sam descended the wide stone steps of the queen's pavilion. His grandmother's home was a much larger version of the buildings that made up both the palace complex and the city of Tamarind. Built on a foundation of thirty-two latti stones, each twice the height of a man and consisting of a stout pillar with a bowl-shaped stone sitting upon it. The pavilion itself ran along a single level. A steep, downward-swooping roof had been covered in banana leaves to mimic the look of the original ancient settlement. But the buildings were made of stone, not wood, a solid foundation that did not require rebuilding after every typhoon, devastatingly common in these parts.

Also within the palace complex were homes belonging to the original founding families and other members of the nobility. Uncle Isko's pavilion was here, as was Hanalei's. Or what had once been her home. It had been returned to the queen after Lord Arihi disappeared and was now used to house important guests.

Sam's pavilion was built upon sixteen latti stones, second only in size to the queen's. But being unmarried, he had no real need of it. And if he was being truthful, he did not care for the proximity to his grandmother's home. It was the next pavilion over. He lived in the bai with other unattached males. There he had the freedom to come and go as he pleased, far away from the watchful eyes of guards and relatives.

His aunt Chesa was a distant relation on his father's side. Years ago, when she had moved from the country and asked to live in his pavilion temporarily, until she found her own suitable lodgings, he had agreed. Uncle Isko had cautioned him. "She will not want to give it up when you wish to reclaim it, Samahti. Tell her no."

"I don't need so much, Uncle." His aunt had been a widow with two children. A daughter who had since grown and married, and a son, Jejomar. They would make better use of his home.

Uncle Isko had shaken his head. "Don't say I didn't warn you."

Sam was remembering his uncle's words now as he stood before his aunt, trying not to gnash his teeth. "What do you mean, Hanalei's not here? Where is she?"

"Surely you didn't expect us to let her stay?" Aunt Chesa wore voluminous green dressing robes. Sam had come early enough in the day that her face was devoid of the heavy layers of paint she normally wore. Her black hair hung loose, puddled on the floor. Penina stood behind her, brushing section by section, her face free of all expression. Hanalei's former nurse was in her middle years, a short, round woman. She wore a simple white dress with a yellow hibiscus tucked above one ear. "Have you forgotten who her father was?" his aunt continued. "You, of all people? She's practically a criminal herself, Samahti. We have a child in the house."

Oke, her new husband, sat beside her, also dressed in green robes. He patted his wife's knee. "Yes. A traitor's daughter. I must question your judgment on this matter, nephew."

The *nephew* made Sam's nostrils flare. His aunt was nearing forty years of age. Her husband was fifteen years younger, barely older than Sam and Jejomar. A man with delicate features and hair like fine black thread. Even the bare feet he propped on the table, Sam's table, were elegant; the soles looked soft as a baby's cheek.

Sam said, "Hanalei would have stayed in the guest pavilion, which is empty and out of your way. And Jejomar is no longer a child. He is seventeen."

Just then Sam caught a glimpse of a figure slinking past the door holding a fishing pole.

"Jejomar!" Aunt Chesa called out. "Where are you off to, darling?"

The sigh was audible from where Sam stood. Jejomar kept one hand on the doorframe and leaned in. "I have business, Mama. And then fishing. I'll bring back supper." He looked at Sam. Nothing in his expression hinted at their argument only hours before. Sam knew he had not told his mother about the canoe or the cost to replace it. Fine. As long as Jejomar's "business" meant paying the agreed-upon fee, Sam would also stay quiet. And then Jejomar smirked, and in that smirk there was a hint of spite. "Your Hanalei's at the menagerie, Sam. The guards took her there this morning."

"Jejomar!" his stepfather snapped. Jejomar rolled his eyes and hoofed it out of there, and a second later, the front door slammed.

Sam turned disbelieving eyes on his aunt and her husband. "The menagerie?" he echoed. Silence. His aunt fidgeted.

Sam was certain he had heard wrong. "You sent Hanalei to sleep with the animals?"

Oke tipped his head toward his wife, claiming no responsibility. Aunt Chesa said, "Not any animal. With the seadragons. I thought it fitting." When Sam only stared at her, she added, "There are *beds* in the menagerie. Or mats. The animal keepers must sleep somewhere. It's not as if we threw her in a cage. Honestly, Samahti, bringing her to our home was thoughtless. And at so late an hour. I've not been able to sleep since." Behind her, Penina continued to brush his aunt's hair, slowly, thoroughly. But her left eye had begun to twitch.

Sam could not choose his relatives, so instead he counted to ten. And ten more after that. Finally, he said, "She came a long way. Did you give her something to eat at least?"

Silence.

Sleeplessness and outrage did not mix well. "With respect, Auntie, your time here was to have been temporary. Yet three years have come and gone. Mara is married, and Jejomar can move into the bai if he wishes. It's time to make other arrangements. Penina." He looked over his aunt's head at the older woman. "A word, please."

Penina dropped the hair and set the brush on a table.

His aunt looked shocked. "Samahtitamah! You can't just throw us into the street!"

"I'm not. There are pavilions everywhere. I'm sure you'll find another quickly."

Oke surged to his bare baby feet. "But those cost squid!"

"*Oke*," Aunt Chesa said under her breath.

Sam did not bother to hide his dislike. "Most things do. Your silver isn't my business."

Auntie Chesa rose. "All this fuss for that girl. As you wish, she may stay here."

Spoken as though she were doing Sam a favor. He pictured Hanalei on the outrigger. *I have nowhere else to go*, she had said. He could tell the words had cost her. He *hated* that he had sent her here and that she had been turned away.

Sam chose his words carefully. "Hanalei is my guest, and your treatment of her has shamed me. I won't bring her here since her presence disturbs you. You may remove your belongings to your new home without disruption."

"Samahti!" Auntie Chesa collapsed onto the chair. The tears fell. "You're cruel to your auntie! I will go to the queen—" She stopped, seeing Sam's face, swallowing her words.

"This is my mother's home," Sam said. "And it is mine. It does not belong to the queen. But you may do as you wish. Penina?"

Penina followed him out of the chamber and out of the house. They did not speak until they had shut the front doors behind them. Sam snatched up his boots from the row of shoes and slippers lining both sides of the door. He sat on a bench and yanked one on.

Penina said, "I am sorry, Prince Samahti. I did not hear anyone come by last night. If I'd known—"

"I know. Don't worry."

A smile trembled on her lips. "She did not die. My Hanalei. How can I help?"

"She needs a place to stay. An inn somewhere, for now. And my grandmother wishes to speak with her . . . She needs clothes—"

"I'll see to everything."

Voices rose, carried through an open window. Sam suspected Oke would strip the banana leaves off the roof if no one was here to watch him. He handed Penina the pouch at his belt, full of silver squid. "If it's not enough, just use my name."

"You are a *leech*!" Aunt Chesa cried. Her voice carried

through an open window. Oke's response was unintelligible. A door slammed.

Shaking her head, Penina took the pouch and disappeared indoors. Sam went his own way, thinking his uncle Isko had been right. The man was always right.

12

HANALEI WOKE TO THE SOUND OF PIGS SQUEAL-
ing. She sat up in a panic, bleary-eyed and wondering,
Where am I now?

In a tiny chamber, it looked like, barely larger than her
cabin on the *Anemone*. The walls were rough-cut stone.
There were no windows. Light came from a torch set in a
wall bracket. She had woken in a bed wearing a sleeping
tunic that did not belong to her. Sleep faded, and memory
returned.

Hanalei threw aside the covers and ran to the door. Half
expecting it to be bolted, the way it had been on the ship, she
was surprised when it opened easily. She startled Bayani,
who had one hand raised to knock; the other balanced a
tray of food. Liko stood nearby. They were in a great cavernous space that was part of the royal menagerie, where
the seadragons lived. Hundreds of fully grown pigs trotted
past her door, herded along by their keepers. Good. She had
not imagined the squealing. Her mind remained sound.

Liko nudged a snuffling pig away from her boot. "They're for the dragons."

Hanalei could feel them nearby. Fifty beating hearts. She could smell them, even with the pigs so close, their earthiness and filth flooding her nostrils. When she had last visited the menagerie, as a young girl, there had been two seadragons living in the pools beneath the mountains. Adjacent caverns held sharks, octopuses, whales. All the other larger water creatures. The rest of the menagerie was kept nearby. Hanalei took the tray, thanking Bayani, and asked, to be sure, "How many dragons are there?"

"Fifty," Bayani said. "Prince Samahti collects them."

Hanalei did not ask why. She had a feeling she knew. "May I see them?"

"We'll take you," Liko said, her expression serious. "But you can't wear that."

Hanalei looked down at herself. The sleeping tunic left her knees exposed. Her feet were bare. She did not wish to know what her hair looked like. Bayani gazed politely at the wall, but the animal keepers snuck glances as they walked past. Two young girls giggled behind their hands.

"Old Catamara left you clothing," Liko informed Hanalei as she backed into the room, self-consciousness coming too late.

"I'll be fast." Hanalei slammed the door shut.

Sam's aunt Chesa had been unpleasant. After Hanalei

and the guards had parted ways with Sam at the city gates, they had set off for the palace complex, guiding their kandayos along coral-paved streets. Familiar, quiet roads with few people about. They rode past pavilions built on latti stones, and as they drew closer to the royal pavilion, the streets grew wider, the homes larger, the torchlight brighter along the maze of pathways. Hanalei stopped beside one home, on the left. It sat upon twelve latti stones.

A powerful longing filled her, to walk up the steps and open the door. To be scolded by a familiar voice. *Are those sandals I hear, Hanalei? Indoors? Take them off at once.* "Who lives here now?" she asked.

"No one all the time," Liko replied. If she heard the tremble in Hanalei's voice, it did not show in her expression. "It's for important guests. The Salamasinian king is visiting with his niece."

At least it was well cared for. It had not been razed, as she had feared. The bougainvillea flourished, red blooms blanketing the walls, neatly trimmed away from the shutters. A candle flickered in one window, in a chamber she had once called her own.

"There was a woman who lived here," Hanalei said. "Penina. Do you know what happened to her?"

Liko and Bayani exchanged a look. They shook their heads.

Four guards stepped from the shadows of the pavilion, looking their way. A reminder to move on. Not far, though. Sam's pavilion was the next one over.

Liko's knock had summoned a sleepy-eyed servant. They had followed the girl through a slumbering house, tiptoeing down corridors and passing large, airy rooms. The guest pavilion was located out back, a miniature of the main house, set on four latti stones. Liko and Bayani had remained outside. For Hanalei, there had been time for a much-needed bath. The servant had willingly filled a tub with warm water and brought in towels, soap, necessary things. But someone must have informed Sam's aunt of her presence, even in the dead of night.

They were not strangers. Chesa had visited Tamarind City a number of times with her children, staying in this very pavilion. Hanalei, as Princess Oliana's page, had crossed her path often. Mostly she remembered Chesa's complaints, about the servants, the food, her chambers, the softness of her pillow. Everything. *Never again*, Princess Oliana had said every time Chesa departed. But of course there was always another time. Chesa was family, however distant, and with family came duty and obligation.

The older woman had stormed into the room as Hanalei was sitting on a mat drying her hair and yawning. Chesa wore a beautiful green dressing gown. Time had deepened the line between her brows and the grooves beside her lips. Her hair was a sparse gray fluff, like bird down. She had always favored long, elaborate wigs. "You are full of nerve, girl," she said. "Walking right into my house."

Hanalei lowered the towel from her hair. "I was invited."

"Not by me." Chesa planted fists on hips. "Do you feel no shame coming here? After what your family has done?"

Hanalei's face burned. Liko and Bayani watched from the doorway. Behind them stood two burly household guards with menacing expressions. Hanalei did not know them. She caught a glimpse of a boy her age lurking in the hall and realized it was Jejomar. Quietly, she gathered her belongings. Yes. She was ashamed. She should not have come here. To this house, or to this island.

Liko tried, "Prince Samahti wished for her to stay—"

"Of course he did," Chesa snapped. "One pretty face, and the boy loses all judgment. I'll deal with my nephew." She pointed to the door. "Go with these men. They'll find you a suitable bed."

They had done as they were told, slinking out of the house like whipped pups. Hanalei had not realized the depth of the insult until she stood between Liko and Bayani outside the menagerie's massive wooden doors.

Aghast, Bayani said, "She can't stay here."

Liko agreed. "I'll take her to my cousin's. She doesn't live far. You go find Prince Samahti. He—"

"No." By then, Hanalei had been tired to her bones. She did not care what sort of bed she was given, or where. She had slept in worse places. "Thank you, Liko. This will do."

Old Catamara had left her clothing, Liko had said. Hanalei did not remember anyone by that name, from before. But there was a pile of neatly folded clothes on top of a chair. After finishing her breakfast, Hanalei inspected them. It was the plain, simple uniform of an animal keeper. The long cream-colored tunic fit, more or less, as did the dark green trousers. She tied a belt made of braided coconut fibers around her waist. Her leather sandals hung from a wall hook. A brief touch told her they were still damp from seawater. That was when she saw a second pair by the foot of the bed. She slipped them onto her feet and found that they were only a little big. A washstand and pitcher sat on a table, alongside soaps and combs and brushes. She tidied up, pulled a comb through her hair, and finding no ties anywhere, left it undone. She had slept with her satchel beneath her pillow. She pulled the strap over her head, then headed for the door, her mind, as usual, full of seadragons.

Fifty seadragons swam about in a massive pool beneath the mountain. Hanalei watched from a platform built high above, cavernous walls all around. Purple and gold dragons, silver and black. Every shade of blue. Others lingered along the floor. Hanalei could make them out occasionally, in spots where sand and silt had not been churned up. Sunlight filtered down through an opening in the mountain. The cavern was further lit by the millions of ghost crabs skittering up and down the walls. Each crab, the length of a thumb, gave off a milky glow. In this part of the menagerie, torchlight was unnecessary.

Directly across the cavern was another platform where the pigs had been led. As she watched, the keepers shoved the animals off the platform two by two. They went squealing, their cries abruptly cut off when the seadragons lunged from the water, snatching at their morning meal.

Guiltily, Hanalei recalled her own breakfast. Bayani had given her a tray with rice and mango . . . and pig. Roasted, shredded, salted. Delicious. There were footsteps behind her. Thinking it was Liko or Bayani, who had stayed over by the walls, she said, "Poor pigs. What a way to go."

"The dragons won't eat anything else." Sam appeared beside her. He was dressed formally in black. A grand tapa cape swept the ground. The workmanship was as fine as Lord Isko's had been. Sand-colored, with abstract patterns stamped in black, a series of dots and half circles, triangles and long, fluid lines that mimicked the waves. A band of hammered gold sat upon his head, and a lei of green ti leaves hung from his neck. "We've tried goat, chicken, octopus, fish. They're only interested in pig."

"That can't be. Seadragons will eat anything. Especially octopus."

"They did at first. But the keepers started to feed them pig. We have more pig than octopus . . . and now they prefer it."

Hanalei tugged at the sleeve of her tunic. She was most comfortable in trousers. Dresses were costly, constricting, and difficult to keep clean when one traveled as much as she did. She owned one dress, for when trousers would not do, but it had been left behind on Little Kalama, so she supposed she now owned none. She had not thought about the dress until this moment, wearing her borrowed tunic and trousers and standing beside Sam, whose clothing had been made for him alone. He looked splendid. She looked like an animal keeper's apprentice. She glanced sideways, then looked hastily away in case her thoughts showed in her eyes. "You look very . . . royal. Are you meeting someone important?"

Sam nodded. "We have guests. I wear what I'm told, or else." He tugged at the ties to his cloak, silk ribbons around his neck. "Hanalei, I'm sorry about my aunt."

"Don't be sorry. She should be able to say who sleeps under her roof. It's her home."

"It isn't," Sam said with some annoyance. A cough had them turning, and Sam's expression cleared. "Catamara.

This is Lady Hanalei, recently returned home. Hana, Cata-mara cares for the dragons."

Liko had called him Old Catamara. Hanalei could see why. The man standing before them was at least eighty years old. He was dressed as she was. His hair was sparse and gray, his eyebrows wild. A maze of wrinkles lined a narrow face and pointed chin. The slight stoop of his back made it so his head came to Hanalei's shoulder.

Catamara bowed at the waist, carefully. "Young prince. Lady Hanalei."

"I'm just Hanalei." He did not sound like a Tamarindi, or even an islander from the Nominomi. She wondered where he was from. "Keeper Catamara. Thank you for . . ." She indicated her clothing, her sandals.

Catamara inspected her, head to toe. "It fits."

Hanalei smiled. "Very well."

Catamara's eyes dropped to Hanalei's hands. His breath wheezed inward. "Dragonscale?"

"Yes."

"Does it hurt you?"

It had, once. "Not anymore."

Catamara stepped toward her, then stopped. Without another word, he turned and shuffled off. Past Liko and Bayani, through a doorway in the stone.

Hanalei watched him go. "He's new."

"Not so new. He came after you left. Eight . . . nine years

ago? He asked to work at the menagerie. I couldn't tell him no."

"Why not?" Someone Catamara's age should be at home, fussed over by younger relatives, napping in the sun.

"Because he saved my life," Sam said. "When I was ten, my grandmother and I traveled to Salamasina. One morning, I was separated from my guards, over by the harbor. Three dragoners recognized me and thought I would bring them an easy ransom. Fetu couldn't help."

Fetu was like her soundcatcher. Part of Tamarind's magic. He would have been a tattoo and nothing more once they sailed past the boundary rock. "What did Keeper Catamara do?"

"He made them stop, with the help of a machete he kept under his cloak."

Sam smiled at Hanalei's expression. "I was surprised too. He's stronger than he looks, our Cata. After, he brought me back to the palace, my arm broken, both of us covered in blood. We made quite an entrance."

Hanalei was hearing the story years later, and still her heart pounded. "Is that how you got that scar?"

"Yes." His fingertips brushed the scar on his neck, a straight line from earlobe to collarbone. "Grandmother offered him anything he wished, but he asked only to return with us. He has a pavilion near the lagoon. Mostly he sleeps here. He's good with the animals."

She did not like the thought of him injured and alone, saved by chance by a stranger. "Does it happen often? People trying to hurt you?"

"Not often. Sometimes."

A look passed between them, before they turned back to the pigs. There were only a few of them left. Most of the dragons had eaten their fill. They were floating on their backs in the water, fast asleep.

Hanalei said, "You're buying up seadragons."

Sam nodded. "As many as I can. For as long as necessary."

"You're hoping they'll mate." It made sense. She understood the reasoning behind it; she just did not think it would work. Not under these circumstances.

"I . . . Yes." Sam was looking over his shoulder at the guards.

"I think they've heard the word *mate* before," she offered.

"Yes, Hanalei. I'm sure they have."

"Well, that is what you're hoping for, isn't it? *Do* they mate?"

Sam cleared his throat. "They mate plenty. That's not the problem."

"No, the problem is there's no dragonfruit."

Sam was frowning. "Why don't you look surprised? What do you know about seadragon mating rituals that I don't?"

Hanalei peered over the railing, deep in thought. "I've been to the menageries on Salamasina and Raka. Both have male and female dragons. They don't produce dragonfruit either, and I've wondered . . . maybe it has something to do with captivity. Perhaps they can't produce eggs in a place where they're not free."

"*Your* egg came from here," Sam reminded her, pointing. "From *that* captured dragon."

Hanalei had recognized her at once. One of the two original seadragons. A deep purple in color with a white frill. She was off to one side on a ledge, alone. And she had not taken her eyes off Hanalei since she had appeared at the rail.

Hanalei's heart twisted. It was not her the seadragon longed for. "It could have been an anomaly. Something rarer than rare. It's like you said, these dragons mate plenty. We should be seeing dragonfruit."

Sam said, after a moment, "Don't tell me that, Hanalei. Not after all this. My mother . . ." He trailed off, distracted by the purple seadragon. He looked at the dragon, at Hanalei. He went back and forth. "She's watching you."

"I noticed."

"She usually ignores the humans." Sam's frown deepened. "Does she . . . She knows who you are."

"I think so, yes." The purple dragon slipped into the water and swam toward them, lingering beneath their platform, eyes on Hanalei. The other dragons made room for her.

Sam's breath caught as the purple dragon began to sing. "She's never sung before," he murmured. "None of them have."

It was the saddest song Hanalei had ever heard. She brought the soundcatcher to her lips and breathed in, not out, capturing every mournful note. Her eyes filled with tears. When the dragon fell silent, Hanalei lowered the soundcatcher and said, "Sam. There's something I need to tell you."

"Prince Samahti." Liko strode up to them. A young boy was with her, about eight years old, wearing the green uniform of a royal messenger. He was wide-eyed with excitement, nearly bouncing off his feet. "One of the tower guards spotted a dragon by the lagoon. Near Asan Rock. They're bringing it in now."

"Alive?" Sam asked.

At the same time, Hanalei said, "What color is it?" They looked at her. "Blue or green? Do you know? Is it alive?" *Please don't say you've killed a green seadragon. Please.*

The boy piped up. "It's a green seadragon, miss. There's a big stick in its neck. Someone's killed it."

13

THE *BIG STICK* WAS A HARPOON. SAM PULLED HIS
kandayo up sharply and swung off, landing directly in front
of his grandmother. Before them was the lagoon—in the
daylight the water so clear one could see white sand drifting along the seabed. Steep, tree-covered cliffs surrounded
it, except for a narrow passage that led to the Nominomi.
And lying partially on dry land, partially submerged in
the shallows, was a seadragon. Its scales were the bright
green of a fern. Its eyes were shut, jaws wide open, teeth like
knives. A dragoner's harpoon jutted horribly from its neck.

The sight had drawn the curious in large numbers. They
gathered around the corpse—villagers, guards, guests of his
grandmother's. The men in tapa capes. The women in colorful dresses, parasols held high to shield them from the
sun. Uncle Isko was there. So was his cousin Jejomar, along
with friends, their fishing poles lying forgotten on the sand.

His grandmother stood well away from the seadragon
beneath the shade of coconut trees. She wore a red dress

and a white plumeria lei. Her gold crown was similar to his, thin and hammered. She watched Sam dismount, then said, drily, "We won't be sailing this morning after all. No one wishes to go out on the water."

Those with her laughed. It was an illustrious gathering of elders, the mothers and fathers of those down by the shore. Among them the kings and queens of Salamasina and Kalama. The viceroy of Sumay, a territory of faraway Langland. The ambassador of Raka, now a territory of Esperanza. His name was Lord Martin, and he was new to both his ambassadorship and the Nominomi. Sam could tell because he wore heavy black velvet and looked hot and miserable.

Sam bowed, trying not to let his anger show. A dead seadragon was a waste. His grandmother's words had been lightly spoken, but the hard light in her eyes showed Sam his feelings were shared. "I'm sorry to hear it. Grandmother, I'll take care of this," meaning the seadragon.

"There's no need. Others will see to it." His grandmother smiled at the man beside her. King Nakoro of Salamasina was a big man with a neat gray beard. Ti leaves crowned a bald head. He wore pale blue robes and sandals decorated with gray pearls. The king had two sons and one beloved niece, Rosamie, who was over by the seadragon. "His Grace has expressed an interest in visiting the ruins at Piti," she continued. "I've said you will accompany him,

Samahtitamah. And anyone else who wishes, of course."

"It's been twenty years since I last saw those ruins," King Nakoro said. "Remember, Samahti? What a ride we had. It feels like a good day to be in the mountains, and away from the sea."

His grandmother looked at her friend with a slight frown. Sam had not been born twenty years ago. The king must have meant Sam's father, who shared the same name. A simple mistake. "It will be my pleasure, Your Grace."

"I'd like to come too." This came from Lord William, Lord Martin's younger brother. He was close to Sam in age. His hair was straight, fine, and gold. A vicious sunburn peeled the skin from his nose, which held up a pair of spectacles. He was skinny as a broom. Like his brother, his clothing was heavy and dark. But William at least seemed in good spirits. "I have a list of things I'd like to see." William fished around in his vest and pulled out a crumpled bit of parchment. "Though I'm not sure I'll have time for it all. It's quite a long list."

"We'll take a look and see how far we make it," Sam told him. "If we fall short, you're always welcome to return."

William beamed and thanked him. Even his brother's severe expression softened. Sam's grandmother gave him a look of approval before saying, "And you, Ambassador. Will you be joining them?"

Lord Martin had been invited to Tamarind because he

was distantly related to the Esperanzan king. And he had a sister who was young, lovely, and unmarried. She was over by the seadragon. "I thought I might visit one of your pepper farms, Your Grace," he said. "I've heard a great deal about them."

"Certainly." The queen's smile was pleasant, but her eyes were shrewd. Ambassadors always wished to visit the spice farms, and to ask probing questions about production and trade routes. Things they did not need to know. Diplomacy often meant striking a delicate balance, she often told Sam. It meant being welcoming while also giving away nothing. "I will show you there myself . . ." The sound of hooves had her looking beyond Sam. Her smile faded away to nothing.

Hanalei reined in her kandayo, spraying sand everywhere, and jumped down. Sam had told her he would return. He had not expected her to follow. Liko and Bayani had come too, along with the boy messenger and half a dozen animal keepers, including Catamara.

It was the first time in ten years Hanalei had found herself in the presence of Queen Maga'lahi. But she was not looking at the queen. Or kissing her hand. Or saying any of the things that needed to be said in such company. His grandmother's eyes flickered. A warning.

"Hanalei," Sam said under his breath.

Hanalei pointed at the dragon. "She isn't dead."

"What?" Sam spun around. He saw ladies inspecting dragonscale, elders examining claws, children peering inside a wide, gaping mouth. A little girl, no older than four, sat on a man's shoulders. She clutched the seadragon's eyelashes with both hands, trying to lift an eyelid. Sam watched the lid rise, long enough to reveal a milky white orb, before it fell back into place.

His grandmother's voice was sharp. "It looks quite dead, Hanaleiarihi. You are frightening my guests."

"Your Grace, please. Look at her frill. A dragon's frill turns black when it dies. Always. And the change happens instantaneously. Those people . . . we have to get them away from there."

Sam saw his grandmother's doubt and her companions' growing alarm. The dragon's frill was green.

Uneasy, King Nakoro said, "Young lady, what do you know about seadragons?"

Hanalei held out her hands, scars on full display. From his grandmother came the smallest indrawn breath.

Hanalei answered, "Plenty, I promise you. That dragon is alive."

Sam had never seen a dead seadragon. He believed her. He turned on his heel and ran. "Get back," he shouted, waving his arms over his head. "Get away from there!"

And saw that he was too late. The crowd turned his

way, puzzled by the shouting. Uncle Isko spread his arms wide—*What's wrong with you?*—even as the seadragon's eyes slowly opened on their own.

For the rest of his life, Sam would relive this nightmare. The way the seadragon's jaw came down on three children, swallowing them whole. Three child-shaped lumps moved swiftly along its throat, even as a red tongue snaked out. The man with the small girl on his shoulders attempted to flee, but the seadragon's tongue caught the child around the shoulders, dragging her back. She disappeared, wailing, into its mouth. Stunned, the man fell to his knees. Rosamie, also, was gone. Uncle Isko shoved her companions out of the way just as the dragon turned on him. With its tongue, it scooped the lord protector into the air, rolled him tight like a rug, and gulped him down.

"Uncle!" Sam yelled. There were cries behind him and cries before him. Shrieking everywhere. A guard's machete lay abandoned on the sand. Without stopping, Sam scooped it up.

"No!" Hanalei cried out. She was running too, not far behind him. "Don't kill her!"

"Stay back, Hanalei!" Sam snapped.

"Sam, please. Please don't kill her."

The last thing he wished to do was kill a seadragon. Another glance showed Hanalei had stopped, both hands clapped over her mouth. Far behind her, guards dragged what looked to be a massive net down the beach, but they were still some distance away. Sam cursed under his breath and shoved the machete's handle into his belt. He whipped off his cape, waving it over his head and yelling at the top of his lungs. "Seadragon! Hey! Hey! Seadragon!"

The dragon swung toward him with a hiss. The first time Sam realized it had two front legs was when it came fully out of the water, onto the sand, and started toward him. Tentatively at first, before picking up speed. Sam's jaw sagged. *Legs? Since when?*

He turned and ran. Away from the crowds and his grandmother. Away from Hanalei. Giving the guards time to cast their net. He could feel the dragon getting closer, the dreadful *thump slither* beneath his feet. He spotted William racing by with Liko, each clutching a small child. With consternation, he saw his cousin Jejomar running in the opposite direction, toward tree cover. And he felt the hideous, wet flap of a dragon's tongue as it whipped him on the head and sent him flying onto the sand.

Spitting, coughing, Sam rolled over to see that the dragon had stopped mere feet away. It no longer paid any attention to him. Its head had swiveled around, frill flying. Farther along the beach came the sound of dragon-song, low-pitched and sad, a mother mourning her loss.

But there was no other dragon to be seen. The song came from Hanalei, who blew into her soundcatcher. The green seadragon looked at her, head tilting to one side and then the other, puzzled. And it was then that Sam saw the tender flesh beneath its chin, unprotected by scales. Grabbing the machete, he leapt, slicing cleanly. A startled grunt followed, and a long sigh. The seadragon collapsed onto the sand, as dead as his uncle and the children, as dead as all the rest.

14

"HELP ME, SAM! THERE ISN'T MUCH TIME."

Sam knelt on the sand by the seadragon, surrounded by a terrible human keening. The pitch raised every hair on his arms. Hanalei's words were followed by a shove to his shoulder, hard enough to jolt him from his stupor. "Time for what?"

Tears tracked their way down Hanalei's face. She placed a gentle hand on the seadragon's frill. It had turned black, just as she had said. Instantaneously. "Some of them were swallowed whole, and sometimes—" She glanced at his grandmother, who appeared, stricken, by their side. "Your Grace, sometimes there's enough air for them to breathe."

Sam exchanged a shocked glance with his grandmother. He rolled to his feet. "What do you need?"

"Others to help. As many as possible." Hanalei backed away, surveying the dragon from frill to tail. It lay parallel to the shore. A scaled underbelly was exposed, facing the trees. "We have to cut her open. We don't have long."

"You there!" his grandmother addressed guards and weeping relatives alike. "Come here now."

No one thought to disobey her. Her words, so imperiously spoken, drew dozens closer. Even the father whose little girl had been swallowed stumbled over, helped along by Bayani. An ashen-faced King Nakoro came to stand beside his grandmother. Sam could barely look at him. His niece, Rosamie, was in this dragon. William and his brother stood on Sam's left. William's eyes were huge behind his spectacles. Their sister was in this dragon. Hanalei waited until they had formed a half circle around her before she called out, "There's a chance we can save them. Some of them. We need to remove her scales before we can cut her open. This way is fastest."

Her, Sam noted, never *it*. Somehow Hanalei knew this seadragon was a female. He watched as she demonstrated, standing along the seadragon's underside. Each scale was green, about the size of a human hand. There were thousands of them, one overlapping the other. Hanalei reached for a scale that was as high as her shoulders. Gripping the curved bottom of the scale, she swung it to the right in a downward arc, and then to the left. Each move made a sound, like teeth snapping together. And then she plucked it free, revealing the pale gray flesh beneath. "You see?" she said. "Be careful. They're sharp."

"Spread out," Sam instructed when it looked as though everyone would congregate in one spot. Along with Bayani, he herded the group so that they were more evenly spaced along the corpse. Some knelt as they plucked, and others removed scales at chest level. With a grunt, Catamara lowered himself to the sand. He pulled from the very bottom. Sam returned to Hanalei's side.

They're sharp. Sam soon learned the truth of Hanalei's words, wincing as a line of blood bloomed on his palm. It was not just him. Yelps and gasps erupted. His grandmother snatched her hand away from a scale long enough to glare at a bleeding thumb, then returned to her task. Hanalei's hands were a blur as she moved down the length of the seadragon. By the time Sam tossed aside one scale, she had removed ten. And she had not cut herself once.

Suddenly, William cried, "It's moving!"

Not the dragon itself; it was well and truly dead this time. Its belly was moving. Sam could see human forms within, writhing, twisting, knees and fists pushing against the seadragon's flesh.

"Hurry!" Hanalei yanked two scales free. The panic in her voice, along with the sight of the desperate, kicking figures, had everyone working harder, in a frenzy.

The next minutes passed in an agonizing slowness, but the number of scales on the sand grew larger. Curses were uttered, followed by mumbled apologies to the queen, who plucked away with grim intensity. The sun blazed hot on their backs. The air was oppressive, a mingling of heat and damp and wilting plumeria. Sweat trickled down Sam's neck. He paused long enough to toss his crown onto the sand, then shucked his tunic over his head and dropped it on top of the crown. Others followed his example; more tunics littered the sand. A heavily perspiring William removed his velvet cape. He reached over, tugged at the strings of his brother's cape, and let it fall. Ambassador Martin did not stop plucking. His hair was plastered to his head, and his face was the red of a boiled crab shell.

Finally, Hanalei stopped. She turned to the queen and Sam, and said, quietly, "We should move them away."

Sam knew why Hanalei wanted them gone. Blood and gore coated the seadragon's mouth. Some may have been swallowed whole, but not all.

"I'm staying." King Nakoro's eyes were damp, and his hands bloodied. No one argued with him.

"Mai Mai, please." Sam did not want her to see what happened next.

"I will go," his grandmother stated, before raising her voice. "Everyone! Come!" She touched King Nakoro's arm briefly, then marched away from the shore.

"My god, my god, how did this happen?" Ambassador

Martin kept saying, and let his brother pull him away. Half the guards followed, herding the crowds toward a patch of shade beneath the flame trees.

"Hana, what can we do?" Sam asked.

Hanalei picked up the machete Sam had dropped on the sand. "When I cut her open, reach in. Pull out what you can."

"How does she know all of this?" someone wondered.

Hanalei did not swing the machete. Instead she made a shallow incision several feet away from the writhing figures. She deepened the cut with quick sawing motions. What sounded like a great pent-up sigh escaped from the opening, followed by a stench that made Sam think of a thousand dead fish. He fell back a step. Several people vomited onto the sand.

"Grab the edges!" Hanalei continued to saw, sweat beading her forehead. "Pull them out!"

Sam breathed through his mouth and grabbed the top flap of skin. Bayani made a retching sound and grabbed the bottom. They pushed and pulled in opposite directions, straining. Out popped a foot. Bare, and coated in a thick purple substance that looked like ube.

Sam grabbed hold of the foot. It froze at his touch, then started to kick, desperately. Trying to avoid a blow to his face, Sam reached in with his other hand, feeling his way around dense innards, until he grasped what felt like another slippery foot. He yanked, falling backward onto the sand and pulling a body with him.

Sam rolled to his knees. It was Rosamie. Eyes wide open, drenched in purple, and coughing violently. Sam pounded her on the back.

"Rosa!" King Nakoro grabbed hold of his niece, knocking Sam out of the way.

Sam turned back to the dragon. Bayani had reached so far inside its guts that his cheek was smashed up against its skin. A second later he stumbled back, followed by a small girl. She was alive but silent, her cheeks bulging. Sam reached down and, with two fingers, cleared purple clumps from her mouth. Coughing followed, and a glad cry rose from the direction of the flame trees. The others still searched. Sam joined them, reaching in with both hands, feeling around. Sweat poured from him. Where was his uncle?

"Careful!" Hanalei warned suddenly.

The split in the dragon widened on its own, and in a sea of terrible smells and thick purple liquid came the rest of its victims, spewing onto the sand. The torrent sent Sam sprawling onto his side and landing hard on one shoulder. He staggered to his feet. Catamara pounded on backs and cleared throats and noses. Sam started to do the same, but a hand reached out of the mass and closed around his ankle.

It belonged to someone trapped beneath two others. Someone who wore a thick gold band on a middle finger. The image of a shark was carved upon it. Seeing the ring, recognizing it, Sam grabbed the hand, then the arm, and pulled his uncle free.

HANALEI HUDDLED BY THE SEADRAGON, IN A crook formed between head and neck, and buried her face in its frill. She could not help the tears from falling. Angry, frustrated, guilty tears. They kept dying. Everywhere she turned, they were dying. Like this dragon here. A beautiful creature lying dead on the sand, gutted like a common fish.

What had happened to the dragonfruit? Just before her death, the seadragon's frill had been her original green. Not pink or rose. Not the color of the heart flower. It meant her eggs had been laid sometime between Hanalei's last sighting of her and this morning. But where were they? With her companion? The blue seadragon? Or had Captain Bragadin managed to get his hands on them without her help? Three eggs with such a man. Hanalei could not bear to think of it.

On the other side of the seadragon came the sound of weeping. Her mind shied away from the horrors that lay close by. She had fled to this crook as soon as the dragon had split open, not able to witness who had lived and who had not. Especially the little ones. She had done what she could.

"Hanalei."

A shadow came over the crook. She lifted her head to find Sam standing before her. He had lost his crown, his cape, and his shirt. Muscles rippled along his arms and chest. Tattooed on the left side of his torso was Fetu. Fast asleep, his wings over his eyes to shield them from the sun. Fetu never stirred before dusk, not for anything. The same purple juices that had ruined her sandals and stained her satchel had soaked Sam's trousers. It spiked his hair. He smelled worse than she did, like a fish hatchery that had never been cleaned, and she remembered he had fallen into the muck. But his face, chest, and arms were no longer purple, courtesy of the now filthy cloth in his hands.

Sam crouched before her. There were cuts and scrapes on his hands. "I thought you'd gone."

"Where would I go?" Hanalei swiped at her tears. "I'm always crying in front of you. I'm *not* a crier, I promise."

"Cry all you want. No one will blame you."

"Did you see . . . Did you find the children?" Hanalei lowered her head to her knees, bracing herself.

"Yes. They're safe. They're with their families."

Hanalei's head snapped up. "All of them?"

"All."

She could have sworn she had seen . . . "What about the others? How many did you lose?"

Sam looked surprised, then understanding dawned. "No one, Hana. Everyone's fine."

That was not possible. "There's blood everywhere, Sam. Someone is dead."

Sam eyed the blood dripping from the seadragon's jaw. "Probably Uncle Isko's. He cut his leg badly, but there's a healer with him now. She says he'll mend." Sam moved aside so that she could see.

Tamarind's lord protector was some distance away, sitting on the sand. White bandaging had been wrapped around his right leg. He kept his head lowered as Bayani poured a bucket of water over him, washing away the last of the seadragon's innards. When Lord Isko turned his head in their direction, Hanalei looked away.

Near Lord Isko was a young woman resting against the trunk of a coconut tree. She was wrapped in a blanket and was being fussed over by an older man with a beard. The one who had asked Hanalei earlier what she knew about seadragons. With a start, she realized she knew who he was. She had seen him at a distance on his home island a year ago. King Nakoro of Salamasina.

Hanalei said, "There was a woman in a green dress. I saw the dragon's teeth . . . Have you found her?"

Sam regarded Hanalei, frowning, then rose and stepped

from the crook. "Hello," he said to someone she could not see. "Will you step here for a moment?"

"Yes, Prince Samahti."

A woman came into view. She wore a green dress, the entire front of it drenched in blood. But the woman herself appeared well, smiling even.

Astonished, Hanalei rose. She leaned against the seadragon for support. "You're not hurt?"

The woman looked down at herself in wonder. "It looks like I should be, doesn't it? But I am not. It isn't my blood."

"Probably Lord Isko's," Sam said again.

"Yes, I think so too," the woman said. "The gods must be watching over us today. I cannot believe no one was killed." A man came by and placed a blanket over her shoulders. He told her the cart was ready to take them home. The woman offered Hanalei and Sam one last smile and allowed herself to be led away.

Hanalei watched her go. Her mind was playing tricks on her. "If no one died, who's crying?"

Sam cocked his head, listening. "Those are happy tears." He reached out and touched the seadragon's frill. "Could we have rescued everyone without killing it?"

"No." Hanalei had begged him not to harm the seadragon, and she could see her death weighed on him. "They would have suffocated. And she wouldn't have survived much longer, not with that in her." The harpoon had not yet been pulled free. It jutted horribly from the seadragon's neck. "I'm sorry I asked it of you." He had nearly died waving around that useless cape, instead of defending himself properly, or running away. If he had died, it would have been her fault.

"I'm sorry too." Sam came close enough to touch the soundcatcher that hung from her neck. The space between them was small, and his shirt was long lost. Hanalei did not know where to look. She settled upon Fetu, on Sam's arm, peeking at her through his wings. "Hana. I have a thousand questions."

"As do I." Queen Maga'lahi rounded the seadragon's head and came into view. Sam and Hanalei sprang apart. They looked at each other, and looked away. With a cough, Sam stepped aside so that Hanalei could stand before the queen.

Hanalei had not, in fact, forgotten protocol. Far from it. In all of her dreams of returning home, of seeing her queen again, she had never imagined a circumstance like this one. Her heart beat faster as she held out a hand in silent question. When Queen Maga'lahi offered her own, Hanalei took it gently, mindful of her injuries; both hands were wrapped to protect her cuts. Hanalei bent low, her forehead hovering over the queen's bandaging. And she stayed that way for a good ten seconds until a twitch of the hand signaled permission to rise.

Queen Maga'lahi's expression was unreadable. "Isko said you favored your mother. But I see much of your father in you. You wear his face."

Hanalei spoke in a rush. "I'm sorry, Your Grace. For what we did. I wish that we had not."

"We?" Queen Maga'lahi's eyebrows climbed. "Why do you assume any blame? You were a child. Your father a man fully grown."

"He took the dragonfruit because of me. I should not be here, standing here. I wish—"

"My daughter would not wish it," Queen Maga'lahi said. "I should never have wished it. Samahti?"

"Yes, Mai Mai."

"How many people were saved from this dragon?"

Sam's eyes were on Hanalei. "Twenty-seven."

Hanalei felt her throat constrict at the number. She had not realized it was so many.

"Twenty-seven lives spared," Queen Maga'lahi repeated. "Because of you, Hanaleiarihi. So do not apologize for your place in this world. We are where the gods wish us to be."

"Yes, Your Grace." Hanalei could see Lord Isko being helped into a carriage. Two golden-haired men were with him. They looked like Esperanzans.

"Now," Queen Maga'lahi said, her words turning brisk. "How do you know this creature is female?"

Where to start? The very beginning would take too long.

But perhaps she did not need to go back so far. "For the last six months, I've been following a pod of seadragons across the Nominomi. Five seadragons, along the old waterways."

Sam and the queen exchanged a look. "Why?" Sam asked.

"Why do you keep fifty dragons in the menagerie?" Queen Maga'lahi asked him. "For the same purpose, I think."

For Princess Olli? Hanalei considered the queen's words. Maybe, deep down, Hanalei had been searching for dragonfruit all along. But there was another reason. "They are my livelihood," she explained. "There's a school on Raka that specializes in the Nominomi. Everything under the sea is studied, written about, lectured on. They write many books."

"I've heard of this school," Sam said.

"As have I," Queen Maga'lahi said. "You were a pupil?"

"Not at first," Hanalei said. "I cleaned the dragon cages. I started when I was fourteen, after I left Captain Bragadin's. Eventually, the teachers discovered I could speak and write other languages, and they taught me how to do more than clean cages." She placed a hand on the dragon. Its flesh had started to cool. "They are not mindless predators. No more so than we are. I will challenge anyone who claims they are. I have seen distinct family relationships, distinct hierarchies. And I have so much to learn still. Studying their physical characteristics alone will take a lifetime."

"Physical characteristics." Sam looked down, at toes and claws. "Such as how some seadragons have feet."

"Yes," Hanalei said. "My teachers are elderly now, some very frail. I began to travel on their behalf. I am paid for the observations and illustrations I send back to Raka. I'm so sorry," she added, seeing their expressions. "I can be very long-winded on the topic. I've been known to put others to sleep."

"It is not boredom we feel," Queen Maga'lahi said. "Or disinterest. Far from it."

"How did you know she's female, Hana?" Sam asked her. "You knew it before you got off your kandayo. Usually, Catamara has to wait until they're dosed with poppy before he can rummage around down there and see. He can't tell just by looking at them."

"These teachers," Queen Maga'lahi said, "they know male and female dragons at a glance?"

"They don't." Hanalei took a deep breath. "Ten days ago, I followed the dragons to Little Kalama. To a grotto there. Captain Bragadin was also following them. He killed three of the dragons, and captured me when I tried to warn them. Two escaped."

"A green one and a blue one," Sam said.

"Yes," Hanalei said. "But before they escaped, this dragon's frill changed color. It turned pink."

It hurt to look at them. To see, first confusion, and then a desperate hope.

"Dragonfruit?" Queen Maga'lahi said, and her voice was no longer steady.

Sam paled. "She wasn't . . . I didn't see any pink."

"The eggs aren't with her anymore," Hanalei said. "They've been laid, very recently. I don't know where."

"Could this captain have them?" Queen Maga'lahi asked.

"Yes." Hanalei pointed at the harpoon. The letter *B* was intricately carved on the handle. "This is his. Captain Bragadin has his initials carved onto all of his weapons."

Sam took a closer look, eyes narrowing. "Of course he does."

"The captain would never have harmed her if she still carried the eggs." Hanalei knew firsthand the pains Captain Bragadin had taken to keep this seadragon from harm. At least while she could be of use to him. "But he could have followed her here to a nest, waited until the eggs were laid, shot her with a harpoon, then run off with the dragonfruit."

"We have guards, Hanalei," Sam said with skepticism. "An Esperanzan dragoner does not get to just sail in and hunt dragons on our island. We would have seen."

"Yes, there's that." Hanalei thought through the possibilities and came up with nothing. She was at a loss.

Queen Maga'lahi asked, "Is it possible this captain does not have the eggs?"

"Very possible, Your Grace," Hanalei said. "Because of the other dragon. Where is he? The male is supposed to protect the eggs once they are laid. It is his one task. At least that is what I have read. Perhaps he is keeping them safe somewhere."

"Where do seadragons nest?" Queen Maga'lahi wondered. "Underwater?"

"Sometimes," Hanalei said. "Or in caves. If an island is deserted, it could build a nest out in the open. Right on the sand."

"You're saying they could be anywhere . . ." Sam stopped in consternation. He was looking up, and someone on top of the seadragon was looking down. The face quickly disappeared. Sam backed out of the crook. "Unbelievable," he said.

Hanalei and Queen Maga'lahi followed. Immediately surrounding the dragon were at least twenty others. Guests and locals, most of the guards. Catamara was on top of the dragon with the menagerie's apprentices. Even King Nakoro was there by the tail, looking sheepish.

Queen Maga'lahi wore a dire expression. "How much did you hear?"

"All of it," Catamara said. The others fidgeted, looking everywhere but at her.

"Quite a bit," King Nakoro confessed. "In my defense, I came over merely to convey my gratitude to the young lady"—here he smiled at Hanalei, who smiled back—"when I was drawn in by this remarkable tale. Dragonfruit, you say! After all this time. Where do we even begin to look?"

"What is this *we*, Nako?" Queen Maga'lahi asked.

Sam pointed across the lagoon. "We could start there."

Hanalei raised her hand to shield her eyes from the sun. Coconut trees lined the opposite shore, tall and graceful. But off to one side the trees were jagged and broken, some snapped in half, leaves drooping in the shallows or on the sand. It looked like something large had passed through carelessly, leaving destruction in its wake.

Hanalei looked quickly at Sam, who said, "The typhoon brought down trees all over the lagoon, but we cleared them out." He looked to Liko for confirmation.

"We finished yesterday," Liko said. "That is new."

"There's a cave over there," Hanalei said suddenly. She and Sam had explored it endlessly as children.

"A big one," Sam said. "Large enough for a seadragon to build a nest. And a short walk from the water, if it has feet."

16

SAM LED THE WAY AROUND THE LAGOON. SOME-
one had found him a clean tunic, though his hair remained
spiked and foul-smelling. Hanalei and the queen rode with
him, along with twenty guards on swift kandayos. Most
carried spears, which were good for throwing when one
preferred to keep one's distance. A good practice with seadragons. They also carried darts so heavily laced with poppy
that one would instantly knock a dragon out. For an hour,
hopefully. Two hours if luck and the gods were with them.
Hanalei had heard Sam give the orders: the darts were to be
used first, the spears only if they had no other choice.

The path they followed was narrow, the coconut trees
dense, the ground beneath a mixture of red clay and fine
sand. When the cave came into view, they pulled their kandayos up short. Someone whistled.

A very large creature had been here. To their left was a
cave opening. From there a path of churned-up dirt and
broken trees led straight to the shores of the lagoon, visible

in the distance. Hanalei swung off her kandayo and headed for the cave.

"Wait, Hana," Sam cautioned.

"Stay where you are, Hanaleiarihi," Queen Maga'lahi ordered. "We don't know what that cave holds."

Hanalei spoke without thinking. "The cave is empty, Your Grace. The dragon is gone."

"How do you know this?" Queen Maga'lahi asked.

On Sam's face was the look he had given her back in the menagerie, when the purple seadragon had watched her every move. *She's watching you. She knows who you are.*

"It is just a feeling."

Queen Maga'lahi looked from Hanalei to the cave. But she only said, "Let us be sure. Viti?"

A small black spider appeared on her neck, as a tattoo, before hopping onto her shoulder. Queen Maga'lahi smiled. "A little help, please, my dear."

The spider crawled swiftly down to the hem of her red dress and dropped onto the dirt. The closer Viti drew to the cave, the bigger she became, so that by the time she disappeared into the dark, she was the size of a lobster.

Queen Maga'lahi walked toward the cave. The guards followed. Hanalei and Sam hung back, out of earshot.

"She's still terrifying," Hanalei said.

Sam's lips curved. "The queen?"

"The spider."

"You shouldn't have tried to catch her with that jar. She's not a firefly, Hanalei."

It was Hanalei's turn to smile. "I was seven."

"Spiders have long memories. Like bats. Fetu," Sam added, tapping his chest. "Wake up. We're going into a cave." An instant later, he grimaced.

"Are you bleeding?" Hanalei guessed Fetu's response had been a scratch, or a bite. He never liked having his sleep disturbed.

Sam pulled at his collar to inspect. "No," he said sourly.

Hanalei turned back to the cave and tried not to smile.

"How often do you sense these dragons? All the time?"

No. She knew only that both dragons had been here and both dragons had gone. "Only sometimes."

Sam glanced at her satchel, which she had not removed once, not even when cutting open the seadragon. It was covered with purple splotches. "Will you let me read your father's papers?"

Hanalei nodded. "You need to read them."

Viti appeared at the cave opening, growing smaller as she scuttled her way across the dirt. Queen Maga'lahi waited until she had returned to her shoulder before saying, "It's safe. Come along."

Half the guards stayed behind to keep watch by the cave entrance. The rest followed Queen Maga'lahi with torches.

Hanalei and Sam entered last. The ground was covered with rocks and pebbles that poked through her borrowed sandals. The queen's sandals were even more delicate. Hanalei watched her stumble slightly over a stone. Sam lengthened his steps, passing the guards. When he reached his grandmother, he held out an arm. "Take my arm, Mai Mai."

"You smell terrible, Samahti."

Unoffended, Sam kept his arm extended. "I've smelled worse."

Hanalei saw the wry expression on the queen's profile before she took Sam's arm. Their affection for one another was as bright as the torches that lit their surroundings. Brighter maybe, because the queen was, by necessity, both mother and grandmother. Hanalei looked away, thinking of her own mother, who had died too young to leave behind a memory for her only child, having succumbed to malaria before Hanalei had taken her first steps. And thinking of her papa, who, for a time, had been the center of her world.

"Your father paid for the month," the innkeeper on Raka had told her, standing in the doorway. A neat, aproned woman, she had been kind and cheerful, right up until the day Hanalei's father had been found in the harbor, his body broken, his purse missing. "The month is over."

Hanalei had clutched a blanket around her shoulders. She was recovering more and more each day from the effects of the poison, though she still tired easily. Her legs were getting stronger. Her arms and lungs too. As for her heart, it would never recover. It was broken. She said quietly, "I don't have any squid." She had looked, searching every crack and crevice in the room. If there had been any silver or gold squid, her father must have taken it with him.

"You don't look poor, girl." The innkeeper eyed Hanalei's dress. Crisp cotton with a tapa overlay. Embroidery along the hems. Penina had made it for her. "Don't you have other family?"

"Just my father."

"What about that ring?"

Hanalei stepped back, drawing the gold seashell ring beneath her blanket. It had been a gift from Princess Olli. The innkeeper said, "Do you want the ring, or do you want to eat?"

Hanalei needed to eat. She looked at the floor. "How much will you give me for it?"

"Two days more. And an extra half day for each dress like that one. After that, I can't help you."

Hanalei slipped the ring from her finger and held it out. "I accept. Thank you."

The innkeeper took the ring. If Hanalei thought she saw sympathy flicker, it was only a flicker. "You have small hands," she commented. "If you need work, there's a man at the harbor who hires children. The work's bad, but he'll feed you. Give you a roof to sleep under." She shoved the ring onto her little finger. "His name is Bragadin."

"Hanalei."

Sam's voice brought her back to the present. They had all stopped and turned to look her way. She had nearly walked into Bayani, who reached out to steady her. How long had her memories distracted her? Sam wore a slight frown, but all he said was, "Which way, do you think?"

The cave branched off in three directions. The passage-ways were massive. A seadragon would be able to come and go freely. Hanalei walked past the group, eyeing each diverging path. She sniffed the air. "Do you smell it?"

"Dead fish?" Bayani asked after a moment.

"That is just my grandson, I think," Queen Maga'lahi remarked.

"Seaweed." Smiling, Hanalei pointed to the path on the right, where the smell was strongest. "This way."

The farther they walked, the stronger the tang of wet, pungent seaweed. The torches cast a light on ancient cave paintings covering the walls. The fruit bat turned up often, along with the tree snake, the coconut crab, the proud kingfisher. Human figures stood near pavilions built upon latti stones. Hanalei lost count of the number of canoes she walked by. Proas, na druas, camakaus, others she could not name. After a time, the passageway opened into a cavern. And in the center of the cavern was a giant nest. It had been built in a shallow sandpit, twenty feet all around, and made from spongy piles of seaweed.

Hanalei ran to the edge of the nest and looked down. *Oh no.* She had expected to find it empty. This was worse. She slid down into the nest, where a solitary seadragon egg lay on its side, cracked wide open. The shell was a deep rose in color. Most of the yolk had been soaked up by seaweed. All that remained was liquid pooled at the bottom of the shell, thick and purple like boiled ube. There was no sign of a baby seadragon.

Sam crouched beside her, tense. "Did it hatch?"

"It's too early for a hatching. I think someone threw a rock at it." Hanalei toed a large stone resting between the half shells. She felt something crawl up her leg and controlled a shriek just in time. A banana spider appeared on her shoulder, all of her eyes on the broken pieces of shell. *Viti.*

Queen Maga'lahi remained at the ledge, looking down. Anger coated her every word. "Threw a stone . . . and then what? Where is it?"

Hanalei said, "A seadragon is small when it hatches, Your Grace. Only a few feet. It could have been carried off. It would have been a simple thing."

The guards were quiet along the rim, torches raised, heads turning one way, then the other, depending on who spoke.

Sam broke off a piece of shell and crushed it in his hand. "What about the other two?"

In every version of the tale Hanalei had heard, a seadragon laid three eggs. Never one more nor one less. But she did not know if that was true. "If there are others, they could have been taken by the same person. Or they could be with the other dragon . . . their father."

Queen Maga'lahi said, "Would it return? This other dragon? To this nest?"

Hanalei thought about it. "I think he will try to find another safe place. The lagoon won't feel safe anymore. He would be able to smell his companion's blood on the shore. And he would be able to smell us in this cave."

"Another safe place," Sam repeated. "On Tamarind?"

"I don't know, Sam. I'm sorry. I would be guessing."

"These are more than guesses, Hanaleiarihi," Queen Maga'lahi said. "You have been studying these creatures. Where would you look next? Where would you go?"

"West," Hanalei said without hesitation. "I would ride along the coast. A westward pattern has been one of their few consistencies."

"Ride, not sail?" Sam asked.

Hanalei tried not to look at Viti, whose stare was unnerving. "You might have to sail eventually, but I would stay out of the water if I could. It's safest. You would be looking for an isolated beach. Or a cave like this one. Caves near the water."

"West along the coast," Queen Maga'lahi said. "Then that is what you'll do. You and Samahti. You leave tomorrow."

17

THEY SEARCHED THE CAVE, EVERY CORNER OF every passageway. Under every rock. Viti helped, but nothing was found of a newly hatched seadragon or the person who might have taken it. The ride back to the opposite shore was made in silence.

And then, two fires.

Hanalei saw the flames through the trees. When they returned to the beach, it was to find a torch had been put to the dragon. She burned brightly along the shore as onlookers watched from a safe distance. For Hanalei, the smell was familiar and sickening.

Keeper Catamara stood off to one side, berated by a young man wearing official-looking tapa robes. The official shook an accusatory finger in front of Catamara's nose and flung his arms about in a full temper. He broke off when Queen Maga'lahi and everyone else drew up on their kandayos. Both Catamara and the official bowed.

"What has happened?" Queen Maga'lahi turned away

from the flames to regard the two men. "Why are you shouting?"

The official bowed again and said, hurriedly, "Forgive me, Your Grace. But this man has just set fire to an enormous amount of gold squid." He pointed to the dragon. "Enormous! I brought workers to collect the scales and remove the fat for oil. He has ruined everything."

"You said burn it," Catamara muttered.

"I said *don't* burn it. Do. Not. Burn. It. I was quite clear."

Catamara hunched his shoulders. "My ears. They don't hear, sometimes." The animal keeper looked so frail and pitiful that the official suddenly found himself the target of many outraged stares.

Sam directed curt words his way. "Keeper Catamara sees to the animals in the menagerie, in death and in life." He glanced at the flames, looking away quickly when the frill caught fire. "Whether she was burned or not was his decision to make."

She, Hanalei heard. No longer *it*.

Queen Maga'lahi looked down her nose at the official. "How old are you, child?"

"I . . . twenty years, Your Grace."

"Twenty. And whom do you suppose you speak to in such a way? In that tone, with those words? Surely not an elder?"

Beside Hanalei, Sam sighed.

The official's mouth opened. The tips of his ears burned. He turned to Catamara and bowed. "I did not mean to speak with such disrespect, Keeper Catamara. My deepest apologies."

Catamara cupped a hand to one ear. "Eh?"

The official's nostrils flared. "I said, *my deepest apologies!*"

Catamara's expression cleared. "Ah. Fine."

Both men were dismissed. Catamara returned to the seadragon. The official marched off to address a group of people standing beside large wooden barrels.

"Samahti, stay until it's done," Queen Maga'lahi said. "One of us should be here."

"I will."

Queen Maga'lahi looked over at Hanalei. "Return with Samahti. You'll stay in my pavilion for the time being."

"Thank you, Your Grace."

The queen departed soon after, and most of the guards went with her. Liko and Bayani joined the onlookers.

Sam dismounted. It was just the two of them now. "You don't have to come with us. Tomorrow, I mean."

Hanalei dropped lightly onto the sand. "It sounds like I do."

Sam kept his eyes on the fire, away from her. "A life here comes with expectations, Hanalei. I won't stop you if you wish to go. You are used to your freedom."

Freedom had its own price, like loneliness. She tucked her hurt away, out of sight. "Do you want me to go?"

"It's the last thing I want." Sam ran a hand along his kandayo's mane, thick, twisting strands the color of jade. "Two men showed up the other day, trying to sell me a fake dragon egg. They were traders."

"What?" Indignation washed over her. "How?"

"They bought a rattler egg on Masina and had it painted." Sam worked through a knot in the mane, his fingers gentle. "It looked real. Then I saw the spots." A faint smile appeared. "A very wise eight-year-old told me once that the shell of a dragonfruit is flawless. Without blemish.."

Hanalei had told him. Long ago, prattling on about seadragons. He had remembered. "Does this happen often? People trying to trick you?"

"Oh yes," he said. "I've met Captain Bragadin. He sold me a pair of seadragons last year. When I bought them, they looked healthy. Their color was good. But the day after he sailed off, their scales turned gray. And they couldn't stop coughing. We keep them separated, in case whatever ails them passes to the others."

"Those dragons are old," Hanalei explained. Captain Bragadin. That charlatan. What crime hadn't he committed? "Well past being able to produce dragonfruit. He must have given them some sort of tonic so that they looked healthy. At least long enough for him to sell them to you."

"So they're not a danger to the others?"

"No."

A vein ticked along Sam's temple. He looked to the water's edge, where the onlookers were strangely quiet for so large a crowd. In their silence, dragon flesh smoked and bones splintered, crumbling along the shore. "I did not intend to kill anything today," he said.

Hanalei placed her hand on the kandayo's mane, beside Sam's. "You'll be lord protector one day, after Lord Isko."

Sam nodded. It had been decided long ago, and it had never been a secret.

"Twenty-seven people are alive because of what you did here, Samahtitamah. It was not just me."

Their fingers did not touch, but she felt some of his tension ease. It was all she could do.

"Hanalei," he said. "The woman with the green dress. What did you see?"

"The dragon bit her. In half. I did not imagine it." When Sam did not respond, "Maybe what she said is true. Maybe the gods are watching over us . . . What?" Her hand slipped away. Why was he smiling?

"One moment you're talking about seadragon mating rituals, sounding very scientific. And the next, you're telling me the gods are watching over us. They are opposites, Hanalei. Which do you believe?"

She had never considered such a question. "I understand science," she said after a moment. "There are rules. But I was born in the Nominomi, just like you. I believe in both."

"Prince Samahti."

A guard approached, asking for a word, and their discussion on science and faith came to an end. "I'll be back," Sam told Hanalei, and the two men went off, deep in discussion about the state of some nearby guard towers.

Hanalei tied both their kandayos to a tree. Sam reminded her of a child's top, spinning in every direction. So much for him to do. Their earliest childhood had been defined by freedom, their only responsibility to keep out of the way and return in time for supper. She wondered when he slept. She was still wondering as she walked down to the shore to stand beside Catamara, who stood closest of all to the dragon.

They watched her burn. Neither speaking. There were tears on the old man's cheeks, and Hanalei thought that here was someone who mourned as she did. Grieved for the dragon as a dragon, and not for what the dragon could give. When Catamara bowed, Hanalei bowed. And she spoke words that were nearly lost among the sound of crackling dragonscale:

May Taga find your spirit and guide you home
to the sea beyond.
In clear water
where danger will never catch you.
Among the coral and caves
where the bounty is full.
Alongside your ancestors
and their ancestors
that loneliness never hold you.
His kingdom your own—

"Beloved child of the gods," Catamara finished.

Hanalei looked at him, disbelieving. The prayer had been drawn from another, words added and removed to honor dragons, not men. But the last line had been Hanalei's own entirely. Uttered for the first time on a dragoner near Little Kalama. Catamara could not have known it.

They regarded one another for some time. Until Hanalei repeated, "Beloved child of the gods."

She did not ask. Later, she told herself. When this day was long past and he did not have tears in his eyes. Then she would ask.

Only after the seadragon had burned to a great pile of bone and ash did Hanalei walk away. The sun had begun its descent, and the crowd had largely gone. Sam stood by the kandayos, speaking to someone. An older woman sitting on a large rock, hands on her knees, waiting patiently. Hanalei stopped.

Penina had been her nurse from her earliest years. Penina had fed her, clothed her, scolded her, loved her. And she had been left behind when Hanalei and her father had gone. Penina rose and waved with both hands, face wreathed in a smile. Hanalei's lower lip trembled, and a moment later she was running.

Penina had found room for Hanalei at an inn, with Sam's silver squid, but with the queen's offer, it was no longer needed. They found themselves in one of the larger chambers of the royal pavilion. Hanalei sat neck deep in a bath. Penina perched on a nearby stool. On her lap was a basket full of hibiscus and plumeria blooms. Red hibiscus, white plumeria. She busied herself plucking petals and tossing them one by one into the bathwater.

"Did you know, Penina?"

"Yes." Penina understood Hanalei's question, had known of her father's plan to steal the dragonfruit. "I had a cousin who had a canoe. He always needed silver, this cousin. So he took you, your papa, and the giant pink egg far away. And he asked no questions."

Not only had Penina known about the theft of the

dragonfruit; she had helped. "Why would you take such a risk?"

Penina tossed a petal at Hanalei's nose. "What risk did I take?"

"Penina."

"There was no risk. Only choices. Help my girl, or don't help my girl. It was simple."

Hanalei took Penina's hand and pressed it to her cheek, then let go. "What are you doing with all these flowers? I don't need so many."

Penina's expression turned stubborn. "I'll give you flowers if I wish. I have missed ten birthdays."

"Only nine . . ." Hanalei trailed off, realizing Penina was right. She had turned eighteen ten days ago. The same day she had discovered the seadragons, in the grotto, on Little Kalama.

"Hanaleiarihi. Did you forget your own birthday?"

Hanalei nodded. There had been no reason to remember.

Penina's eyes turned bright. She tipped the entire basket over the tub. The flowers tumbled into the water, red hibiscus and white plumeria, making Hanalei laugh.

Penina had brought clothing. Not an animal keeper's tunic or a dragoner's stark black uniform. She brought dresses. She brought skirts and pretty blouses. Delicate sandals and embroidered nightgowns. Clothing Hanalei had once taken for granted. Tonight, she wore a white lace blouse that revealed her shoulders and collarbone. Her skirt was a cheerful yellow, as bright as a ripe banana, and her hair had been brushed loose. Around her neck was a single strand of plumeria. It was as they shared a meal that Penina returned to their earlier conversation.

"The day you left, I was afraid," Penina said. "So many things went badly."

"What sort of things?"

"Lady Rona, for one." Penina poured coconut milk over a bowl of diced breadfruit. "She overheard us and threatened to go to the queen. Your father begged her to keep his secret."

Hanalei remembered that conversation. They had not guarded their words near a sleeping child. *She will kill you if she finds you, Arihi. You can never come home.*

"Then we learned there were four soldiers guarding the egg," Penina said. "Not two like we thought. Your papa came away limping and bloodied, but with the dragonfruit." She set the pitcher aside and reached for her spoon. "And my cousin was late with the canoe. He went to the wrong cave. We waited for two hours behind a rock, and you were speaking in your sleep, in your papa's arms. There was no way to quiet you. I thought Lord Isko would find us.

Surely, I thought, this was the end."

Hanalei's supper remained untouched. How desperate her father must have been, how determined. "Did Lord Isko know you helped us?"

Penina swallowed before she spoke. "I think so. When you left, they took away our pavilion. I was sent to work in the prison kitchens. I didn't have to sleep there, but it was no fun, hm?"

That mean, vindictive man. She should have left him in the dragon. "I am so sorry."

"Me too," Penina said. "But your prince, he tours the prison five, six years ago, and he sees me. He says, 'Why, you are Hanalei's Penina,' and brings me to his home." She pointed her spoon at Hanalei. "Eat."

Alongside the breadfruit were roasted vegetables and white rice. And a whole fish, fried and crisp, laid out on a platter.

Hanalei picked at her supper, saying absently, "Sam isn't my prince."

"Not for long," Penina agreed. "Twenty young ladies in and out of this pavilion. He'll be one of theirs soon."

Hanalei stopped picking. "Twenty?"

"All with good skin," Penina remarked. "The queen is getting older, my girl. Princess Oliana still sleeps, and Prince Samahti—"

"Needs daughters." *Or his mother well again.* Hanalei set her spoon down, her appetite lost.

She had noticed the visitors, at the shore and throughout the pavilion. She had not thought anything of it. The queen's home had always been filled with guests. It was strange to think of Sam marrying. Strange and unpleasant. "Does Lady Rona still live in the city?"

"No. A tidal wave killed her."

Penina's revelation came so matter-of-factly, it took a second for the words to sink in. Hanalei gaped. "When?"

"Nine years ago. During a typhoon. It was a bad one."

"What about— Where is your cousin?"

A shadow came over Penina's face. "He did not come home from Raka. No word, no canoe. Nothing."

Her father, Lady Rona, Penina's cousin. Three deaths, all tied to the sea. "Penina, do you think—"

"Yes." Penina set aside her spoon. "I think the seadragons belong to Taga, who is one of the meaner gods. And I think that when we take what belongs to the gods, they want something in return. They are not so different from us that way. Who knows what became of that captain."

"What captain?"

"Erromondo. He was part of Princess Oliana's guard. Do you remember?"

"Yes." Of course she did. Captain Erro had guarded them

on the last journey across the archipelago. He had been a particular favorite of Sam's. Always ready with a joke. Endlessly patient with a young boy and his questions. Lord Isko had gone away to tend to a broken heart. But he had left Erro, his second-in-command, in charge. "What does he have to do with anything?"

"Ten years ago," Penina said, "Captain Erromondo was to take the three eggs from the menagerie and bring them here, to the queen's pavilion."

Hanalei knew what happened next. An earthquake had rocked the city, overturning the carriage and leaving two precious dragon eggs cracked open on the street. It was that night her father had stolen the last remaining egg. "Was the captain blamed for those broken eggs? It was an earthquake."

"He wasn't blamed for that. It was after." Penina held a cup in both hands but did not drink from it. "The driver was hurt when the carriage overturned. He was bleeding on the road, calling for help. Captain Erromondo did not help him. Instead, he fell to his knees and started to eat one of the dead dragons. Right there on the queen's road, with everyone watching, and wearing the uniform of a royal captain. There was blood on his face and hands. Dragon bone in his teeth. Some said he looked like a wild animal."

Hanalei sat frozen. She could picture all of it. Penina had described the scene too well. "What happened to him?"

Penina shrugged. "The dragon was dead. No use to anyone, so he wasn't punished for stealing."

"Like my father would have been."

Penina nodded. "Lord Isko took away Erromondo's captainship. For actions unbecoming. Then we heard he left the city. And who can blame him? People pointed at him in the street, made jokes. You can still hear the songs today, about Erro the Egg Eater."

Hanalei winced. He was not the only one who had feasted on dragons. What sort of name would she be given? What kind of songs would be sung? "Where did he go?"

"Who knows?" Penina said. "Home maybe. His family had a pavilion somewhere past Nama Maguro, before the village of Pago Maya. No one I know has seen him." She reached out and covered Hanalei's hand with her own. "The guards at the lagoon are no good with secrets. Everyone knows about the new dragonfruit, and that you'll help Prince Samahti find it. You cannot do this, Hanalei. It isn't safe."

"How can I say no?" Hanalei's purple-stained satchel was on a nearby chair, ready, once again, to spill its secrets. "My choices are like yours. Do I help Princess Oliana, or don't I? Simple."

Penina snatched her hand away. "You're eighteen and think you can throw my words back at me?" And when Hanalei started to smile, Penina said, "The last time an egg was stolen, three people died. Is that what you want?"

Hanalei's smile faded. She thought of Sam. "Of course not."

"Then you must find another way. You and your prince. Because if you take something from the seadragon god, Hanalei, my girl, he will take something from you. And you will not get it back."

18

THOUGH HE LIVED IN THE BAI WITH THE OTHER unmarried males, chambers continued to be kept for Sam in the royal pavilion. He made use of them, as it would be quicker to bathe here before seeking out his cousin Jejomar, who was an embarrassment and a disgrace.

Sam's apartments opened up onto a courtyard at dusk. He passed a series of connecting gardens, veering behind statuary and potted palms whenever he heard female voices, mothers and daughters around every corner. Plumeria blossoms scented the air.

He would not have been the only one to have seen Jejomar fleeing the dragon. Running away when so many had stayed to help. Even Lord William! William, the ambassador of Raka's fragile brother, had stayed.

And yes, understood, seadragons were scary. Maybe Jejomar could be forgiven for running . . . but he had not come back. Had not returned to check on the living, to help in any way. And that was why Sam was going to find him and wring his—

Sam whipped behind a statue of the god Olifat just as a group of ladies appeared around the corner. The statue was twice the height of a man, built on a pedestal. Olifat wore a fierce expression and no clothes. He held an outrigger between both hands as though preparing to crush it.

"Yes, Mama, I am *trying*" came a testy voice. "I am wearing my best dresses, and I spend hours on my hair each day. It's not my fault Prince Samahti keeps disappearing."

"Did you see how he slayed the dragon?" a second female asked, wistful and dreamy. Sam drew farther behind the statue, careful that no part of him was left exposed. "The prince is so brave and handsome. And he does not seem to care for Anaa, Mama. May I have him?"

"Your sister comes first" came a third female voice, older, exasperated. "Anaa, you must try harder. I hear the prince is fond of the ukulele. Perhaps you can play—"

"I *hate* the ukulele." The women rounded another corner, their voices trailing away.

Sam stepped from behind the statue, only to come face-to-face with Uncle Isko and Bayani. His uncle wore black robes, left open to reveal one trousered leg and one bandaged leg. He leaned heavily on a cane.

"Hiding behind statues, Samahti?" Uncle Isko said drily. "Has it truly come to this?"

The man was everywhere you did not wish him to be. "Uncle. How are you standing? Here, let me carry—"

"Stay where you are. I am no invalid to be carried."

"You shouldn't be on that leg."

"I offered already, Prince Samahti," Bayani said.

Uncle Isko gave him a look, then turned back to Sam. "Where are you off to?"

"My aunt's."

"Ah." Uncle Isko shifted his cane from one hand to the other. "Do you know, I've never seen that boy run as fast as he did this morning. Not in all his seventeen years."

Sam wanted to return to his hiding place behind the statue. Jejomar's embarrassment was his embarrassment. Who else had seen?

"That reminds me, training starts in a month," Uncle Isko said. "New soldiers. I'll see to it your cousin has a place."

Sam had begun his training at the age of five, at his uncle's side, but most started at fourteen. "I don't think a soldier's life is for him. And his mother will not like it." Neither, he knew, would Jejomar.

Uncle Isko's expression darkened. "His mother has had a say for far too long. That boy is coddled, and if he is not taken in hand, he will rot from the inside out. I will speak to his mother." He tapped his cane once. "I'm off to supper. I'll make your excuses to your grandmother and your lady guests. Again."

"Thank you."

Uncle Isko walked on, with some difficulty. Over his shoulder, he said, "Let us cross Lady Anaa from our list. It is baffling. What sort of person does not enjoy the ukulele?"

Sam found his aunt Chesa at the back of his pavilion, standing before an open fire, burning things.

No one had come to the door. When he removed his boots and let himself in, he found empty halls and chambers. Where was everyone? He went to find Jejomar, but the smell of smoke and flames had him running toward the rear of the pavilion. He came to a halt when he saw Rangi, his old cook, peeking out a back window.

"She told us to go," Rangi explained, worry in her voice. "She was screaming, Prince Samahti. Throwing things." She made room so that Sam could see. "But I thought someone should stay."

"Thank you." Night had fallen completely. His aunt Chesa wore a dark dress and no shoes. Her hair was different from this morning. It no longer fell to her knees, but was short and sparse, floating about her head in tufts. Aghast, he said, "She cut off all her hair?"

"No, that is her normal hair," Rangi assured him. "You've only seen the wigs."

Guilt washed over him, warring with the outrage he felt

on Hanalei's behalf. "I told her she didn't have to leave right away."

Rangi patted his arm. "I don't think that's it. Or not all of it. She was upset after you left this morning, but we've seen that sort of mad before. Then Penina left. And then Master Oke left—"

"Her husband left her?"

"For good this time." Rangi lowered her voice. "He said he wasn't moving into some hut by the city gates. And she screamed at him for spending all her squid. And then Master Jejomar came home upset over the seadragon at the lagoon. And it has just been a very bad day for this family," Rangi concluded, shaking her head.

"What is she burning?" Sam asked.

"I didn't see. Maybe Master Oke's things?"

That made an awful sort of sense.

A well-rested Fetu poked his head out from Sam's collar, yawning. Rangi smiled. "Hello, Fetu. Are you hungry?" She plucked an orange from a bowl, and Fetu hopped onto the table, chirping. "Prince Samahti, why don't you leave him with me? You know your auntie isn't fond of bats."

Sam agreed. A pair of sandals was always kept for him by the back porch. He put them on and went to the fire. "Aunt Chesa." He touched her arm. She jumped, startled, though he had been calling her name. "Come away, Auntie. Are you hurt?"

"Hurt?" Aunt Chesa looked down at her bare feet, covered in dirt and grass. "No."

Sam could feel her trembling as he led her to the porch. She sat down on the back steps, said, "We are ruined," and burst into tears. Helplessly, Sam patted her shoulder, murmuring useless things, but she only cried harder. He looked around to see Rangi framed in the window. *Help,* he mouthed. Rangi came out and settled beside his aunt, rubbing her arm consolingly.

Sam went to put out the fire. A rainwater basin had been built behind the guest pavilion, shielded from view by a wall of tangled bougainvillea. The basin was full, due to the recent typhoon. Sam used a bucket to throw water onto the flames. Fetu found a much smaller pail and helped, diving into the basin and flying over the fire. Man and bat made repeated trips until nothing remained but the smell of smoke.

Sam sniffed. Smoke and something else. He wondered what else his aunt had burned besides her useless husband's belongings. The night smelled strange. Strange in a familiar way, though he could not think why. He set the bucket down, checking one last time for any missed embers, then returned to the pavilion. Fetu, perhaps remembering his aunt's aversion to bats, vanished beneath Sam's shirt. The kitchen was empty. He could hear his aunt and Rangi farther down the hall. He went in the other direction, stopping before a chamber that had been his, and knocked. There were retching sounds from within and eventually a familiar voice, full of irritation.

"Mama, I'm fine," Jejomar called out. "Leave me alone."

"It's me. Open the door."

Silence.

"Jejomar, let me in."

Shuffling sounds followed. The door opened to reveal his cousin, pale and sweating. The smell of sickness wafted from a bowl placed on the floor by the bed.

"What's wrong with you?" Sam demanded.

"Something I ate maybe." Jejomar's response was vague. He sighed when Sam placed a hand on his forehead. "Ah. That feels nice."

Sam took his hand away. No fever at least. "Sit down," he said, determined not to feel sorry for him.

Jejomar had moved into the chamber years ago, but there were still signs it had once belonged to Sam. A pair of ukuleles hung from hooks on the wall. Small wooden carvings lined the windowsills. Kandayos mostly, with flowing manes, and a pair of seadragons. Carvings of the original dragons from the menagerie.

Jejomar lowered himself carefully into a chair. "What are you doing here?"

"Making sure you made it home safe." Sam went to stand by an open window where the air was fresher. "That was a long run from the lagoon."

Guilt flooded Jejomar's face. He looked at the mat beneath his bare feet. "I should have stayed to help. I thought about it."

"As long as you thought about it. That's the important part." How were they related? How did they share a drop of the same blood? "No one died, if you wondered."

"It was a big seadragon!" Jejomar said defensively. "It had teeth! What did you need me for anyway?"

"We could have used the help—"

"Oh please. You didn't need me. I'm sure you took care of everything with your *stupid* bat and your *stupid* machete. We can't all be as brave as you—"

"There are babies braver than you," Sam snapped. Fetu popped up from Sam's collar and bared his teeth. "Infants in their mothers' arms are braver than you—"

"I know." Jejomar dropped his head into his hands. "I'm sorry. Sorry, Fetu."

Fetu, only a little mollified, became a tiny bat-shaped marking on the back of Sam's hand.

Silence filled the chamber. Jejomar looked pathetic. And he was ill. Now Sam felt bad, which he resented. "What did you eat?"

"Bad fish," Jejomar said.

"Is anyone else sick?"

"I don't know."

"He needs rest, Samahti." Aunt Chesa stood in the

doorway, her eyes and nose red. There was still grass and dirt on her feet.

"I'll go," Sam said.

"Jejomar can't move into the bai, not now." Aunt Chesa brushed away tears with the back of her hand. "I'm alone and can't do without him. I know you'll see that finding other lodging is impossible. I'm too distraught."

Jejomar lifted his head. "Mama."

"Your husband can't just leave," Sam said. "He's your husband. I'll find him and bring him back."

"I don't want him here. I won't make him stay if he doesn't wish it."

Sam would be happy never to see Oke again. "What were you burning, Auntie?"

Aunt Chesa looked at Jejomar, then looked away. "It's a private matter."

And a humiliating one, Sam saw. Her wigless state made her appear smaller, older. He was not accustomed to thinking of his aunt as someone to protect. Only tolerate. Better to let this go. "Stay until you've found someplace suitable. But please, no more fires."

His aunt nodded stiffly. She left without having spoken a single word to her son.

Jejomar slumped even further down into his chair. "You shouldn't have done that, Sam. Poor relations are like barnacles, don't you know? You'll never get rid of us now."

"OLIANA," QUEEN MAGA'LAHI SAID. "MY LOVE, there's someone here to see you."

Hanalei looked down at Princess Oliana in her bed, unable to hide her shock. *Nothing is different*, Sam had told her when she had asked after his mother. He had meant it, for time and illness had not touched her. The hair Hanalei had once brushed remained black as lava stones. Spiraling curls reached her knees. Her face was free of line and shadow, the fishhook scar on her cheek was as vivid as ever, and there was the smallest of smiles on her lips. A stranger would not have believed her to be a woman in her forty-fifth year of life.

Across the wide expanse of bedding, Queen Maga'lahi wore a deep blue dress; hammered gold bangles covered her arms from wrist to elbow. "You look surprised, Hanalei-arihi."

An understatement. "I am, Your Grace. I don't understand."

They were not alone in the chamber. Directly overhead, Fetu hung upside down from a beam. Sam and Lord Isko were at a table, sorting through the contents of Hanalei's satchel. The lord protector's bandaged leg had been propped up on a chair, and a polished cane lay within reach. Through the open windows came the busy, persistent chatter of sand crickets.

"No one understands," Queen Maga'lahi replied. "Why she will not wake or eat or drink. Or even grow older."

Hanalei gasped. "She doesn't eat?"

"She won't keep anything down," Sam said. "It hasn't harmed her, or helped her. We've brought in healers from all over the Nominomi. Doctors from Langland and Esperanza. No one has seen an illness like hers."

Hanalei could not decide which felt worse. Grief or guilt. It should have been her in this bed. "I am so—"

"Don't say you're sorry," Lord Isko said without looking up. "It's a waste of everyone's time."

Sam eyed the lord protector. The queen frowned. But no one spoke. Not even Hanalei. She had saved his life today and he had not said a word about it. As much as she wished to, she could not tell this surly, ungrateful elder what she thought of him, especially in front of the queen. Instead, she asked, "May I hold her hand?"

"You may," Queen Maga'lahi said.

Hanalei perched on the edge of the bed, careful not to

jostle, and took Princess Oliana's hand in hers. It was warm, with familiar callouses along two fingertips. The scars on Hanalei's own hands were a stark reminder of all that had come to pass since she had last been in her company. "Lady. It's Hanalei." She kissed Princess Oliana's knuckles, then pressed her forehead to them, fighting back tears. She did not want her first words to be accompanied by weeping. "It's Hana. I know you can hear me."

The queen's gaze sharpened. "You sound sure, Hanaleiarihi."

"I am sure."

"How?" Sam asked.

"I heard you," Hanalei told him. "You came every day. You brought your carvings to work on, to pass the hours. Or you brought your ukulele. You slept on the floor sometimes."

Lord Isko snorted. A deliberate, rude sound meant to rile. Hanalei had had enough. "I understand, Lord Isko. You couldn't be any clearer. You don't want me here."

"I don't recall saying those words." Lord Isko sat back. He looked like a man who wanted an argument. Suddenly, Hanalei did too.

"You don't have to." Gently, Hanalei placed Princess Oliana's hand on the bed. She did not want to accidentally bruise it in her anger. "You think I'm here for some terrible, secret purpose."

One eyebrow went up. "And? Are you?"

"I'm not." Hanalei kept her voice even, her tone respectful. "You're lord protector. You're supposed to think the worst of everyone. But I've never lied to you, sir. You've never allowed it. If there's something you wish to accuse me of, here I am."

"Very well," Lord Isko said, and it was like there was no one else in the chamber. "You have been gone from Tamarind ten years. More years than you lived here, I might add, and in the company of a man of dubious reputation. Then one day you fall from his ship into Tamarindi waters, and are conveniently saved by a handsome, gullible prince."

From Sam: "I resent that, very much."

Lord Isko ignored him. "Would you blame any lord protector for wondering where your loyalties lie? After all, look at where you are now, and with whom."

Surrounded by a prince, a princess, and the queen of Tamarind, who watched and listened and said not a word.

"I don't blame you," Hanalei said, because she understood. Lord Isko would have been right to worry—if she had been the sort of person who wished this family harm. "I have only my word, and I cannot make you accept it. I was on the *Anemone* unwillingly. Captain Bragadin and I do not 'keep company' with one another. Far from it. I have sailed past Tamarind six times over the last few years—on other ships—and I have never disembarked, not once." She turned away from the incredulity on Sam's face. "I would not have come this time, except . . . I saw something I shouldn't have. And then I saw Fetu." For as long as she could remember, Fetu had always meant safety. And Fetu had always meant home.

In the silence that followed, there was a solitary chirp, and Fetu dropped straight down from the beam. Hanalei caught him and held on tight, though she did not look away from Lord Isko. Sam went to stand by an open window, his back to them all, looking out into the darkness.

It was the queen who spoke. "What do you mean, Hanaleiarihi? What did you see?"

It was a relief to finally tell someone. "Your Grace, have you heard of a ship called the RES *Lagoon*?"

"Should I have?"

"It's a dragoner, Mai Mai," Sam said without turning. "Captained by Augustus, the Esperanzan king's youngest son."

Lord Isko said, "What about the *Lagoon*?"

"Captain Bragadin was searching for the dragonfruit," Hanalei said. "Prince Augustus was following. Two dragons surfaced near us, very hungry, and to keep them from sinking his ship, Captain Bragadin ordered incendiaries fired on the *Lagoon*. The ship went down with everyone on it . . . and it drew the seadragons away from us."

There was an appalled silence. Sam turned around. "Drew the seadragons away. Do you mean . . . ?"

"Yes. There were no survivors."

Queen Maga'lahi pressed a hand to her throat. "That captain is an Esperanzan. He killed his own prince? Fed him to the fish?"

"Not only him, Your Grace," Hanalei said. "There was a woman on board. I didn't recognize her, but Captain Bragadin called her Augusta. He said she was the prince's grandmother."

Queen Maga'lahi and Lord Isko exchanged astonished looks. "I have met her," the queen said. "Long ago. Yes, Hanaleiarihi, I can see why you felt the need to leave that ship."

"I saw you struggling with someone," Sam remembered. "Was it Captain Bragadin?" When Hanalei nodded, his expression tightened. "How did you get away?"

Hanalei looked at her satchel. "It's at the very bottom. Watch your fingers."

With his leg propped up, the satchel was beyond Lord Isko's reach. Sam crossed the chamber and reached into her bag, removing a solitary scale the size of a hand. It had come from the gold seadragon, struck down by a harpoon on Little Kalama. Dried blood crusted one edge. Hanalei had forgotten it was there, and had neglected to rinse it clean.

"You cut him," Sam realized.

"It was horrible." Hanalei kept Fetu close, pressing her nose against fur. She remembered the slash from cheekbone to lip, and Moa telling her to go. She had jumped, frightened. And Sam was there.

"But necessary," the queen murmured. "Well done, child."

There was no such admiration from Lord Isko, who wanted to know, "Where did the ship go down? Exactly where? Exactly when?"

"Nine days ago," Hanalei said. "Between Kalama and Masina, along the main waterway. Someone would have seen the wreckage. Or what was left of it."

"Do we tell their ambassador?" Sam asked. "Lord Martin should know."

"Tomorrow," Queen Maga'lahi decided. "After you've gone, I'll tell him. If he wishes to speak to Hanalei, he'll only delay your journey."

Sam returned to his chair. "Bragadin wants these eggs as badly as we do. Following them into Tamarindi waters would mean nothing to him, not after what he's already done."

Hanalei was in agreement. Captain Bragadin would not care about boundary rocks or maritime laws. What was trespassing after murder?

The queen addressed Sam. "You're thinking about the villages."

"They should be warned," Sam said. "And we need more guards patrolling the western beaches."

"Agreed," Lord Isko said. "I'll write the message. Samahti, you send the bat."

"Fine."

Plans were discussed. Queen Maga'lahi was called away. She took her leave after granting Hanalei permission to stay by Princess Oliana's side. Lord Isko did not protest, but he did not leave either. He and Sam remained at their table, poring over her papers. She could tell when they came to the part about her feeding on the dragon. Their expressions reminded her of Moa reading the same papers on the *Anemone*. *Is this a true story?* Moa had asked. And *This is disgusting.*

They moved on and she heard words like *darts*, *nets*, and *maps*. She left them to it. It was a relief to not have to do everything herself. The burden was a shared one this time, not hers alone, and a weight she had not known she carried lifted off her shoulders and off her heart, making it easier to breathe.

She braided Princess Oliana's hair. Sitting cross-legged on the bed, she brushed and braided, chatting the entire time. In her heart, she knew the princess could hear her. She spoke about cheerful things mostly. Her travels, and the people she had met along the way, and seadragons. Fetu curled up on the princess' pillow, a wing just touching her hair, snoring. Every once in a while, Hanalei would look over to find Sam and Lord Isko listening too.

Sam came over. He sat in the chair the queen had left, peeling a banana left on a tray. A moment later, Fetu was awake and perched on his knee, waiting. Lord Isko remained at the table, writing feverishly.

Hanalei kept her voice down. She did not want Lord Isko to hear. "Are you angry with me?" She had seen his face when she had spoken of sailing past Tamarind. Sailing on and never stopping.

Sam's eyes met hers across the great expanse of bed. "I'm sad, not angry. I wish you'd come home sooner." He broke off a piece of banana and offered it to Fetu. "I know why you didn't."

Hanalei tied a length of ribbon around a braid, taking her time. It wasn't until the fruit was nearly gone that Sam spoke again.

"You're worried about tomorrow."

"Aren't you?"

"A little. Especially after what happened to your father and Lady Rona, to Penina's cousin—"

"How did you know about them?" Hanalei asked, startled.

"Are you truly asking?" Lord Isko said from the table,

where he should not have been able to hear them.

With a quick smile, Sam pointed to his own ear. *Like a bat,* he mouthed. Out loud, he said, "I wouldn't go near those eggs if there was another choice. But buying up sea-dragons, hoping for dragonfruit, what has it got us? I don't know how much longer she can be like this. These eggs are a chance for her."

"Would she want you to take such a chance?"

"No." Sam gave Fetu the last of the banana and left the peel on a tray.

"Samahti." Lord Isko held out a tiny rolled-up scroll, the length of a fingernail.

Sam set Fetu beside his mother, then went to retrieve the scroll. When he returned, he tucked it into the pearl cuff on Fetu's leg. "Give them the message," Sam instructed his marking. "And make sure they feed you. Then find us on the road. I'll be watching for you, my dear."

Fetu chirped. He hopped from Sam's shoulder to Hana-lei's to Princess Oliana's, before flying out the window and into the night.

Once the sound of bat wings had faded, Sam told her, "My mother used to say that the cure for worry was action. She was right, Hana. Hope's not working." He leaned down and kissed his mother on the cheek, beside her scar. "I'm her son, but I'm not a child to protect any longer. I'll do what needs to be done."

Sam spoke with guards in the courtyard while Lord Isko came to the bed and placed a hand briefly over Princess Oliana's. He offered the satchel to Hanalei, who sat in a bedside chair.

"You're welcome to keep it longer, if you need to."

Lord Isko lowered the satchel. "There are pages I wish to have copied," he acknowledged.

"As you like."

Lord Isko gripped his cane with his other hand and frowned at her. "I haven't thanked you. For today."

"It isn't necessary. Especially if you don't mean it." The last part would not have met with the queen's approval, but she was not around to hear.

Lord Isko just stood there, waiting. As though it was her turn to speak, which it was not. Even so, the silence was too much for her. Hanalei returned his frown with one of her own. "Princess Olli used to say that we do not keep a tally with the people we care about. Our family, our friends. We help them because we love them, and we expect nothing in return. I don't require thanks, Uncle. I am very happy you're safe."

Lord Isko's breath hitched, and the sudden brightness in his eyes stunned them both. He glared at her, then swung away and made for the door. It slammed.

Seconds later, the door opened and Sam stuck his head in. "Why is uncle drying his eyes with my handkerchief?"

Hanalei wrapped both arms around herself. She said nothing.

"Never mind," Sam said, after a moment. "I think he might have deserved it. Sleep well, Hanalei."

"Sleep well, Sam."

Much later, Hanalei changed into the nightdress Penina had left for her. She fetched a pillow and blanket from a chest and placed it at the foot of the bed, where a page always slept. She blew out the candles. Sleep came easily, and with sleep, dreams.

Curious. I don't remember saying anything about loved ones and keeping tally. Are you certain it was me?

I made it up. He sent Penina to the prison kitchens. I wanted him to feel bad.

The laugh that followed was one she had not heard in a very long time. A hand brushed her cheek. Hanalei took the warmth of it with her, into the dawn when Penina came for her, and by the time she woke fully, the dream had been forgotten.

20

THE HOUR WAS EARLY, AND THE AIR ALREADY blood hot. Sam passed through the quiet courtyards of the royal pavilion, dressed in the dark green of the queen's guard. The only difference was the hammered gold band worn high on his right arm. He entered a stable teeming with activity. Guards saddled their kandayos. The cook readied his cart. Guava and breadfruit in banana leaf baskets. Pots and pans stacked one atop the other. The smell of nutmeg and kandayos everywhere. Over by the water troughs, Catamara rolled up an enormous pile of dragon netting. He was helped by two apprentices, a boy and a girl, both about twelve years old. To Sam's surprise, his grandmother was there.

She wore Tamarindi green and a crown of jade and pearl. He kissed both her cheeks. "You didn't have to wake so early."

"Sleep today of all days?" His grandmother held out her

palm. On it was what looked to be a tiny birdcage, two inches tall. Only it did not carry a bird, but a spider. Viti. "I wished to give you this."

Sam did not reach for the cage. He had Fetu. He did not want to be responsible for another. "I can't take your marking."

"It's not for forever. Just for this journey. She won't be a marking for you, Samahti," she added, understanding part of his dismay. "Simply another pair of eyes should you need it."

Sam took the cage reluctantly, holding it up between thumb and forefinger. Eight pairs of eyes blinked back at him. "Have you ever been apart from each other?"

"Once. Long ago."

Sam waited, but she said nothing more. He tucked the cage into the pouch at his belt. Whatever he meant to say next was forgotten when two figures entered the stable, arm in arm, laughing.

"No," Sam said in consternation. "What are they doing here?"

He spoke of William, the ambassador of Raka's brother, with his spectacles and dark velvet clothing. And Rosamie, the king of Salamasina's niece. She wore impractical white from neck to toe. Cockleshells edged her dress along the sleeves and hem. They rattled with her every move. Sam could hear them from across the stable. A straw hat sat on her head, the brim two feet wide at least. There was no sign of her uncle, Nakoro.

"They asked to join you," his grandmother informed him. "A grand adventure, they said. It is not every day one goes off on a dragon hunt."

Sam's sideways glance was full of skepticism. "You're telling me Rosamie wishes to hunt seadragons?"

His grandmother smiled. "Those were her words. Your presence may have had something to do with it. Isko did not see the harm in their company. Why do you scowl so? He said the suggestion came from you. Something about building alliances."

"I don't know what he's talking about." His uncle was very conveniently not here to ask. "Mai Mai, I don't have time to look after guests."

"They're not children. Let them see to themselves." His grandmother watched their approach, seeing the velvet, hearing the cockles. "Well," she murmured. "They might need looking after, just a little. Do your best, grandson."

The pair came up to them, and greetings were exchanged.

"You look lovely, Rosamie dear," his grandmother said. "But you may end up regretting that white. I do not think Samahti is bringing along a washwoman."

"Oh." Nonplussed, Rosamie looked down at the delicate

embroidery and the spotless, billowing skirt. "Not even one?"

"None, Lady," Sam confirmed, willing her to change her mind.

A cloud passed over Rosamie's features, before she brightened. "I brought plenty of others. I've come prepared. And anyway, my white can't be worse than William's velvet. Look at him."

All eyes inspected William, who said ruefully, "I didn't pack my own trunks. A mistake I'll never make again." The feather in his cap had collapsed in the heat. It stuck to his ear and neck. Sweat dotted his temples and the bridge of his nose. He pushed up his spectacles only to have them immediately slide down again. "Thank you for allowing me to join you, Prince Samahti. I didn't sleep a wink last night, I couldn't contain my excitement. If I can be of any use to you, I would be pleased to help. And if for any reason I become a bother, any bother at all, you may toss me to the side of the road and I'll make my way back. There will be no bitter feelings, I assure you."

William's words had the sound of a speech practiced over and over. He was nervous. Sam's irritation melted away. For him, this was no great adventure. But he had no wish to be someone else's joy killer. And he appreciated the sincere interest William had shown for his island. It was not always so with visitors. "I hope you'll be able to cross a few things from your list, Lord William. Can you ride a kandayo?"

"Um." William eyed one being saddled nearby. The kandayo was young, not long away from its mother's side. Pale green from mane to hoof. "I can manage a horse. They look similar."

"They are," Sam said, distracted by the appearance of another.

Hanalei walked into the stables alone. She wore a riding tunic and slim trousers, both the color of the deep, a blue so dark it was nearly black. A banana leaf hat with a short brim would keep the sun from her eyes. Soft leather shoes encased her feet and ankles, protection from snakes, scorpions, anything that slithered and stung. A saddlebag hung from one shoulder. Everything was practical, not a cockleshell in sight.

"There you are, Hanaleiarihi." His grandmother beckoned. "Come meet your traveling companions."

Introductions were made and more greetings exchanged. William was quick to offer gratitude on behalf of his sister, recovering from yesterday's encounter with the seadragon.

"How old is your sister?" Hanalei asked him.

"Sixteen, Lady. And fond of the sea until yesterday. I'm not certain how we're going to get her home."

"Home is Raka?"

William nodded. "The ambassador's residence there. We share it with our brother."

"I've walked past many times," Hanalei said.

William's eyes dropped to her hands. He would have seen her scars back at the lagoon. He knew where they had come from. "You are braver than I am, Lady Hanalei," he said with a smile, holding out his own hands to show her. "I only have these scrapes, and I wept all night."

Hanalei's smile lasted only a moment, until she turned to Rosamie. Who was not smiling, and who shifted so that her arm brushed against Sam's.

"Thank you," Rosamie said simply.

Hanalei glanced from Sam to Rosamie. "You are very welcome, Lady."

Sam did not move away from Rosamie, for he did not wish to cause her embarrassment. He wondered if that was what diplomacy was mostly. Keeping his mouth shut and not doing many of the things he wished to do in certain company. "Bayani," he said as the guard walked past. "Find our guests some mounts. Nothing with a temper."

Rosamie and William went off to choose their kandayos. Hanalei would have gone too, except Sam's grandmother asked her to stay. She handed Hanalei a dagger, its handle made of carved wood, inlaid with black pearl.

"We can't have you running about using dragonscale as

a weapon," his grandmother told her. "It's a bit too ancient epic for my liking."

Sam smiled as Hanalei took the dagger, holding it as though it were made of spun glass. "It's lovely, Your Grace," Hanalei said. "Thank you. But what if I lose it?"

"It is a gift, and yours to lose," his grandmother said. "I've read your papers. I've seen your father's words. That you are still with us is extraordinary."

"I wish I'd never left."

"I as well." His grandmother placed a hand on Hanalei's cheek. "We are defined by our hardships, Hanaleiarihi, and how we face them. We are made stronger or weaker by those we hold closest to us." She dropped her hand. "Look after each other. Come home safely."

"Yes, Mai Mai."

"We will, Your Grace."

"And, Samahti?" When Sam straightened from his bow, he saw that his grandmother's attention had turned to a far corner of the stable. She was frowning. "Watch over your cousin as well. Why does that boy always look like he's up to something?"

Jejomar was saddling a kandayo, partially hidden by the animal's girth. His shoulders were hunched slightly, his head low, which was likely why the queen thought him so shifty-looking. He wore plain riding clothes. A bulging satchel lay at his feet.

Sam knew what the answer to his question would be. He asked it anyway. "What are you doing here?"

Instead of replying, Jejomar looked over at Hanalei, who knelt beside Catamara, inspecting dragon darts. "Hello, Hanalei."

"Hello, Jejomar." Hanalei glanced over with a half smile. "Your beard is gone."

Sam wondered when she had seen Jejomar's beard, then realized they must have crossed paths that first night, before his aunt Chesa chased her away. At Hanalei's words, Jejomar's hands flew to his chin, no longer covered by wisps and straggles. His eyes widened. He patted his cheeks, his ears, as though searching for something.

Sam said, "Did you forget you shaved your beard?"

Jejomar dropped his hands. "Yes. I forgot."

Sam exchanged glances with Hanalei and Catamara. The latter mimed sneaking a sip from a flask before continuing his conversation with Hanalei.

Sam repeated, "What are you doing here?"

"I'm coming with you."

Who wasn't? Did everyone think this was some kind of excursion? Sam already had William and Rosamie to watch over. He did not need another. "Not this time, cousin."

"I won't cause trouble, I swear," Jejomar said. "Please, Sam. Auntie Olli was always nice to me. I want to help. I'll do anything you want."

His mother has had a say for far too long. That boy is coddled, and if he is not taken in hand, he will rot from the inside out.

Sam eyed his cousin. Along with his wispy beard, Jejomar's spots were gone. Strange. He could have sworn they were there just yesterday, picked over and scabbed. "Did Lord Isko send you?"

"No." Jejomar looked genuinely baffled. "Why would he? Lord Isko hates me."

"He doesn't hate you. It's just how he looks."

Across the stable, William leaned against his kandayo and yanked off his cap, fanning himself with it. His face was flushed, fair hair sticking to his head. Sam felt a terrible foreboding. This would end badly. William was going to faint before they even reached the city gates. He would fall from his kandayo and break his neck, and they would have to bring his body back to his ambassador brother. It would be tragic, for Sam found he liked Lord William. Also, his death would delay their search.

Sam turned to his cousin. "Anything I want?"

Jejomar, whose shoulders had begun to droop, straightened. "Anything! What?"

Sam said, "That man over there, his name is William.

He's the ambassador of Raka's brother. New to the islands."

Jejomar whistled. "You don't have to tell me that. Is he wearing velvet?"

"You see the problem. He needs looking after, and I don't have time—"

"Leave it to me." Jejomar picked his bag off the ground and hung it from the saddle. "I'll take him to Penina. She'll find him something to wear. Will you wait?"

"Not for long."

Jejomar grinned. "Thank you, Sam." His cousin practically skipped across the stable. Sam watched him tap William on the shoulder. They spoke, Jejomar pointing to Sam, then at the velvet. William grinned good-naturedly, and the two quickstepped it out the stable door.

One disaster averted. What else? First, he inspected the pouch at his belt, making sure Viti had not fallen out. Next, he went about the stables, checking everything that needed to be checked. He went over the day's route with Liko, who had marked it down on maps. He poked his head inside the cook's cart and left with a mouthful of nutmeg bread. He checked the straps on Rosamie's kandayo, then admired William's new travel clothes, as plain and serviceable as Jejomar's but with a straw hat. When he came full circle by the dragon nets, it was to see Hanalei standing with her back against her kandayo, watching him.

"What's in the pouch?" she asked.

"Why?"

"You keep looking inside. Is it gold? How much do you have in there?"

"It's not gold."

"Then what?"

Sam reached into the pouch and pulled out the cage.

Hanalei came closer. "The queen gave you *Viti*?"

"Not forever. Another pair of eyes should I need it."

Hanalei was looking at him, seeing far too much. "Two markings now. Are they heavy?"

She did not speak of ounces or pounds. A spider and a bat, they weighed nothing. Fetu would be off delivering his messages for another day or more, and Sam felt his absence keenly. But sometimes Fetu was more burden than bat. A constant reminder of his mother's illness, and of his own failure to find a way to save her. Sam hated even thinking it. It felt mean and selfish. Disloyal. He loved that bat.

But now there was Viti. And with his grandmother's marking came the weight of a queen's expectations. Find the dragonfruit, save his mother, preserve the family line. The responsibility was his and his alone. *Are they heavy?* Hanalei had asked.

"A little," Sam admitted.

Hanalei held out her hand. "You don't have to do everything alone. I'll carry her for you."

Sam felt something in his heart shift, something different

from before, when they were children. He did not give her the spider. He bowed over her hand and kissed it. If the stables fell silent, if every eye turned in their direction, he did not notice. When he straightened, Hanalei was looking at him wide-eyed.

She tugged her hand away, self-conscious. "What are you . . . ?" she began, then tipped her head, listening.

So did Sam. They had heard it at the same time. Deeply touched, he realized, "It's a wish-you-well."

Hanalei smiled at his expression. "They were starting to gather when I came in. It sounds like ten times the number I saw."

Outside, someone was singing. A woman's voice lifted high. She sang a wish-you-well, a song from the old times, heard when the proas and camakaus sailed away en masse, for battle or to explore, to search for a better life. Her voice was joined by others, until it sounded as if the entire city of Tamarind had come to send them off.

Liko hurried up to them, her expression harried. "Lord Isko is outside. He says it's time for us to go."

"We're going," Sam said. "Liko, where did all these people come from?"

"It's Lord Isko's doing," Liko answered. "He sent messengers around Tamarind, last night and this morning. He made sure everyone knew when we were leaving and why. In case they wanted to wish us well."

Hanalei waited until Liko had gone before murmuring, "Beneath that grump, he's as soft as Fetu."

"Don't say that to his face."

"Never."

They smiled at each other, and once again, Hanalei held out her hand. *We are defined by our hardships, and how we face them. We are made stronger or weaker by those we hold closest to us.* Very carefully, Sam returned Viti to his pouch and said, "No. It's fine. I can carry her."

21

WHEN POSSIBLE, THEY KEPT TO ROADS WITHIN view of the water. Sand and sea always to their right. They passed village after village, pavilions on latti stones, nestled under the shade of towering jacarandas.

Any fears Hanalei had that the dragon had gone were laid to rest early in the day. There were sightings everywhere. Villagers described a blue seadragon swimming parallel to shore, just beyond the shallows where the young ones played and the families did their wash. Its length was terrifying, sixty feet at least.

"Did it carry anything?" Hanalei asked. "In its claws? Did it come ashore?" The response had been a dumbstruck silence. That the seadragon had legs, and had traveled on land as recently as the day before, had not come as welcome news. No one had seen anything. The seadragon had swum low to the surface, only its frill and back exposed to the air. If it held anything in its claws, no one had been able to see it.

The sightings left the islanders rattled and avoiding the water. The fishermen and fisherwomen in particular were deeply unhappy. Their livelihoods depended upon being able to sail their canoes into open sea, and to remain there for much of the day. Hanalei knew their misfortune would trickle onward. To the merchants with no fish to sell. To the wives and mothers sent home with empty market baskets.

"Fetu brought your message," a young tree guard named Kaipat told them, just outside the city of Nama Maguro. They remained on their kandayos, the guard too, on a narrow strip of beach. Behind them, a lookout post was nestled high up in the fronds of a coconut tree. "We have darts and nets. Everyone here knows about the dragonfruit, what it means for your mother, Prince Samahti. We'll keep our hands off our spears."

"Good," Sam told him. "You haven't seen it?"

"No," Kaipat answered. "I heard it swims near shore. But why? My grandfather was a tree guard forty years. He never saw one come so close."

"I'm no dragon scholar. Good thing I brought one with me." With a crooked smile, Sam looked over at Hanalei.

Her kandayo stood slightly behind him, to his right. She had been studying his profile as he spoke. The curve of his ear, the straight lines of his nose and jaw, like a carving, and when he turned his head toward her, she looked hurriedly away. "He may be looking for somewhere to build a nest," she said to the guard. "But I don't think he'd stop here. There are too many people around."

"Lady Hanalei," Sam said, as an introduction. The others shifted restlessly, eager to dismount and seek out Cook and his cart. Hours had passed since breakfast.

"Hanalei?" It was an uncommon name, even on Tamarind. The startled look on the tree guard's face told her he knew who she was, and did not know quite how to greet her. As a lady? As a disgraced lord's daughter? Sam's next words made the decision for him.

"That is what I said, yes."

Kaipat dipped his chin hastily. "Lady Hanalei. Er, welcome home?"

"It is good to be home."

Kaipat turned his attention back to a safer topic, like seadragons. "You think it's looking for a beach with no people?"

"Or a cave. One near the water."

"There are plenty of those once you get past Pago Maya," Kaipat told her.

Sam said, "Like that one?"

He was looking at some cliffs in the far-off distance. Seeing them, Hanalei felt a shiver run along her arms. They reminded her of the mountains that housed the royal menagerie. When the waters were high, a boat, or animal, could travel from open sea directly into the mouth of the cave. "Yes," she said. "Like that one."

Lord William was beside her, studying the cliffs. "Is it just me, or does that mountain look like . . . um . . . like a lady?" He tilted his head so far to the side Hanalei heard it crick. His spectacles fell off. Jejomar caught them in midair and handed them back to him.

"She's called the Sleeping Lady," Sam told William. "In the right light, she looks just like a woman on her side, fast asleep. It's just past Pago Maya, a village on our way." To Kaipat: "What about the harbor? Any dragoners?"

"Four," Kaipat said. "Three sailed off at first light. But the last captain is dragging his feet. The harbormaster's been at him all morning."

"Dragoners?" Hanalei said.

"They've been told to go," Sam explained. "Lord Isko thought it best not to tempt them."

Foreign dragon hunters. Uneasy, Hanalei asked Kaipat, "Do you know which ships they were?"

"Two were from Sumay, Lady, and one from Langland. I don't know their names, but the one that's still here is an Esperanzan."

Hanalei and Sam looked at one another. Sam asked, "Which Esperanzan?"

"The *Compass Rose*, Prince Samahti."

Not the *Anemone*. Good. Hanalei wondered where it was, and what its captain was up to.

William remarked, "It must be a new dragoner. My tutor made me learn the names of all Esperanzan ships. I've never heard of the *Compass Rose*."

"Never?" Sam asked. When William shook his head, Sam told the tree guard, "The harbor's not far. Let's take a look." He turned his kandayo around, calling out to Cook on his cart. "A good place to stop?"

Cook gave an agreeable nod. He pointed to a clearing across the road. "Good as any, Prince Samahti."

That settled it. Sam rode off with William, Jejomar, and Kaipat. Hanalei heard "When did Fetu leave? Did you feed my bat?" And Kaipat's answering laugh. "He wouldn't give us the message until we fed him. He left before dawn." "Probably in the trees, then, fast asleep," Sam said, before they rode out of earshot.

Everyone else dispersed, sliding off their kandayos and following the cook's cart. Most carried their drinking water in long joints of bamboo. Some poured the water over their heads to cool off. Rosamie appeared by Hanalei's side, a picture of misery. Her white dress stuck to her in damp patches. The cockleshells at her hem continued to rattle, but the sound was listless, as if they too were done in completely by the heat. Hanalei could not see Rosamie's hair beneath the giant hat, but she guessed it was soaked through. Hanalei removed her own hat and fanned herself with it.

"That sleeping lady is naked." Rosamie eyed the mountain with a frown. "Someone should plant trees in certain places. It's indecent."

Hanalei found herself smiling. Lady Rosamie was not the first person to think so. "Every fifty years or so, someone plants trees. And someone always cuts them down." Always in secret, in the dead of night. The tree cutters were never caught.

Rosamie turned her back on the mountain. She pointed to the sea. "Is it safe? I heard you can tell."

Hanalei stopped fanning herself. Who had told her that? Sam? The thought bothered her. She shoved her hat into her bag. Three dolphins swam and played just beyond the shallows, jumping over one another in graceful arcs. The squeaks they made sounded like laughter. "It's safe. Otherwise, they would not be here."

"Good." Rosamie walked off, not to the cook's cart, but down the beach toward a large boulder covered with trees.

"Where are you going?" Hanalei called.

Rosamie kept walking. She did not turn around. But Hanalei heard the words *shade, water, dying*.

"What about lunch?"

Rosamie lifted a hand in a single, disinterested flick. "Do not care" came drifting back.

Hanalei wasn't hungry either. But she was curious about King Nakoro's niece, who was so clearly meant for Sam. Sam, who needed to marry. Hanalei fetched the bamboo filled with water from her saddlebag, and followed.

"You're spoiling my chance," Rosamie informed Hanalei, through her hat.

When Hanalei rounded the boulder, she discovered a secluded patch of sand and sea. The flame trees growing on top of the rock provided a welcome shade. Rosamie's dress had been discarded, tossed onto another rock. She floated on her back in the shallows, wearing only her shift and her giant hat, which she had placed squarely on her face.

Hanalei would have loved nothing more than to dive into the cool waters of the Nominomi, but she was not about to fling her clothes about with so many others nearby. She made do with removing her shoes and stepping ankle-deep into the shallows. "Your chance for what?"

Through the hat: "You know what."

Hanalei kept her voice neutral. Or thought she did. "I've only been home two days. How much could I have spoiled?"

Silence.

Rosamie whipped her hat from her face as she stood. It was Hanalei's first good look at her. She was very pretty, though cross, her face round and her black hair cut very short, at chin level. "All of it, I think. I've never seen a hand kissed the way yours was today. You made William blush. Just like when he saw the Naked Lady."

"Sleeping," Hanalei said absently. She could still feel Sam's kiss, hours later.

"Whatever. Lady Hanalei—"

"I'm just Hanalei."

"You don't use your title?"

"Not in a long time." Hanalei could see herself falling lower and lower in Rosamie's regard. She tipped her head back and drank from her bamboo.

Rosamie slapped at the water, scaring away some fish that had come too close. "My mother says a title is like armor. The way clothing can be. She says ladies need as much armor as we can carry, if we're to make any headway in the world."

"Armor is heavy." The dolphins had also come closer to their little cove, making Hanalei smile. "Where is your mother? On Salamasina?" She remembered meeting Rosamie's uncle, but no one else.

Rosamie returned the hat to her head. "My mother is gone. She died last summer."

Rosamie had spoken of her parent in present terms, not past. Her grief was there for Hanalei to see, now that she was looking. Silently, she held out the bamboo.

Rosamie came out of the water. She took the bamboo and flopped onto the wet sand by Hanalei's feet. After drinking her fill, Rosamie wiped her mouth with the back of her hand. "I heard Princess Oliana was like a mother to you. Was she?"

"Yes." Hanalei sat beside her. "My mother and the princess were friends since they were girls. My mother died when I was a baby. I don't remember her. Princess Olli is who I remember."

Rosamie's words were subdued. "I know your story, Hanaleiarihi. The dragonfruit saved your life, but your troubles did not suddenly go away."

"No." Instead there had been more troubles. No father, no silver, no home.

"Then what will you do differently this time? What is your plan?" She studied Hanalei's face. "There is no plan."

"There will be."

"When?" Rosamie challenged. "After everyone who matters is killed?"

Hanalei looked away. "If you're so frightened, you should go back."

"I am not fright— What is it?" Rosamie asked when Hanalei jumped to her feet, scanning the water.

Hanalei looked and listened. She could not hear them anymore. "The dolphins are gone."

22

THE *COMPASS ROSE* WAS A DRAGONER LIKE ANY other. Painted black with a rounded hull. An Esperanzan flag hung limp from its mast. The ship was anchored at the far end of the harbor, past empty fishing boats both large and small.

"They won't go," the harbor guard told Sam with visible frustration. "They say, 'There's a hole in the boat, it needs to be patched.' And when it's patched, they say, 'Our shipmate has gone to the village. We are waiting on her return.'" He threw up his hands. "We could drag it ourselves, use the big hook, but your bat's message said to stay out of the water."

"Are they playing cards?" Sam asked as their kandayos ambled their way toward the *Compass Rose*, which did not look like a ship preparing to depart. A table and chairs had been placed on the dock, near the stern. Four dragoners slouched about, tossing cards and coins onto the table. Two others stood nearby with their fishing poles in the water.

William brought his kandayo beside Sam's. "That is brazen."

"They tried to bribe one of my men into letting them stay," the harbor guard said. "I'd toss the lot of them in shackles, Prince Samahti, but I know you want them gone."

"I do," Sam said. "Let's see what we can do to hurry them along. She could use some air anyway."

"She?" the harbor guard said.

"Air?" Jejomar asked.

Sam reached into the pouch at his belt and pulled out the miniature cage. He tossed Viti lightly into the open. In the moment it took her to drop to the ground, the spider had grown five feet in height and far more in length. Eight legs skittering and scraping along the wooden planks.

The startled shouts came from Sam's own party and from the dragoners, who leapt to their feet. Playing cards flew into the air. Fishing poles toppled into the water.

"Get your captain," Sam ordered.

In response, the dragoners scrambled up the ladder to the deck. The ruckus brought more dragoners to the railing. Dozens of them. They peered cautiously down at Sam and his party.

"The queen gave you her spider?" Jejomar exclaimed. "A little warning, cousin!"

"That is Queen Maga'lahi's spider?" There was awe in William's voice, even as he prudently moved his kandayo a safer distance away, behind Kaipat. The harbor guard pressed a hand to his chest, as if to calm a galloping heart.

Sam did not answer. He watched the dragoners part for one of their own, an islander about Sam's own age, neither tall nor short, dressed in black. Their captain, Sam guessed.

He smiled down at Sam and waved. "Hello! Greetings. That is a big spider."

Sam did not return the smile. "You've overstayed your welcome, and our patience. It's time for you to go."

"Yes, sure. We have supplies to load, not many, but as soon as—"

"Viti," Sam said.

Spiderweb shot from his grandmother's marking straight to the side of the ship. Viti yanked. The *Compass Rose* tilted sharply toward her. Half the dragoners sailed overboard, their cries cut off as they plunged into the water. Those who managed to remain on board grabbed desperately on to rails and poles, until Sam gave the order and Viti released her web.

The ship righted itself with a great groan. Thumps and curses filled the harbor as the dragoners dragged themselves out of the sea and onto the deck. Behind Sam came the sound of wheezing laughter. He kept his own expression neutral. When the captain reappeared at the railing, hair standing straight up on his head and rubbing an elbow, his smile was nowhere in sight.

Sam said, "Get your people, and go."

"Yeah. We're going." The captain swung around, then stopped and spun back to glare down at Sam. "Why should you get the eggs? The sea belongs to everybody."

"Beyond the boundary rocks, it does," Sam acknowledged. "Hunt whatever you like there. Here, you are in Tamarindi waters. And every drop belongs to the queen."

We'll see. The captain did not say the words out loud. He mouthed it, then turned away and disappeared from view.

Sam and his party remained on their kandayos as the dragoners returned dripping wet to their ship. Men, women, a boy aged fourteen or fifteen. The last shouted a string of curses at them, but only after their ship had sailed too far away for retaliation.

"What a brat," Jejomar commented.

"Sailing under an Esperanzan flag," William said, red with embarrassment. "My apologies, Prince Samahti."

"You're not their keeper, Lord William." A much smaller Viti crawled up Sam's leg and back into her cage. "Thank you, my dear." He returned her to his pouch. And to the harbor guard: "Take down the name of the ship. Let's not have them back."

"No," the harbor guard agreed. "I wonder what their

captain is like. Worse, if that's the sort of crew he keeps."

Sam looked at the *Compass Rose* growing smaller in the distance. "That wasn't the captain?"

"No. He ate some bad octopus, they said. Never left his cabin. That one, he goes by the name Moa."

When Sam returned to the beach, it was to find Hanalei all alone by the shore. Everyone else stayed far back on the road, most on their kandayos, ready to flee. For in the water, between the shallows and the deep, was a blue seadragon.

"Wait, Prince Samahti," Liko said, when he would have gone charging across the sand. "I don't think she's in any danger—"

"You don't *think*?" Sam glared at Liko, at the rest of his guards. Why were they all just standing there?

Catamara placed a hand on Sam's kandayo. "Look, young prince. Watch."

"I'm all right, Sam," Hanalei called out. She did not turn from the sea, but raised a hand in a backward wave to offer reassurance, just as a strange thing happened. Part of the dragon's frill rose, straight up into the air.

Sam slid off his kandayo, boots landing hard on the ground.

Rosamie's voice was hushed. "Is it— Did it just wave back at her?"

Hanalei looked over at them, eyes huge. Clearly wondering the same thing. Sam watched as she turned back and raised her other arm. The dragon's frill rose again. It rose when her arm went up and dropped when her arm came down. Hanalei raised both arms. Two sections of frill rose.

"Catamara," Sam said, his voice unsteady. "What am I looking at?"

"It looks like your lady has made a new friend."

"We heard a scream," Liko said, subdued. "And saw Lady Rosamie running from that rock over there."

"It scared away the dolphins." Rosamie clutched a blanket around her shoulders, knees exposed, feet bare. Her dress had gone missing, but she still wore her hat. "And when it saw Lady Hanalei . . . they just stared at each other. Like they knew one another."

Sam thought of the dragon back in the menagerie, who had watched Hanalei, had seemed to recognize some part of her.

Hanalei kept both arms raised. She moved them slowly from side to side, like palm fronds waving in a breeze. The seadragon did the same, frill undulating, and Hanalei laughed.

"Why isn't she afraid?" Jejomar asked no one in particular.

Sam was terrified enough for the both of them. "Take

this." He shoved the reins at Bayani and made his way across the sand, slow and cautious. His heart thundered in his ears.

"Did you see?" Hanalei asked when he drew up beside her, water lapping at his boots.

"I saw." Sam touched her back lightly, resisting the urge to grab her and run. Far away, where she would be safe. "Hana, that dragon can come out of the water."

"He isn't going to hurt me."

"You don't know that for certain." Sam could hear the others behind them, creeping closer.

"I do know it." The face Hanalei turned up to him was smiling, and it was sure. She took his hand, startling him, and yanked it straight up in the air. Every bit of frill snapped upward in response, making her laugh. "I think he remembers me from Little Kalama. He knows I tried to warn him."

This dragon was playful, Sam conceded. Like a child. Nothing like the fifty sober seadragons back at the menagerie. Because this one was free, his conscience told him. The others were not.

"I've been waiting for him to show his claws." Hanalei looked down at their entwined fingers and dropped his hand hastily. "Do you think he's holding the eggs? Wait," she said without stopping for breath. "Let me try this." And she somersaulted across the sand twice.

The seadragon dove into the water, disappearing momentarily, before shooting straight up in the air. It spun twice before falling back into the waves. Fast, but long enough for everyone to see that its claws held nothing. Instead, two bright pink eggs were visible from a center pouch. A collective gasp rose behind them.

Sam felt as if the air had been kicked out of his lungs. "He has them."

Hanalei looked as stunned as he felt. "He's a marsupial."

"Like a kangaroo?" William's voice drifted over, baffled.

"The pouch," Hanalei said. "That's how he's been carrying them. I've never seen a pouch on a seadragon before."

Not one but two dragonfruit. And they were so close. "Catamara," Sam said. "Can we use the darts?"

Hanalei's smile faded. Her excitement, her pleasure in this beautiful animal, all gone. Because of him.

"No." Catamara came to stand beside them. "We could hit the eggs. Too dangerous."

Frustrated, Sam said, "Then we'll have to follow. Take them once they're in a nest." He glanced sideways at Hanalei. "If there were another way, I would do it."

"I forgot," Hanalei said, stricken. "For a moment I forgot why we were here. You never forget."

"She's my mother."

The seadragon watched and waited, head tilting one way and the next. Hanalei no longer had the heart to play. Behind them, Jejomar and William threw their arms over their heads, waving madly, but the dragon did not care for them. At last, he turned away, frill flying, and swam off slowly, heading west.

23

THAT EVENING, THEY MADE CAMP IN A GROVE OF mango trees. It was a good spot, close enough to the Nominomi to smell the sea-salted waves, far enough away to flee inland should the guards by the shore call a warning. Ten open-air pavilions offered shelter from sun and rain. They had been built around a common area, one with firepits and stacks of chopped wood left behind by fellow travelers. Each pavilion was small but comfortable, with space for four sleeping mats. Hanalei shared hers with Rosamie.

"How were you not frightened?" Rosamie knelt on her mat, rummaging through a jewelry box made of inlaid pearl. "You didn't even scream. I must have screamed enough for both of us."

"You did," Hanalei told her, earning a dirty look in response. She sat cross-legged on her own mat, pulling a comb through damp hair. Or trying to. It felt like there were knots upon knots, and the constant yanking and tugging was giving her a headache.

The sun had nearly gone, but the cooking fire and torchlight cut through the gathering darkness. From where she sat, Hanalei could see the entire camp. Those who were not settling into their own pavilions sat by the fire, where, by the look and smell of things, supper was nearly ready.

They had just returned from nearby bathing pools. Hanalei had changed into a pale blue skirt and blouse, clean and crisp. Dear Penina. Hanalei did not know how she had found clothing that fit her so well, so quickly. Rosamie also wore a skirt and blouse, in white. Unlike Hanalei, she wore jewelry. Plenty of it. Gold glinted at her wrists and ears and ankle, along with a shell choker around her throat.

"Well?" Rosamie pressed. "Why weren't you scared?"

To Hanalei, the answer was simple. "He didn't feel dangerous to me."

"It's a seadragon." Rosamie closed the box with a snap. "Aren't all seadragons dangerous?"

"They are not. It would be like saying, 'Aren't all men dangerous?'"

The look Rosamie gave her was withering. "It's not the same thing at all, Lady Hanalei."

"How is it different?" Hanalei countered. "A man will

say, 'I'm hungry,' and kill a chicken." She pointed her comb at the open fire where chickens and pigs turned slowly on their spits. "No one ever feels too badly for the chicken. When a seadragon is hungry, it will hunt an octopus or a whale or sink a ship because, to them, humans are food. But I have never seen one terrorize for the sake of terrorizing. The way a cat sometimes does. That is not in its nature."

"You were not the one swallowed by a seadragon." Which Rosamie had been, only yesterday.

"We hurt her first," Hanalei reminded her. "There was a spear in her neck. She was dying. What would you have done in her place, if you were cornered and scared?"

Rosamie regarded her for a long moment. "You're very odd," she said finally. "I wonder if that's why Prince Samahti likes you so much. He's drawn to strange women."

Hanalei laughed. "And you're drawn to insults because you know I'm right."

"Oh hush. And give me that." Rosamie came over and snatched the comb away before kneeling on the mat behind her. Hanalei braced for a vicious hair-pulling, but Rosamie was surprisingly gentle, patiently unraveling the knots and tangles.

"My uncle says you work for some sort of school. Does that mean you're poor?"

Hanalei had just begun to think she liked Lady Rosamie

of Salamasina, despite everything. But at her question, the feeling went away. "Poor?"

"Yours is one of Tamarind's original families," Rosamie said, as if Hanalei were unaware of her own family history. "But you work for your supper, and even though you've returned home, you're not wearing a single piece of jewelry. Even the apprentices wear gold." They watched two girls walk by the pavilion, hands over their mouths and giggling over some shared amusement. One was an apprentice in the menagerie. The other labored for Cook. Gold hoops gleamed at their ears.

"I lost my home," Hanalei said, and felt an ache in her chest. She had never said so out loud before. Hearing it spoken made it feel real, something that could not be undone. "It's being used for important guests. I suppose the gold is gone too. I haven't asked."

The comb stilled. Hanalei turned her head to the side in question.

"Our pavilion is near the queen's," Rosamie said. "The room I'm in has a most absurd bed. The headboard and posts are carved with—"

"Seadragons," Hanalei finished with a faint smile. "My father had it made for me."

Papa. Hanalei would not wish away a single memory of him. Only the hurt that came with such memories.

"Will you bring him home?" Rosamie asked quietly. "Your father?"

Hanalei did not understand the question. How could she? "He's buried on Raka." In a foreigner's graveyard. Far from the island of his birth.

Rosamie worked on another knot. "My mother died in Esperanza. We had gone to seek care for her with a special doctor there. My island's customs are like yours, like Raka's. Our dead must be buried immediately. But with my mother, the elders made an exception."

"What sort of exception?"

"I was allowed to have her ashes brought home for burial. It was how I met William and his brother. We were on the same ship."

"They allowed a cremation?" Burning the dead was not their way.

"I was shocked too. But I had to ask. My mother was an islander, a daughter of the Nominomi. It snows on Esperanza. I couldn't leave her there, in the cold." Rosamie pulled the comb through Hanalei's hair without it catching on a single snarl. "I'm sorry I called you odd."

Hanalei looked over her shoulder, smiling. When she turned around, Sam was there, standing by the steps.

His hair was damp and he had exchanged his dusty soldier's uniform for a clean one. A gold cuff gleamed around his upper arm. He gave a little bow. "Hanalei, Lady Rosamie. How is your pavilion? Comfortable enough?"

Rosamie leaned around Hanalei to beam at him. "As comfortable as home. Thank you for the netting."

While they had gone to bathe, a mosquito net had been set up over their mats, propped up in the center by a wooden pole. For now, the gauzy fabric was rolled back, secured to the pole with ribbons. Before they slept, it would be unfurled, the edges tied to loops on the mats' corners. A quick glance at the other pavilions showed Hanalei that theirs was the only one with a pole and net.

"Tamarind's mosquitoes are vicious, especially once the sun sets." Sam looked over at Hanalei, who said, "Thank you for the netting, but I'm going to sleep on the beach tonight."

"The beach?" A frown creased his brow. "Why?"

"To help with the watch. I might know before the others if there's danger—"

"You might. Or you might not. It's safer for you here."

"Sam."

"What if you're wrong?" Sam asked. "How do I tell my grandmother I let you become fish food? I'm sorry," he added for Rosamie's benefit. "I don't mean to bring back bad memories."

"Oh." Rosamie's eyes darted back and forth between

them. "Please don't apologize."

Feeling thwarted, Hanalei said under her breath, "A seadragon is not a fish."

"I know it's not a fish, Hanalei" came Sam's testy response.

"Look over there," Rosamie said brightly. "Supper's ready. I'll just go . . . I'm going." She returned the comb to Hanalei and hurried to the steps, leather sandals tapping lightly against wood. Sam helped her down the shallow steps, earning another smile in return.

Once she'd gone, Sam commented, "You made another friend. That's two today."

"Maybe." Hanalei could usually tell when someone did not like her, but she did not know what to make of King Nakoro's prickly niece, who was sometimes kind and some-times not. "You don't have to keep scowling. I'll keep away from the water."

"Good." Sam leaned against a column. "And someone should tell you, you're not poor."

Startled, Hanalei glanced over at the open fire, where Rosamie had settled beside William and Jejomar. "How long were you standing there?"

"Have you forgotten our laws?" Sam asked, ignoring her question. "When your father married your mother, every-thing he owned became hers. Upon her passing, it became yours. Since you personally committed no offense to the crown, and because there was no confirmation of your death, it could not be touched."

Hanalei saw his lips move and heard his words. Still, she asked, "What does that mean?"

"That the pavilion in the city is yours to do with as you like," Sam told her. "The same with your homes in the mountains and in the south. They have been looked after. You have your cinnamon shares. The profits from those are managed by my grandmother's own spice masters. Your personal belongings, including all jewelry, are in a vault. You're not poor, Hanalei. You have more gold than I do."

In her wildest imaginings, she had not thought her possessions would be kept for her. Especially the pavilion in the city, where she had spent the most time. The pavilion was hers. "This is good news," she managed.

Glaring at her, he said, "It's excellent news."

"Then why are you upset?"

"I'm not."

"You are."

"I'm . . ." Sam trailed off, realizing, "I am."

They looked at each other across the pavilion. Hanalei brushed her skirts to one side, making room for him on the mat. He came over and settled beside her, legs drawn up, elbows on knees. He did not speak right away and Hanalei did not press him. Conversation and laughter drifted over from the fire, mingling with the sound of sand crickets.

"I hate that you've been hungry," Sam said at last. "That you've gone without when you did not have to."

"I feel the same. About you."

Sam turned his head, looked at her. "I've never gone hungry."

Not for food. But maybe for other things. "I didn't realize it yesterday, but most of the people by the lagoon, they weren't from here. They were visitors. Like Lady Rosamie and Lord William. Sam, where is everyone?"

He should have been surrounded by friends. Young men and women who had grown up alongside him in the royal court. They had been Hanalei's friends too: Siboyas and Hori, Tupaia and Fian. So many others. She had not seen them by the shore, or in the queen's pavilion. And though Hanalei had asked him where everyone was, she already knew the answer.

To the adored child, send them on journeys. An old Tamarindi saying. It was a tradition among the families that once a son or daughter turned eighteen, they would travel beyond the Tamarindi archipelago. Most had already done so, but this time it would be without strict parental supervision. A chance to see the Nominomi and the oversea kingdoms as men and women. No longer children. The journeys usually lasted six to twelve months, sometimes longer. Sam's friends had already left. He should have gone with them.

Sam did not meet her eyes. "They're traveling."

Hanalei said quietly, "But not you."

"How can I leave, Hana? I'm needed at home."

He was her old friend, and she found herself shifting closer so that her arm touched his. "You won't always be. Not as much. When your mother is better, where will you go first?"

"I haven't thought about it."

"Liar."

She heard the smile in his voice. "I have a list," he admitted. "It's a long one. When my mother is better—"

The sound of something breaking brought her head off his shoulder. They looked to the fire. Liko had jumped to her feet with a cry. She was slapping at her skin—her arms, her chest, the back of her neck.

"Hey!" Bayani had also leapt to his feet. "What's with you, Liko?"

"What's happening?" Hanalei asked.

"I don't know." Sam pulled Hanalei to her feet. Within moments they were at the fire.

"Bugs." Liko spun like a fire dancer. She slapped at her skin. "They're everywhere."

She must have flung aside her plate. Food had gone all over the place. Mostly on Bayani. His tunic was covered in sauce. But also on Rosamie and William, who picked bits of chicken from their clothing and hair. Hanalei looked at Liko's arms, realizing, with a start, what she was looking at.

"Move back," Sam said to the others. "Liko, stop."

Liko did as she was told, though her eyes were panicked. She held out both arms so that all could see the marking that raced up one arm and down the other.

"It's small." Jejomar peered over Sam's shoulder. "Is it a cockroach? It looks like a cockroach."

"My marking is a *cockroach*?" Liko squeezed her eyes shut.

"Jejomar," Sam said.

Hanalei stepped around Sam, smiling. "Liko, open your eyes. Look. It's a fire maiden. A firefly."

Liko opened her eyes just as the firefly rose from her skin, a tattoo transformed into a living, sparking creature. There were *oohs* and *aahs* and startled laughs as the lone firefly turned into two, doubling and tripling until dozens swooped among them.

Hanalei held out a finger. A firefly landed on the very tip, a tiny light twinkling in and out.

Rosamie came over to inspect. "But is it real? Or an illusion?"

"It's real," Hanalei said. "Hold out your hand." When Rosamie did, the firefly fluttered from Hanalei's finger to hers. They laughed.

"A fire maiden." Liko's expression was full of wonder. "It feels strange under my skin."

"Like bugs crawling," Sam said with a smile. "I remember."

"I remember too." Cook sat by the fire with Catamara. On his arm was the image of a ko'ko' bird. "Soon you won't notice."

By then, hundreds of fireflies lit the night sky. Bayani flapped his hands about, shooing away the ones that flew too close to the flames. Liko asked, "How do I make it stop?"

"Hold out your hand," Sam instructed, "and call it back. It's your marking. You tell it what to do."

"It will listen?"

His reply was rueful. "Most of the time."

Liko turned in a slow circle, taking everything in. She held out a hand and said, "Come back?"

In an instant, all but one firefly vanished. It returned to Liko's wrist. Its light dimmed and it transformed into a simple tattoo, flat and unmoving. Rosamie dropped her hand, disappointed.

"You don't think it's too small?" Liko asked, studying her wrist. "Lord Isko has a shark."

"The queen has a spider," Sam reminded her, and saw her expression clear. "It's an honorable marking, Liko. Useful too. A good one to have around, in the dark."

Once the excitement died down, supper continued around the fire. Only Liko was absent. She sat on the steps of her pavilion, sparks of light flitting about her head.

Here by the fire, the conversation flowed freely. William laughed at something Jejomar said. They pored over what looked to be some sort of list. Rosamie's empty plate lay at her feet. Her face was tipped toward the darkening sky. She preferred the night, Hanalei was coming to realize. Happier beneath the moon than the sun. Catamara shared a pipe with Cook and some of the guards. They passed it back and forth, cheeks puffed out like apples from the smoke.

The chatter dipped as a colony of bats broke through the trees, wings flapping. Beside Hanalei, Sam searched the sky, looking for one bat in particular.

"When do you expect him?" Hanalei asked. "Tonight?"

"Tonight's too soon. Tomorrow, hopefully." His smile was slight. "I'm used to having him close."

William looked over when he heard Fetu's name. "May I ask a question, Prince Samahti? About your bat?"

"Yes."

William set his list aside, half sitting on it to keep it from blowing away. "Well, we're trying to find the dragonfruit, to save your mother. Who I very much look forward to meeting! But once she's well again, won't she want her marking back?" William looked around as Jejomar nudged him and the others turned his way. He added hastily, "I'm terribly sorry. That was nosy, wasn't it? My sister says I should count to fifty before I speak—"

"No, it's a good question." Sam reached for his cup. "My mother will want Fetu back. I've always known it. He has never been mine to keep."

"Won't you miss him?"

"Very much," Sam said. "But he won't be far away."

Rosamie leaned around Hanalei to ask, "Do you think you'll have a marking of your own, Prince Samahti?"

"No, Lady," Sam said with certainty. "Markings usually skip a generation in the male line of my family. My father had one. If I have a son, it's likely he'll have one too."

Hanalei picked at her supper. No marking had appeared on Hanalei's mother, but her father's had been a shark. Just like Lord Isko's. As a small girl, she had ridden on the back of her father's hammerhead, laughing, arms clutched around fin as it whisked her around the shallows. It was one of her earliest memories, and one of her happiest.

"Are the types of markings hereditary?" William asked. "Do the same ones keep turning up in the same family?"

"Sometimes," Sam answered. "I don't remember there ever being a firefly in Liko's family. But there are plenty of spiders in mine." He reached into his pouch and set Viti free, tossing her onto the grass. She sat there beside his boot, eyes blinking, taking everything in. "It's a lucky marking for a queen to have."

"Because of how big they can get?" William asked.

That," Sam agreed. "And because they can sense danger. Ill intent, malice."

William's eyes widened. "You mean, Viti can tell if someone means you harm?"

"Sometimes, yes."

Jejomar stood, holding his empty plate. He looked down at William and announced, "Tree climbing."

"I beg your pardon?"

"Your list," Jejomar reminded him. "Didn't you say you wanted to learn how to climb a tree?"

William's expression cleared. "Yes, of course. It's number three on my list."

There was a scar on Jejomar's neck. Hanalei hadn't noticed it until now. Curious, she leaned forward for a closer look, but he turned aside, pointing to some coconut trees not too far away, beyond the mango grove. "Those are good for learning," Jejomar said. "They're not too big, not too small. I'll get a torch."

"You mean now?" William pushed his spectacles higher on the bridge of his nose.

"We won't have time tomorrow," Jejomar said with a shrug. "It's not hard. You just need strong arms and firm knees."

"Well, all right then." William got to his feet, smiling. "I'll give it a go. Though I have neither of those."

Rosamie brushed at her skirt. "I'm coming with you. To supervise."

"Do you know how to climb trees, Rosamie?" William said with some surprise.

"Every islander does, William. I think it's a law."

"I should go, too, Prince Samahti." Bayani rose, drumstick in hand. "In case anyone needs catching."

Sam eyed Bayani, and the others who were suddenly eager to finish their meal and watch William try his hand at tree-climbing. In no time at all, the campfire had cleared. Only Hanalei, Sam, and Viti remained. And Catamara, who now had the pipe all to himself.

Hanalei reached for Viti and set the spider on her knee. "That was strange."

Sam watched the torches disappear into the trees. "Climbing a tree is not that interesting."

They looked at one another, then at Viti, then Catamara, who blew smoke into the air. "That is the trouble with a quest like yours, young prince."

"What do you mean?" Sam asked.

Catamara shrugged. "There are only two eggs left. And you are not the only one here with a mother." The old man puffed away on his pipe, smoke drifting ever so slowly toward the heavens.

24

SAM LAY FLAT ON HIS BELLY, PEERING THROUGH blades of wild beach grass. The sand rolled out before him, bright and fine as poured salt, sparkling beneath the morning sun. It was a day meant for swimming or fishing. Or it would have been, were it not for the seadragon asleep on the water. It lay atop a rock that rose from the deep. Tail submerged. Pouch turned to shore. Two pink eggs nestled within.

"You're sure?" Beside him, Catamara brushed aside some grass that poked at his face. He wore green, like Sam, along with a battered straw hat. "This is what you want to do?"

"I'm sure."

Catamara warned, "If the boy misses . . ."

"We have to try, Cata. If it swims off, it might not come back. Bayani's a good shot." It was their first sighting in two days. As day turned to night and night to day, Sam had begun to panic, afraid he had allowed the dragon to slip through his fingers. He could not take the chance again.

They were surrounded by half their party, all lurking in the grass. Behind them, a guard platform had been built in the trees. Hanalei had wanted to observe the dragon from up high. She was there with Bayani, having climbed a rope ladder, though Sam could not see them, hidden as they were among the leaves. A large bell hung from a branch, secured by thick rope. It was a warning bell, struck by the guards when danger was near.

The others remained across the road with the carts and kandayos. The animals could not be expected to stay quiet, and Sam did not want to risk scaring the seadragon off. Just then, the dragon yawned and rolled, showing its back to them. It was what he had been waiting for. A small bit of protection for the eggs.

Sam lifted a hand. He could not see Bayani, but Bayani could see him. He braced himself. With luck, and the grace of the gods, it would all be over soon.

The arrow never flew. There was a sharp cry overhead and when Sam looked up it was to see Hanalei falling from the tree, surrounded by nothing more than air and sunlight.

His heart seized. "Hana!" he shouted, on his feet and running, knowing he would be too late to break her fall. Hanalei's arms windmilled. She grabbed frantically for the bell rope, catching hold long enough to check her fall and set the bell ringing, before landing on the sand with a thud.

Sam dropped to his knees in front of her. He had to shout to be heard over the clanging. "Are you hurt?"

"Just my ears," Hanalei said, though she rubbed her shoulder and bent her arm, wincing.

The others were not far behind Sam. Rosamie ran over from across the road, surprisingly fast, followed by Jejomar and William. Bayani rappelled down the ladder, bow hanging from a shoulder.

"Let me see." Sam felt her arm gently, and when she did not flinch, he knew her elbow socket had not been pulled free. She would likely bruise where she had landed. His mind shied away from how much worse it could have been.

"I'm fine. Nothing's broken. I'm very sorry, Sam."

Hanalei was staring out at the Nominomi. When he followed her gaze, he saw the seadragon looking right at them. As the ringing faded, it slipped into the water and headed out to deep sea.

Gone. Again.

Catamara's hand came down on his shoulder. "Bad luck today. Next time."

Sam closed his eyes briefly. Helping Hanalei to her feet, he said, "I'm glad you're not hurt. I might need to sit down."

"Prince Samahti." Bayani stood slightly apart from the others, a grim cast to his features.

"We'll get another chance," Sam told him. "Let's head out. After I sit. Maybe it'll turn up again today."

"It's not that . . ." Bayani looked at Hanalei , who ducked her head and said, "Apologies, Bayani. I couldn't think of what else to do."

Sam looked from one to the other. "What happened?"

"Lady Hanalei didn't fall," Bayani said, his voice heavy. "When she saw me aiming for the dragon, she knocked my bow away. And then she jumped."

The chatter around them dropped away. Sam turned to Hanalei. Sam expected to see outrage on Hanalei's face, to hear a denial. Instead, her shoulders inched higher around her ears. All he saw guilt. "You rang the bell on purpose," he said.

"I'm sorry, Sam."

Sorry? "Was this your plan all along? Save your precious dragon? Never mind anyone else?"

"No! Of course not! Sam, those eggs aren't safe—"

"You've always known it, and yet you came anyway. Why?"

"Not to kill him. To keep him close. If I could just have more time to figure out—"

"We don't have it, Hanalei! What time? When those eggs hatch, they'll be useless. Who are you trying to save here?"

"You!" Hanalei said. "You'll get hurt. I love your mother.

I want to help your mother. But I won't risk you."

Their voices were rising. And then suddenly they weren't. Sam said, very quietly, "It's not your decision whom to risk. You say you want to help. So help. And if you can't, or you won't, just go."

No one spoke to Sam, which was for the best. His mood was foul.

He set a bruising pace as they rode west. They could have been heading east, toward home, with two dragon eggs in their possession. They had been so close. He had meant what he'd said to Hanalei. It was his mother who mattered.

Who are you trying to save here?

You! I won't risk you.

He should not have yelled at her. Not in front of the others, not at all. If the situation were reversed, he would not want to risk her either.

Sam leaned forward, his kandayo's mane whipping against his face. It felt as if the sky were falling in on him. It was not just Hanalei or the dragonfruit. Three days had passed since they had left Tamarind City, and there had been no sign of Fetu. Where was his marking? What could have happened to his bat?

It was not until they stopped for their midday meal that Sam surveyed the party and realized instantly who was missing.

"Where is she?"

Hanalei was nowhere in sight. And neither, he saw, was Rosamie.

Catamara sat beside Cook on his cart. He looked down at Sam, disapproval on his face, and said, "You told her to go, so she went."

25

"WELL, WHAT NOW?" ROSAMIE ASKED.

Entry Forbidden. Hanalei regarded the wooden sign nailed to the trunk of a coconut tree. The words had been slapped on with red paint that had dripped and splattered before it dried. Hanalei thought instantly of blood. Beyond the sign was a lane choked with grass and weeds. No one had traveled down this road in a very long time. She nudged her kandayo forward. "This looks like the right place. Come on."

"I was afraid you'd say that." With a sigh, Rosamie brought her kandayo alongside Hanalei's. Her features were in shadow, shielded by the brim of her hat.

"You didn't have to come with me. Why did you?" Sam would not care if she was gone, but Lady Rosamie was a different story. He would be in big trouble for losing such a guest.

"How could I let you slink off like that? It isn't safe to go

off on your own . . . What?" Rosamie demanded at Hanalei's sudden smile.

"I've been on my own a long time, Lady Rosamie."

"I forgot about that part until now. Besides, I thought
Prince Samahti would feel bad and come after us. What's
taking him so long?"

"He shouldn't feel bad. I deserved it." Hanalei had deliberately warned the seadragon away. If Princess Olli never
recovered, it would be her fault and no on else's.

"Wallowing is not going to help us. Tell me why we're
here. Who is this Captain Erro and why are we going to his
pavilion?"

"He was a royal guard," Hanalei said. "Lord Isko's
second-in-command. He was there the day I was poisoned."

"A guard? He must not have been a very good one."

"What happened wasn't his fault. He was good at what
he did. And he was kind to us children."

"Was he dismissed after the poisoning?"

"Not for that." Hanalei tried to recall what Penina
had told her over supper. "Ten years ago, the captain was
responsible for escorting the three dragon eggs from the
menagerie to the queen's pavilion. But there was an earthquake. Two eggs fell from the carriage and broke open,
killing two baby dragons. Instead of helping the injured
driver, Captain Erro threw himself in the mud and started

eating one of the dragons. Right there in front of everyone."

Rosamie made a face. "He was dismissed after that."

"Yes," Hanalei said. "We're going to his pavilion because I wish to test a theory."

She had not left Sam's party immediately. She had been riding at the very back, feeling a terrible guilt, mortified by what she had shouted for all to hear. *I won't risk you!* She had groaned every time she thought of it, had not even been aware of what she was doing, until Rosamie leaned over on her kandayo and whispered for her to stop.

And then she had remembered Penina mentioning Captain Erro's home. It was somewhere in these parts. She had broken off from the group, followed by Rosamie. After asking for directions from three different people and leading the kandayos down a number of wrong paths, they had found their way here.

Rosamie asked, "What sort of theory?"

"Captain Erro risked his livelihood to eat the dragonfruit. He disgraced himself and his family. He must have wanted something very badly."

Rosamie tipped her hat back, enough for Hanalei to see understanding dawn on her face. "*Every wish demands a price.* You want to know what price he paid."

"*If* he paid one. We could find nothing. I hope we do."

They passed more signs nailed to trees. One said *Be Gone with You* and the other, simply, *Leave*. The grass and weeds brushed the undersides of both kandayos.

"Lady Hanalei," Rosamie said. "I think we're going to find something."

They should have heeded the signs. The pavilion suffered from terrible neglect. Gaping holes in the thatching, a foundation of crumbling latti stones. Which was strange because latti rarely crumbled. The stones were built to last many centuries.

Hanalei and Rosamie dismounted, leaving the kandayos to graze. Around them were trees downed in past storms and left to lie where they fell. Coconut trees, flame trees, jacarandas. The place looked abandoned.

"No one lives here," Rosamie said.

Hanalei felt a crushing disappointment. They had come all this way. "He must have gone years ago—" She froze. Over by the pavilion, a man stood beside a latti stone, his arm raised.

In the next instant, Hanalei felt a shove and went tumbling into the tall grass. Rosamie followed, shrieking. Something heavy fell on them.

"Stay down!" The heavy something was Sam. A loud *thunk* sounded above them. Hanalei spit out a mouthful of grass and turned her head. A machete was half-buried in a tree trunk.

"Stop!" Sam shouted.

"Can't you read?" The man hollered back. Hanalei saw metal flash in his hand before it sailed toward them. A dagger lodged beneath the machete. Rosamie shrieked again.

Hanalei elbowed Sam in the gut, rolled to her feet, and dove behind the tree. Sam and Rosamie were right behind her.

"I said get lost! Go on with you!"

"Plumeria!" Sam yelled back. "Plumeria!"

Rosamie looked at him, mouth open. *Plumeria?* But for Hanalei, an old memory surfaced. She shouted, "Captain! Plumeria!"

Silence.

Hanalei peered out from behind the tree. The man had stepped away from the latti stone. His hands were by his sides. Despite the heat of the day, he wore gloves. He looked haggard, black hair grown past his elbows, a full black beard. His trousers and tunic were stained and patched. Still, Hanalei recognized Captain Erro.

Sam pulled her back. "Hana. Lady Rosamie. Are you hurt?"

They shook their heads.

"Good. Stay here."

Sam stepped cautiously into the open. Hanalei poked her head out again, but she could go no farther. Rosamie had a firm grip around her ankle.

Captain Erro said, "That is an old password."

"I am an old friend," Sam replied.

The captain's smile held no humor. "Is that what we are, Prince Samahti? Old friends?"

In response, Sam raised a hand high. "Put your weapons away. I don't want him hurt."

The tall grasses shifted around them and a dozen guards stepped forward. Bayani carried his bow. Liko and the others held machetes and knives, lowered at Sam's order.

Hanalei tugged at her ankle. Rosamie's grip tightened. "Stop. We're supposed to stay here."

"Let go." Another tug. Rosamie released her leg with an exasperated sigh.

"Why are you looking for me?" Captain Erro demanded.

"I wasn't," Sam replied, as Hanalei came to stand by his side. He glanced down at her, his expression unreadable. "I was looking for someone else."

"Hello, Captain," Hanalei said.

Captain Erro's gaze snapped to hers. "And who are you? Besides a trespasser?"

He did not recognize her. Well, ten years was a long time. "My name is—"

"Hanalei," Captain Erro said, astonished. He took a single step forward. A warning from Bayani kept him from taking another one. "You are Lady Hanalei."

"Yes, sir."

"How . . . ? The dragonfruit. It worked for you."

She nodded. There was an intensity to the captain's gaze, fierce and unblinking. It made her deeply uneasy. Enough to inch closer to Sam, though she knew how angry he was. His anger was not as scary as Captain Erro's. Without looking at her, Sam took her hand in his and kept it there.

Captain Erro's eyes dropped to their clasped hands. "Where is your father? What happened to him?"

Sam's hand twitched.

"Why do you think anything happened?" Hanalei asked.

Captain Erro's lips twisted. A bitter, knowing smile. "Something happened." He looked around at the guards. "Get rid of them if you want to talk. I dislike an audience." He swung around and disappeared around the side of the pavilion.

Hanalei stepped away from Sam, her hand falling free of his. "What's wrong with him?"

"I don't know."

Liko was helping Rosamie to her feet. Bayani was coming their way. Sam told him, "Wait for us at the end of the lane. Take Lady Rosamie with you. We'll meet you there."

Bayani looked unhappy with the order. "Someone should stay with you."

"He's right," Rosamie said. "That man just threw a machete at us!"

"I'll stay." Liko surveyed the tall grass surrounding the pavilion. "He won't know I'm here."

"He'll know," Hanalei and Sam said at the same time. Sam added, "He won't hurt us, and I think . . . I think we need to hear what he has to tell us."

Liko and Bayani knew better than to argue. Within moments the guards had retreated down the path, taking Rosamie and her kandayo with them. Hanalei's animal was left to graze.

Hanalei and Sam headed around the decrepit pavilion, skirting pottery shards and deep pits in the dirt, the sort that would break an ankle if one did not take care.

"You shouldn't have left," Sam said abruptly.

"You told me to go."

"And? Suddenly you listen?"

"I listen!"

"What if you had missed the rope? Hm?" Sam's ire grew with every step. "You miss the rope and crack your head open at my feet, what then? You're used to no one caring if you live or die, Hanalei. You're not on Raka anymore." He fell silent as they rounded the back of the pavilion. Captain Erro stood before a trio of nutmeg trees. On the ground were thousands of fallen shells. Never harvested, left to rot.

They approached, boots crunching over newer shells, squelching over the mush of older ones. They stopped beside the captain. Hanalei's questions were momentarily forgotten, distracted by the trees themselves. Human features had been carved onto the trunks. On one, a beautiful woman, her features delicate and her lips full, smiling slightly. The rest of her form was merely hinted at. A curve here and there suggested a skirt and a slender arm. A bare, elegant neck. The carving on the center tree was that of an old man. Face weathered, deep lines. At the base of the trunk were two feet clad in sandals. The man's face and feet were beautifully detailed, the rest of him left undone. The third tree showed two boys. The older was about ten, gangly and smiling, and holding the hand of the younger, who looked to be three or four.

Off to the side was a fourth tree. It had fallen to the dirt, perhaps uprooted in the recent storm. If there was a carving on it, Hanalei could not see it. The trunk had been covered with a long sweep of banana leaf.

Sam was also staring at the carved figures. "I didn't know you were such a fine carver."

"You were the artist," Erro said, his tone odd. "Even as a boy. I've never carved a thing in my life."

Hanalei and Sam exchanged glances behind Erro's back. "What has happened here, Captain?" Sam asked. When he did not answer, Hanalei spoke.

"You asked about my father. He was killed on Rakakala,

not long after the dragonfruit . . . helped me."

Captain Erro showed no surprise at her revelation. "You lost your family."

"Yes, sir."

"So did I, Lady Hanalei."

A nutmeg dropped from the middle tree, making Hanalei jump. It rolled to a stop by Erro's boots. He bent and picked it up with his gloved hand, pressing it to his lips.

"Captain." There was an edge to Sam's voice. "What happened here?"

"I had debts," Erro said. "When I was younger, I did foolish things. Promised squid I did not have. And it made it so dangerous people came my way, and my family was no longer safe. When you are at the mercy of bad people, they make you do bad things." He placed the shell at the base of the tree, among all the others. "When the dragonfruit broke on that roadside, I did not see the harm in taking a little bit for myself."

Hanalei tried to make sense of what he told them. "What did you ask for?"

"To be free of my debt. The burden of it."

Sam turned to look at the crumbling pavilion, the ruin all around them. "And were you?"

"I suppose it's a matter of perspective," Erro said. "The nutmeg tree, for instance. It's a profitable tree, no? Spices can bring a man great wealth. You would know."

Sam studied the neglected trees. "If they're cared for, harvested. Then yes."

"I'll never harvest these trees. I won't part with a single seed." Erro looked around and whistled. A dog came trotting out from the tangle of grass. A small, cheerful, mangy creature. Erro crouched, began tugging off one glove, finger by finger. Hanalei half expected to see scars like hers, or burns, but there was nothing there. His skin was unmarred. When Erro held out a hand, the dog licked his fingers. It let out a single puzzled *woof*. And then it curled up on the ground, covered its eyes with a paw, and went to sleep.

Erro rose as the ground shifted. Hanalei and Sam backed away, watching as a hole opened beneath the dog. The animal dropped several feet into the space, and when the ground shifted again, it was to cover the animal with dirt. Hanalei and Sam backed up some more. A tendril appeared in the same spot. In the span of seconds, the tendril grew, from a stem to a small nutmeg tree to one just as large as the ones beside it. Bushy leaves and plump seeds covered thick branches. On the trunk appeared a faint carving of a cheerful, mangy dog standing on two legs, paws raised, tongue hanging out one side of his mouth.

Hanalei was vaguely aware of her mouth hanging open, and of Sam's. As one, they looked from the brand-new tree to the older ones.

"Your family," Sam said, his voice not quite steady. Hanalei covered her mouth with both hands.

Erro nodded. "*Every wish demands a price.* Isn't that how the saying goes?" He laughed, a sound that lifted the hairs on Hanalei's arms. "Everything I touch with my bare hands turns into a nutmeg, this tree that I hate. This tree that would free me from debt if I only harvested it. The gods have a wicked sense of humor, I think that is safe to say."

The captain had deliberately harmed his dog. He could have just explained. Hanalei snuck a glance at the tree covered with banana leaf.

Erro saw her looking. "My mother. Struck down during the last typhoon."

Sam went right up to the middle tree, his face inches away from the old man's. Not touching. "When did this happen?"

"Ten years ago," Erro said.

Sam said quietly, "Do you never leave here?"

"There's no need. I am self-sufficient."

Sam stepped away from the tree. "Does no one visit? Friends?"

"I left them behind on Tamarind."

Tears pricked Hanalei's eyes. She had come here to test a theory. And now wished that she had not. There was comfort in ignorance, in not knowing. The truth before her was a wretched one.

"Captain," Sam said, "you shouldn't have gone through this alone. Why didn't you tell someone?"

A bitter laugh. "Who would I tell, Prince Samahti? Who would have come?"

"Lord Isko would have come," Sam said, and Hanalei knew it to be true. Captain Erro's behavior had been unbecoming to a royal guard. But he had harmed no one. Lord Isko could be hard, but he would not have forsaken one of his men. He would have tried to help.

At the mention of Lord Isko, something flashed across Erro's expression. They both saw it.

"He already knows," Hanalei said.

"Yes." Erro's gaze was fixed firmly on his two boys. "He came and he went. Years ago."

"Why did he leave?" Sam asked.

Silence.

Sam said, "You said your debts made you beholden to bad people. You did bad things for them. What bad things?"

Captain Erro's expression wavered. "Please go."

And suddenly Hanalei understood.

Sam said, "Wakeo was behind my mother's poisoning. But we never learned how the poison made it into my mother's supper. Into Hanalei's. We only knew it had to have been done by someone they trusted."

"The prince made me do it," Erro said, his voice low.

"He told me it was my family—"

"Or mine," Sam finished.

"Yes. Lord Isko found out and he came . . . I was not supposed to survive that day. Then he saw what happened here and he said . . . he would not kill me. Living was a far more suitable punishment."

Like Hanalei, Sam kept a dagger at his belt. He gripped its hilt, his knuckles whitening.

Captain Erro said, "I wish you would."

"No" was Sam's response. "I don't want you to die either."

Erro bowed his head. "Forgive me, forgive me. There's nothing you can do that would be worse than what has already been done."

"I can burn your trees down," Sam told him.

Erro went still.

"While you watch. I can make it worse."

Hanalei placed a hand on Sam's arm. She could feel him trembling beneath her fingers. "Come on, Sam. Let's go."

Erro saw her hand just then, covered with scars. His eyes widened. She wondered if he had ever once spared her a thought. Princess Oliana's page, no one of consequence. She led Sam around the pavilion, to her kandayo. It was the only one there. Sam swung on behind her. When she settled against his chest, she could feel the pounding of his heart.

"I'm sorry, Hana."

"For what?"

His words were low, full of self-reproach. "You've tried to tell me, over and over again, and I have not listened. Forgive me."

It did not matter. What did she care about being right? Every wish demands a price. What were they supposed to do now?

26

THEY ARRIVED LATE IN THE AFTERNOON IN THE village of Pago Maya. Weary, hungry, and increasingly disheartened. There was the problem of the dragonfruit, for one. And there was concern for Fetu, who should have appeared by now. Even the apprentices watched the sky with grave expressions, hoping to spot the familiar, flapping wings.

Pago Maya had been built on a hill to protect the village from flooding. The first chief had grown weary of rebuilding pavilions after every typhoon. The present chief, Umere, greeted them on the steps of his pavilion, alongside his family. Diplomacy ruled in Pago Maya. Hanalei was treated as a guest whose infamous father and sudden reappearance were touched upon, then politely ignored.

As Sam went off in one direction with the chief, Hanalei heard him say, "My bat is missing, chief. Was he here?"

Chief Umere's voice was a rumble. "Fetu? Yes, two nights ago. He stayed to eat and pass along your message. What do you mean 'missing'?"

"I told him to find me on the road, but no one has seen him."

"He'll turn up, Prince Samahti. Perhaps Fetu misheard and went back to Tamarind instead. He'll turn up, you'll see."

Their voices faded away. Hanalei went off in the opposite direction with Rosamie, toward the bathing pools, thinking that Fetu had never misheard anything in his life. He was a bat, with a bat's excellent hearing. Where could he be?

She was soon distracted by the pigs. They were everywhere. Black-and-white-spotted pigs, both large and small. The fully grown ones turned on spits. The babies were allowed to roam freely along village roads. Napping on patches of grass, like cats and dogs would in other villages, on other islands.

Rosamie carried a small bowl of lemons. She nearly lost her hold on it when she tripped over a pig. "Are they pets, or are they supper?" she asked, looking around in bafflement. The animals were indifferent to their presence, making no effort to get out of their way.

"Both." Hanalei picked up a fallen lemon and returned it to the bowl. "The children are taught not to get too attached to the piglets. In case they become supper." Seeing Rosamie's expression, she added with a shrug, "It is their way."

The bathing pool was fed by a small waterfall and

shielded from the rest of the village by boulders. The bougainvillea grew wild among the rocks. The scent from the blossoms was heavy and pleasing. It was just the two of them there. Hanalei set her bag on the grass and shook out one of the dresses Penina had packed for her. She threw off her clothes and hat and dove into the water, welcome after the long ride.

Dirt and grime were easy to wash away. She wished it were as simple to scrub away the memory of Captain Erro. She remained underwater as long as she could, picturing two small boys carved into wood, until her lungs protested. When she surfaced, it was to find Rosamie sitting beneath the one tree that offered shade. Fully dressed. Her floppy straw hat remained on her head. She rubbed her eyes like a tired child would, with both fists.

"Do they hurt?" Hanalei asked.

Rosamie dropped her hands quickly. "I'm just tired."

"You could ride in the cook's cart sometimes," Hanalei suggested. "To rest your eyes. It's dark in there."

Rosamie's expression grew guarded. "That isn't necessary."

Hanalei made no comment. She turned and swam to the end of the pool and back. When she returned, Rosamie was waiting.

"How did you know?" she asked Hanalei quietly.

"It's common on Raka." Hana dug her toes into the sand

and pebbles. The water came to her chin. "More than it is here. When I was in the workhouse, there were two boys who couldn't see color. The sun hurt their eyes. They wore big hats when they worked outside. And when they could, they worked at night." She skimmed the water's surface with both arms. "The woman who weighed the dragonscale each day, she always wore the same color. Black. She said it made dressing simpler."

They both looked at Rosamie's dress. It was white. A different dress each day, but always white.

Stricken, Rosamie said, "I wasn't going to steal it."

Hanalei stopped skimming. "Steal what?"

Rosamie wrapped her arms around her knees and buried her head on them.

"Do you mean the eggs?" Hanalei came closer, water lapping at her shoulders. "I'm the last person to throw stones at you. Look at who you're talking to. But I don't think Sam . . . Prince Samahti, will just give you one."

Rosamie spoke to her knees. "He will if I can get him to fall in love with me. He will if there's one extra."

You're spoiling my chance, she had told Hanalei. Had she meant Sam or the dragonfruit, or both? "What would you use it for?"

Rosamie lifted her head. "It isn't for me."

Hanalei waited. A mosquito buzzed by her nose. She swatted at it.

"My uncle," Rosamie said at last. "Something's wrong with him. He forgets things, and it's become worse and worse. He forgets who I am and who my cousins are. Others are starting to notice. I thought if I had the dragonfruit . . ." She trailed off in misery.

"You said yourself it was dangerous. Why would you take such a chance?"

"He's my family," Rosamie said, "and my king. He's worth any risk." She selected a lemon from the bowl and sliced it in half with Hanalei's dagger, the one Queen Maga'lahi had given her. "I don't know what I was thinking. I know you have to tell him."

"Sam doesn't need to know everything . . . What? Have you done anything wrong? Do you plan to?"

Rosamie set the dagger aside. She wiped away a solitary tear. "I never thanked you for saving my life that day."

"You did. Back in the stables."

Rosamie sniffled. "I didn't mean it then."

Hanalei smiled, and Rosamie, after a moment, returned it. "Come here. Tip your head." When Hanalei did as she was told, Rosamie squeezed both lemon halves onto her hair. It was not enough. She had a lot of hair. In the end, Rosamie ended up slicing four more lemons.

"Do you see some color?" Hanalei asked curiously. "One of the boys could see almost all of them, just not red or green."

"None," Rosamie said. "I see light and shadow and texture. I can tell when a banana is ripe because of how it smells, not because I can see green or yellow. Yellow, green, purple, blue. They are just words to me."

Hanalei had turned away from Rosamie, combing lemon juice through her hair with her fingers, when Rosamie asked, "Did it hurt?"

Hanalei looked over her shoulder. "My hands?"

"That tattoo." Rosamie was studying her back. "It must have taken months to finish. You know I'll never be fond of seadragons, not after being eaten by one. But yours is extraordinary."

27

HANALEI DID NOT TELL HER. SHE MUMBLED SOME-thing about it not hurting at all, then threw on her dress and fled the bathing pool, leaving Rosamie staring after her.

Dusk had fallen, and the pathway lay in shadows. She trembled the entire way back to the chief's pavilion. When had her marking appeared? How could she not have felt it? Or known in some way that it was there? Liko had felt her firefly. She reached behind her, under the neckline of her dress, trying to touch as much of her back as possible. There was nothing to be felt but skin.

Someone was running up the path behind her. Hanalei yanked her hand free of her dress. There was huffing breath and a sudden dull thud, followed by a squeal. "Stupid pig!" and "Lady Hanalei! Lady, wait."

It was Rosamie, who ran up and grabbed her by the shoulders. "I didn't realize what I was looking at, and I think— Did *you* realize?"

Hanalei shook her head.

Rosamie dropped her hands. "How are always so calm? I would have fainted. I still might."

"I feel very close to fainting," Hanalei said in a small voice.

"Here, take my arm." Rosamie guided her to a tree stump on the side of the path. Her voice was just above a whisper. "I've never heard of a seadragon marking. Have you?"

"Never." The largest had always been a shark. Her father's shark. Lord Isko's.

The fires had been lit. Hanalei could see them through the trees. The others were gathering for supper. There was laughter and conversation. Someone was playing the drums.

Rosamie said, "Will you tell Prince Samahti?"

"Not yet. Not here."

"Move over," Rosamie said, sitting beside Hanalei on the stump. "You're shaking. So am I, to be honest. We'll just sit here and collect ourselves. Until we can pretend in front of the others."

They sat for a good twenty minutes, in silence, listening to night fall around them. Hanalei could hear Sam's voice, deep and pleasant and familiar.

Her heartbeat slowed, and the trembling faded to nothing. "Thank you, Lady Rosamie."

Rosamie laughed, the sound high-pitched and uneven.

"It's just Rosamie, Hanalei. I think we are past the grand titles, you and I."

There were nine bonfires in the clearing, each with a turning spit or a large, bubbling pot. Hanalei walked beside Rosamie, her thoughts in turmoil, and so when she passed a group of villagers sitting around a fire, she smiled politely and did not stop. It was only seconds later that she realized she knew one of them. A woman in black holding a bowl, face turned slightly away as if she did not wish to be seen. She wore a crown lei, the ti leaves so lush they covered her forehead. But Hanalei knew that face, just as she knew there was a tattoo beneath that crown. A sunrise pattern, of Rakakalan design.

Vaea, the *Anemone*'s navigator. And if she was here, where was her captain?

Something was not right with this village. Sam had felt it the moment they arrived, but he could not figure out what it was.

The men had been directed to a separate bathing area, a bubbling creek that ran behind Pago Maya, winding its way through coconut groves and cycads. He shared the creek with Jejomar and William. The sun was setting and the mosquitoes were beginning to swarm in earnest.

"Something's strange here," Sam said to his companions. "Something feels wrong."

"It's the pigs." Jejomar stood waist deep in the creek. He pointed to a trio of piglets snuffling nearby. "That's what's strange. Why do they have so many?"

"They're quite numerous," William agreed. He snatched his spectacles from the grassy bank, beating one of the piglets to it.

"It's not the pigs," Sam said absently. "They've always been here. It's something else." He swatted at the mosquitoes. This bath needed to be quick or he would be chewed alive. He looked around. "Who has the soap?" He caught the sliver Jejomar tossed his way.

Sam made use of it, until every bit of travel and dust was gone from him. William was sitting on the bank, wrapped in a drying cloth and looking over a piece of parchment.

"Is that your list?" Sam asked him.

"It is."

So many worries weighed on Sam's mind. Captain Erro. Fetu. His mother. Then there was the dragonfruit. Somehow, he had to find a way to use its magic while avoiding its menace. Those eggs weighed heaviest of all.

William's list felt like the opposite of worry. Something cheerful and light, a thing to look forward to. Sam asked, "What else is on it?"

"Well," William said, "I can climb a tree now, thanks

to Jejomar. I've also heard your waterfalls in the south are magnificent."

"They are," Sam said.

"And we didn't have time before," William said, "but I should like to learn how to crack open a coconut. In case the need arises."

Sam could not help a smile. "You're in good hands. My cousin would win prizes for coconut cracking. If such a thing existed." He looked over at Jejomar, who wore trousers and no shirt and was rummaging through Sam's, not his own, bag. "What are you doing?"

Jejomar held up a black tunic. "Could I borrow a shirt?"

Drily, he asked, "Borrow or keep?"

Jejomar smiled. "I'd give it back, Sam. What do you take me for?"

"It won't fit you."

In response, Jejomar put on the tunic, which fit perfectly. He spread his arms wide. "See?"

When had that happened? Lately, it felt like Sam blinked once and Jejomar grew an inch. He blinked again and suddenly his cousin had calves made of muscle. He did not spend enough time with Jejomar. He had not been paying attention. Guilt had him saying "Keep it."

There was a rustling along the treetops. Sam looked up, hopeful, but it was only a pair of kingfishers. Not a fruit bat.

Jejomar was also looking at the treetops. "I can ride

ahead tomorrow and look for him," he offered. "Make sure he made all his stops."

"You would do that?"

"Why not? Fetu's family. He'll turn up, Sam."

He was not used to being comforted by Jejomar. His cousin was trying. "Take Lord William with you, and one of the guards."

Jejomar agreed and left with William. Sam dressed, then joined Chief and Lady Umere. It was not until later, sitting before their fire, that he realized what was bothering him.

There were no children here.

No older children and no babies, no little ones of any age. On Tamarind, the young did not eat separately from their elders. They ate together. Even when a prince visited. Especially when he did. How had it taken him so long to notice?

There was something else. Chief Umere was older than Sam's grandmother by a good twenty years. A stern, taciturn leader. He was often the first to leave a gathering, even if it was his own, preferring to seek his bed out early and rise at dawn. But this evening, he was laughing and drinking, slapping backs and telling jokes, showing no signs of departing. Lady Umere smiled pleasantly and inquired after Sam's mother and grandmother. In return, Sam asked after her great-grandchildren, watching her smile falter. It returned so quickly Sam had to ask himself if he had imagined it.

"You are kind to ask," Lady Umere said. "They are in the south, visiting our daughter." She passed him more food. Pork, chicken, rice, mango, all heaped on a plate.

Jejomar and William joined them. Not long after that, Hanalei and Rosamie did the same. He took one look at Hanalei's expression and said, "What's wrong?"

"Captain Bragadin's dragoners are here." Hanalei's eyes were on their hosts. "I recognized eight of them. One at each fire."

"Don't turn around," Chief Umere ordered. His tone was desperate, but his lips were smiling. He lifted his cup high, as if giving a toast. "Please. Smile. Pretend, pretend."

Sam's heart thudded even as he smiled. "Why are there dragoners in your village? Chief, where are the children?"

Lady Umere offered a plate to Hanalei, who accepted it with a smile. So much smiling. "Bragadin took them to his ship," Lady Umere said. "Just past the cove. They came two days ago, demanding we repair their dragoner. It's taking on water. It seemed simpler to help them so that they would go. Then your bat arrived with your message, that you would be arriving soon. And Bragadin took the children. He warned us if we told you they were here, we would never see them again."

The night was warm; even so, Sam felt a chill along his arms. Fetu would have warned him, if he could have. "Where is my bat?"

"Forgive me," Chief Umere said, and gulped down the rest of his drink. He wiped his mouth with his sleeve and laughed. "That Bragadin knew he was yours. He made us do it." His eyes flickered to a neighboring fire, where a large pot bubbled.

28

FETU.

His mother's marking. His constant companion. His friend. Sam did not allow himself more than a split second's grief. The cure for worry was action. The same could be said for grief.

"Hanalei."

"Sam. Oh, Sam. Fetu." Hanalei wore a pleasant expression, a smile that matched his own. But her eyes were filled with tears.

"No weeping, Hanalei. Not yet. Give me your soundcatcher."

Hanalei blinked rapidly. She tugged the soundcatcher from her neck, brought it to her lips, and breathed in once, before passing it to him.

Sam's attention was fixed on the chief and his lady. "Tell me everything. Start from the beginning."

No one who watched would suspect anything was amiss. They would see conversation and laughter and drinks being passed around. Rosamie clinked her cup against Hanalei's. Two friends enjoying each other's company. Jejomar and William dug into their supper. Everyone played their part.

The chief informed them that, in addition to the dragoners planted among the fires, there were three lookouts watching from the trees. They would have to be subdued first so that they did not have a chance to run off and warn Captain Bragadin. Sam repeated every word, clearly, for the sake of the soundcatcher. The drums made it difficult to hear. He stumbled only once, when the soup was served at the neighboring fire. Bowls were passed around and Bayani, after his first spoonful, smacked his lips in appreciation. Bile rose in Sam's throat. Hanalei slipped her hand in his, and he held on tight, a moment's solace before he let go, afraid he would crush her fingers.

Liko stood guard beneath a breadfruit tree. When Sam finished speaking into the soundcatcher, he beckoned her over. She leaned down to better hear him above the drums and guitars. "Don't look any different. We're being watched." Sam held up his empty plate. Liko took it; her expression remained unchanged when she felt the soundcatcher beneath the plate. "Bring the guards on the beach their supper. Take Bayani with you. Listen to this together."

"Yes, Prince Samahti," Liko said, as though he had ordered her to do something as simple as ready his kandayo. She went away, handing Sam's empty plate to a passing servant, the soundcatcher nowhere to be seen. She said a few words to Bayani as she passed him, and he rose with an obliging expression, leaving his half-finished bowl of soup behind. They went to a table piled high with food, took two plates each, and shuffled along the queue. Rice, pork, tuna, octopus, guava, starfruit. The plates grew high with food. Only when they teetered under the weight of their bounty did Liko and Bayani move on, heading to the beach.

Sam asked, "How did a dragoner get past the watch?"

"There's a new tree guard in place," Chief Umere said. "I learned she will sometimes look the other way. For a price."

Sam raised a cup to his lips, to hide his expression. Another soldier bought. Like Captain Erro. "Where is this guard now?"

"No one knows. She did not show up to her watch."

Liko reappeared with Bayani, who returned to his seat at the nearby fire, not looking Sam's way once, not once. He did not touch his soup again. Liko paused by Sam's side and said, "The lookouts are taken care of."

"Thank you."

After Liko went back to her post, Sam turned to Hanalei, who was no stranger to the *Anemone*, and said, "Describe them for me."

Hanalei began with the dragoner farthest away. "At the bonfire by the footpath, there's a woman in black wearing a ti leaf crown. She's Bragadin's navigator. To the left of that fire is a man named Papeete. He's the big one with the curly hair; he's holding a pipe. To the left of that is a boy, about fifteen. His hand is wrapped in bandages . . ."

Rosamie spoke. "He's been staring at you the entire time. He makes my flesh creep."

"Mine also," Hanalei said, remembering his giggle as he tried to open her cabin door. "His name is Ant, and he's extremely unpleasant. To the left of that fire . . ." She described the rest of the men and women in detail. When she finished, she asked Sam, "What will you do to them?"

"Me? Not a thing." Viti came crawling out of the pouch onto his leg. Sam said, "All of them, all at once." He could smell the soup from the neighboring fire, and added, very quietly, "Make it hurt, my dear."

Viti hopped onto the grass. Rosamie yanked her skirt aside as the spider crawled past her. Viti would be difficult for others to see in the dark, on the ground. Sam never lost sight of her. He saw the moment a single spider became two, then four, six, then eight. Each went their separate way. Just as they drew up behind the dragoners Hanalei had pointed out, the spiders grew in size, several feet tall, and bit. A single, vicious bite at the base of the spine.

Sam stood and watched. The dragoners had no time to cry out. Their bodies seized and their backs arched, so much so he thought they would snap. Bowls and plates fell to the ground, followed by Captain Bragadin's dragoners.

The drums fell silent, and the villagers of Pago Maya turned to Sam. These were parents and grandparents, terrified for their missing children.

Sam said to the chief, "The ship is by the cove, you said?"

It wasn't the chief who answered, but a male voice from the trees. "I have no weapons. My hands are up. Keep that spider away from me."

29

"HIS NAME IS MOA," HANALEI SAID, TRYING TO ignore the marking that wound itself around her torso, out of sight beneath her dress. "He's one of Bragadin's."

"Not anymore." Moa was on his knees by the fire, where he had been shoved, hands clasped behind his head. Bayani's machete hovered an inch from his ear. Every eye that watched the dragoner was a hostile one.

"We've met," Sam said, to Hanalei's surprise.

"When? Where?"

"At Nama Maguro. He was on the ship that refused to go. It wasn't called the *Anemone* then."

Sam stood before Moa, boots planted wide, arms crossed. He kept his back to the fire, where Jejomar and William removed a giant pot from the flames. William's face was flushed, from heat or exertion or both. Jejomar wept openly. Hanalei's own throat was scratchy with unshed tears. Fetu.

"Bragadin made us paint it." Moa kept looking at his fellow dragoners. They had been laid out like a row of corpses, alive but stunned into stillness. A large, watchful Viti guarded them, legs rustling and twitching in the grass. "He said you would be looking for the ship, after you talked to Hanalei."

A glance from Sam had Bayani flicking his wrist. Blood bloomed on Moa's earlobe. "It's Lady Hanalei," Sam informed him.

Hanalei felt the soft scrape of dragonscale against her hip. She pressed a hand against it. Her marking went still, as if surprised it was not alone, before resuming a leisurely study of its new home. Hanalei shot a panicked glance across at Rosamie, who watched her with wide eyes.

"Yes. Fine. *Lady* Hanalei," Moa snarled, bringing her attention back to him. "Do you want to know where your babies are, or will you keep wasting time?"

"What do you mean?" Chief Umere, who had been listening off to one side, stiffened. "They're by the cove, on your ship. We're going there now."

The chief had wasted no time issuing orders. Kandayos were being readied by the steps of his pavilion, along with carts to carry the little ones.

"They're not there," Moa told them. "Bragadin took them away. They're going into your mountain, to that sleeping lady."

Into the fraught silence, Sam spoke. "Why there?"

"Because that's where the dragon is," Moa said. "It's hurt.

We hit it with the harpoon but didn't kill it. It hasn't come out. Bragadin wants to get to the eggs before they hatch."

Lady Umere wrung her hands by her husband's side. "I don't understand. Why does he need the children?"

Moa's eyes shifted to Hanalei, who burst out, "Don't you look at me, you wretch. *You* tell her."

"They're a lure." Unable to look Lady Umere in the eye, Moa directed his answer to a spot above her shoulder. "Bragadin plans to steal the eggs once the dragon's attention is on them. I came to tell you."

"Out of kindness?" Sam said.

"Believe what you want," Moa said with his own simmering anger. "I kill seadragons. Not children."

Sam said to Hanalei, "You know him well?"

"No. Barely at all."

"Do you trust him?"

In one day, Moa had gone from guide to jailer. Hanalei snorted. "Absolutely not."

"Hey." Moa glared at her. "I saved your life."

"Saved?" Hanalei returned the glare. He had not stopped her from jumping from the *Anemone*. But whose fault was it she had been captured in the first place? "You're the reason I'm here."

"That's what I meant. Yeah?"

"Enough." Sam grabbed Moa's collar and yanked him to his feet. "You're coming with us. And here's a warning for you, dragoner. If we don't bring every one of those children home, you're not coming back either."

It appeared as if every villager had followed them to the water's edge, but when it was time to depart, Sam took five others with him, no more: Hanalei, Bayani, Liko, Moa, and Catamara, who insisted on tending to the injured dragon.

"We'll take a look first," Sam told Chief Umere. "See what has to be done. If we need help, I'll send for it."

"We'll be ready," Chief Umere said. "Prince Samahtita-mah, there are thirty children in that cave. The youngest born two months ago. Please . . ."

"I'll bring back thirty. Not one child less."

The first canoe carried Liko and Catamara, with Moa at the oar. Hanalei took the hand Sam offered and climbed into the second outrigger. Bayani swung in after them, carrying a bow and arrows. After setting them aside, he sat on the bench and reached for the oar, his face averted.

Bayani did not see the fists Sam clenched at his sides, or the effort it took him to loosen them. Hanalei did. She moved away so that Sam could slip past her in the narrow space and crouch before his guard.

"Bayani. Look at me."

Bayani's face crumpled. "Forgive me, Prince Samahti. Fetu—"

"You didn't know." Sam touched his forehead to Bayani's

and kept it there. "So don't say sorry."

"But—"

"Do you know why you're here now?" Sam asked him.

"No."

Sam knocked his forehead against Bayani's, a single hard tap. "Because Bragadin is in that cave. And I want someone with me who's just as angry as I am."

Knuckling away his tears, Bayani admitted, "I'm really angry."

"Good. Then let's go."

Bayani took up the oars, and they followed the first outrigger into calm waters.

Hanalei's marking wound itself around her upper arm, like a bangle constantly spinning. Her mind was in turmoil, and her heart veered in a hundred directions, from grief to worry to anger. To a deepening sense of wonder. That she had a marking at all, and that her marking was a seadragon.

A cape dropped over her shoulders. The short ceremonial tapa Sam had worn to supper. "You're shivering."

She was, but not from the cold. Securing the ties at her neck, she said, "Thank you."

Sam came to stand beside her. Some distance ahead was the Sleeping Lady outlined by the light of the moon. The other outrigger had slowed; it now sailed directly to their left. Singing drifted from the shore. Hanalei recognized the hymns of their childhood. Prayer song.

Staring straight ahead, Sam said, "You thought the gods were watching over us back at the lagoon. Do you still think they listen to us, Hanalei?"

Not tonight they don't was her first bitter thought. Tonight, their backs were turned and their hands clamped firmly over their ears. Determined not to hear.

And yet.

She had prayed over the years, sometimes, when loneliness got the better of her. She touched her shoulder where her marking rested. A solid, reassuring presence. A companion. *Do the gods listen to us?* "Sometimes they do."

"Mostly they don't. I'm coming to realize."

Hanalei could not bring Fetu back. And she could not grieve with Sam as she wished, not with the others watching, and with a dangerous task ahead. She could only reach out and take his hand . . . and hold on tight when she felt him trembling.

The outriggers lingered at the mouth of the cave. The opening itself was a great black hole. Tangled vegetation surrounded it, and the greenery rustled with the creatures that sheltered within. Hundreds of eyes peered out at them. White eyes and yellow ones, a few disconcerting red. Hanalei comforted herself by imagining the eyes belonged to birds. Harmless little birds and nothing else. She asked,

"Does anyone know this cave?"

"I went in once," Liko said from the other boat. "With my father. But I was very young. I don't remember it."

"I came with Lord Isko a few years ago." Sam eyed the opening, drawing on memory. "It has a single passageway that doesn't break off. It goes on for miles. Two, I think. About halfway in, there's a ledge to the right. We can leave the boats there and go on foot. The passage will open up into a cavern. Very large. We should see what we're up against before we let anyone know we're here." His next words were for Moa. "You said the dragon was struck. Where?"

"Here." Moa tapped his chest, to the right of his cold heart. Scowling, he hunched his shoulders against the angry looks aimed his way. "You asked."

Sam was frowning. "Can it survive such an injury? Cat-amara?"

"No." The animal keeper said with certainty. "It will be in a lot of pain, and it will die soon."

"*Is* it still alive? Hana, can you tell?"

"I think he is." Hanalei could sense the beating hearts of four seadragons. A once mighty heartbeat, now faltering. Two tentative hearts beating—baby dragons in their shells. And her own marking, whose heart beat in rhythm with her own. "But not for long."

Sam said to Moa, "If this is a trap, dragoner . . ."

"I have sisters," Moa said. "Three of them. She'll tell you." He jerked his head in Hanalei's direction. "I kill sea-dragons. Not children."

Sam looked at Hanalei, who nodded once. She had met Moa's sisters back on Little Kalama. Sweet little girls. It proved nothing. There were bad seeds in many families.

Sam regarded the cave opening, as welcoming as a grave-yard. "Let's go. No torches. We're going to have to find our way in the dark."

30

"HEY. THERE'S SOMETHING IN THE WATER."

The words, whispered and anxious, came from Moa. Not five minutes had passed since they had left the starlit sky behind them. Hanalei turned toward the sound of his voice, but there was nothing to be seen. Few places were darker than a cave without a torch.

"What is it?" Sam kept his voice low. He stood somewhere to Hanalei's left.

"How should I know?" Moa asked.

"I feel it too," Bayani said. There came the sound of an oar skimming the surface, followed by a soft thud.

"A log?" Hanalei asked.

"Plenty of logs," Bayani commented, ten thuds later.

"Liko," Sam said with some urgency, "we need light. Not a lot."

"I . . . oh." Liko cleared her throat. "Some light, please, little ones."

Ten fireflies appeared, directly over Liko's head, before swooping between the two boats. Moa choked back a gasp. The light was meager, but it was enough to make out the bodies floating in the water. Dozens of them. Islanders and those from the oversea kingdoms, what was left of Bragadin's crew.

"I don't see any injuries." Sam knelt at the side of the canoe, inspecting the bodies as they drifted past. At this speed, it would not be long before they reached the cave opening and dispersed into open sea. "How did they die?"

Catamara was also kneeling. He reached over and grabbed a dragoner by his tunic. Hanalei saw his red beard. She pictured him standing on the deck of the *Anemone*, alive and well.

What color is the color of the heart flower?

Pink, you idiot.

Catamara brought the dragoner's face close to his own and sniffed. "This one smells like rum." He let go and reached for another. "This one too."

Hanalei and Sam exchanged a glance. "Poison in the rum?" Sam asked.

"It's been done before," Catamara said. "A coward's weapon." He looked over at Moa. "You're lucky, young pirate. If you live past tonight, you should rethink your life's choices."

Moa leaned over the side of the canoe and vomited.

"Let's go," Sam said.

Bayani took up the oar. Liko, after a glance at the retching, heaving Moa, took up the other. The fireflies winked out, plunging them back into darkness.

As they drew deeper into the cave, Hanalei found they no longer needed the fireflies. Light appeared ahead.

"Torches?" she asked.

"Ghost crabs," Sam explained. "Just like in the menagerie. Look, there's our ledge."

In no time at all, the canoes were tied to some rocks and left behind. The ledge that ran along the side of the cave was narrow. They hurried along in single file, quick-stepped and silent. Sam led the way, stopping only once. He pointed first at Moa, then at poor Catamara, who lagged behind, clutching at his side. Moa grimaced. He retraced his steps, kneeling long enough for the old man to climb onto his back. They continued on. The light grew brighter and brighter, and when the cavern came into view, Hanalei saw the ghost crabs Sam had spoken of. Teeming masses covered the cave walls, each emitting a milky glow.

The crabs made it possible to see the horribleness laid out before them. A massive cavern. A great pool of water. A dry, sandy ledge. On the ledge was the blue seadragon, dying. A harpoon jutted inches from his heart, just as Moa had described. Most of the dragon's scales had fallen off, exposing patches of gray flesh that rose and fell quickly in a pant. The remaining dragonfruit were no longer in his pouch, but he had kept them close, his body curled around them. Both eggs appeared unharmed, the rose-colored shells intact. The seadragon's eyes were half-open and turned to the ship that was anchored in the water, invitingly close. Captain Bragadin's *Compass Rose*, formerly the *Anemone*. Its side hatch had been left open. Through it came a child's voice, wobbly, scared. "Hello? Is anyone there?"

Sam raised a finger to his lips, then looked across the cavern, where, slightly ahead of them and watching from behind a boulder, Captain Bragadin was. His back was to them, but there was no mistaking the way he stood, or the way he held his head.

Hanalei leaned in to hear Sam's quietly spoken instructions. "The dragon could still be dangerous. I can't risk him going for the ship. I'll head there with the darts. Catamara, you come with me. You too," he said to Moa. "Liko, Bayani, go back for the boats. We need to get the children out of there."

Bayani hesitated, sending a venomous look in the captain's direction.

Understanding, Sam said, "The little ones first, Bayani."

Bayani nodded. He hustled after Liko, who had not waited around.

"What about him?" Moa asked, meaning the captain.

Catamara looked at Hanalei, whose skin suddenly itched. Her marking had begun to move again. Up one leg and down the other, winding slowly around her chest. When she held up an arm, she caught a glimpse of dragonscale. The ink rich and black, the detail fine.

Hanalei's voice shook slightly. "I'll take care of Captain Bragadin."

Now Sam and Moa were staring at her.

"How?" Sam wanted to know.

"With what?" Moa scoffed.

Catamara smiled.

Hanalei's marking flashed across her face. She felt it, like wind whipping past. Moa's eyes bulged. He nearly fell over, and Catamara's hand shot upward, covering his frightened yelp.

Sam opened his mouth, shut it. He came closer, shocked, but at least he knew what a marking was. "Hanalei . . ." He took her hands in his, gently, and together they watched scales coil around her arms, from wrist to elbow to shoulder. "That is no firefly."

Laughter bubbled inside of her, threatening to spill over.

"Does it hurt?" Sam asked.

Hanalei turned her arms over. "No. It itches."

"Hello?" A small voice called out again, from the ship. "Is anyone there?"

"Come," Catamara ordered. "Rescue now. Love later."

Sam leaned over and kissed Hanalei. Her marking froze in perfect astonishment, somewhere around her ankle. "Be careful," Sam told her. And then he was gone, dragging a still-gaping Moa away, his neck craned to look back at her. Catamara paused long enough to say, "Trust your marking, Lady. She will help you."

She?

Hanalei allowed herself a moment to touch her fingers to her lips, before she kicked off her sandals and removed Sam's cloak. She sat on the ledge, feet dangling over the side, then slipped beneath the water completely. Her marking was no longer just a marking. She felt it leave her skin. A seadragon swam directly beneath her, her scales as real as the dragons Hanalei had spent a lifetime around. Its frill brushed against her face; she held on tight to it as they dove deeper. When Hanalei resurfaced, dripping wet, it was onto the ledge behind Captain Bragadin.

Who had been busy. In the short time it had taken Hanalei to swim across the cavern, he had rolled out a small catapult. It looked like the weapon once bolted to the very top of his ship. Before she could take a step, Bragadin released the lever. A single cannon shot forth, striking the hull. Wood splintered and childish shrieks erupted. The ship listed sharply.

"Get up, you stupid lizard," Captain Bragadin muttered,

his back to her. "Move. I did all the work. All you have to do is eat."

The ship listed even more, and the cries from within grew louder. Hanalei looked behind her. There was no sign of Liko and Bayani. Across the way, Sam's head was barely visible above some rocks. And Hanalei knew with a terrible certainty that the canoes wouldn't arrive in time, not before the hull sunk beneath the surface.

Sam knew it too. He ran from his hiding place and dove into the water. When Moa followed, there was a startled oath from Captain Bragadin. He stumbled to the water's edge, hurling vile curses across the way. The blue dragon lifted his head slightly, but that was all. He had no interest in a ship full of children. Or in anything except protecting his eggs.

"Captain," Hanalei said.

The curses stopped. Very slowly, Captain Bragadin looked over his shoulder. When he faced her completely, Hanalei fell back a step, for he painted a grisly picture. His head was wrapped in bandaging, over eye and lip and chin, where Hanalei had cut him with the dragonscale. Blood seeped through the cloth. He looked at her, soaking wet, then looked behind her. "You're a brave one. Not even a dagger to protect yourself?"

The queen's dagger was strapped to her arm. Hanalei pulled it free. "Do I need a dagger?"

"You have some nerve," he marveled. "Between the two of us, who has been more wronged? Come closer, Hanalei. Come see what you did to my face."

He wouldn't make her feel guilty for defending herself. "You frightened me, back on the ship. I wouldn't have hurt you otherwise."

"Touching. And yet my eye is still gone. Where is Vaea?"

"Also gone." Hanalei lied just to watch him flinch. She had learned a lesson or two from him about cruelty.

"How?" he demanded.

Hanalei had a clear view of the water behind him. Sam had reached the ship, which had turned almost completely on its side. He slid along the hull—too fast!—before catching himself at the hatch opening. He disappeared within.

"I said how?"

Hanalei pictured Vaea lying prone from a spider bite. She would be fine in a matter of hours. Imprisoned but fine. Which was more than could be said for Fetu. Thinking of him brought on a fresh wave of fury. "Your navigator was bitten by the queen's own spider. Then eaten, slowly. Digested, slowly. She's still being digested, I imagine."

"You're lying."

"I am not. Prince Samahti was fond of his bat. You're not the only one who can be vindictive."

Captain Bragadin's face had lost all expression. "I should have killed you years ago, when you first showed your face."

"Your mistake."

A familiar, hateful smile appeared. "And yours is standing here all alone, without your prince to save you."

Hanalei looked at him, really looked, and was no longer afraid. "We're the ones you preferred, weren't we? The ones who had no one—"

The captain was standing by the miniature catapult. He wrenched it toward her and hit the lever. At the same time, Hanalei felt herself knocked to the ground by something heavy and wet. She did not see the cannonball, but she felt the heat of it overhead, heard the harmless splash in the water. She rolled away as her seadragon rose up behind her. She was a beautiful animal, with scales the palest pink, jaws wide open.

Captain Bragadin's mouth opened. His scream never came. The dragon swooped down, and he was no more. And Hanalei learned an important truth about her new marking. She did not like to swallow her food whole. She preferred to take her time, and chew first.

31

"GOOD GIRL."

Shaken, Hanalei reached up and patted her seadragon on the nose, a nose as rough as coconut husk. Her eyes were brown, with long sweeping lashes, and her frill was the soft white of a plumeria blossom. Two dimples appeared, to Hanalei's delight, before she remembered where they were and why.

Rescue now. Love later.

"Come on. We have to help."

Hanalei climbed onto her dragon's back. She could hear the canoes approaching, the slap of oars against the water's surface. Liko and Bayani no longer bothered with stealth. They would be here soon. Across the way, Catamara leaned against the blue seadragon, stroking his skin where the scales had fallen off. The animal did not seem to care that Catamara was so close to his precious dragonfruit; his chin rested on the sand and his eyes were indifferent slits.

Of Sam and Moa, she saw nothing. She guided her dragon around to the ship's hatch. "Sam!" she yelled, then jerked back when a small boy appeared in the opening, handed up by Sam, who said, "Take him."

Hanalei took the crying boy and looked around for Liko and Bayani, whose canoes had stopped at the cavern opening. Their mouths hung open. Hanalei beckoned them over, calling out, "She won't hurt you!" and found she had to repeat her words for the poor boy's sake. His cries were now accompanied by terrified hiccups. She passed him down to Liko.

When Hanalei peered down into the hull, she saw dozens of children in water up to their knees and shoulders, depending on how tall they were. The older ones carried the younger ones in their arms and around their necks. A little girl sat on Moa's shoulders. Another on Sam's. He passed her up to Hanalei, saying, "The chief said there were thirty altogether. Make sure we have thirty."

"I'll make sure."

Bayani crawled onto her dragon, on his hands and knees at first. The ship listed again. After that, there was no time to think about anything but the children. Sam lifted a child to Hanalei, who gave the child to Bayani, who leaned down from the seadragon, swinging the child into Liko's arms. Hanalei counted as they passed from her arms to the safety of the boats. Three, four, five, six . . . eighteen, nineteen, and so on. When both canoes were full, she settled them onto the back of the dragon, murmuring assurances the whole way. "This is a nice seadragon. My marking. She won't hurt you. I promise."

A dripping wet Moa climbed out after the last little girl. Sam hung on to the opening with both hands. By then, the ship had tilted so far to one side that behind him was a long drop to the other side of the hull.

Hanalei grabbed his arms and pulled.

Sam didn't budge. "How many?" he asked. "Count them."

Hanalei looked over her shoulder. Ten in the first canoe. Eleven in the second. Eight on the dragon. *That wasn't right.* "Twenty-nine. Wait. I'll count again."

"I have twenty-nine," Moa said grimly.

"Twenty-nine," Liko called out.

"Lady." Bayani knelt beside her. "There's only twenty-nine."

Hanalei tightened her hold on Sam's arms. His neck was craned. He was searching behind him, into the black. When he looked up at her, she knew what he was going to say before he said it.

"Let go, Hana."

She could not argue. Hanalei did as he wished with her heart in her throat. Sam slapped something into her hand.

"She's wet. She'll be mad," he warned. And then he fell, his eyes on hers until the darkness engulfed him. It was a long time before she heard a splash.

Hanalei swung one leg into the hatch. "I'm going to help—"

"Hey." Moa held fast to her arm. "We don't know your dragon. You need to stay here. And look. What's that old man doing?"

On the ledge, the blue seadragon appeared almost as if in a trance. His tail slapped gently against the sand. Catamara, who had not moved, moved now. His hand waved behind his back, urgently. *Go. Go at once*, his hand told them.

Hanalei yanked her arm free of Moa. She said to the guards, "Take the boats and come back."

"What about them?" Moa said, meaning the children on her dragon. They were wet and cold and scared.

"When Liko and Bayani return, they'll go."

"Hanalei," Moa said. "Whatever that old man is doing, it might not last. We have to go."

Hanalei felt herself crumpling in front of twenty-nine frightened children. She hated how reasonable Moa sounded. "I'm not leaving him." There was no sound coming from the hull, and no way to see. In her hand was the pouch he had given her. He had given her Viti.

"I'll stay." Moa elbowed her aside. He straddled the side hatch opening, holding on to the edges so he did not fall in.

"I'll watch for your prince. You go."

"Moa—"

"Go."

He had said the same thing to her back on the *Anemone*, when he had not stopped her escape. Moa had done bad things. But not always. She had to hold on to that. Hanalei took her seadragon and left.

Trust your marking, Catamara had said. *She will help you*. Her seadragon moved slowly, and with care, so her young riders did not tumble. The light from the ghost crabs gradually faded away.

"It's very dark," a little voice said.

"It is, isn't it?" Hanalei said. "Liko, are you near?"

"Here, Lady." A light appeared to Hanalei's left, a solitary firefly that multiplied. Before they knew it, hundreds of bright twinkling fireflies came to life. A welcome distraction. Hanalei took the pouch from her belt. *She's wet. She'll be mad.* Hanalei had braced herself, so that when Viti sprang out, fangs bared, she did not scream. The little spider jumped onto her shoulder. "Sorry, Viti," she murmured. Viti's response was a tiny prick on her neck. Not painful, just uncomfortable enough to make a point, before the spider settled down.

Hanalei looked over at Liko. *Thank you*, she mouthed.

Smiling slightly, Liko stuck her oar in the water, guiding them out of the cave and into the night.

The stars were out, which made it easy to see the crowd at the shore. Hanalei kept her seadragon out of range of any spears or harpoons until Liko and Bayani were able to explain that she was no threat.

A girl, about ten, had buried her face in the dragon's frill. She raised her head and said to Hanalei, "Is she really your marking?"

"She is."

"Does she have a name?"

"Not yet. She's very, very new."

The girl looked wistful. "I've always wanted my own seadragon."

And Hanalei, worried as she was for Sam, had to smile. "Me too."

Only when Liko waved did Hanalei bring her dragon in with the last of the children. She handed them down to those who had waded into the shallows. Mothers and fathers, village elders. Rosamie and William. Later, she would remember that Jejomar had not been among them. She gave the last little girl over to Chief Umere.

"One's missing," she told him quietly. "Prince Samahti is still looking. I'm going back."

The long night had taken its toll on the weary chief. "My grandson, Tane. He isn't here."

"We'll find him." As she turned her dragon around, Chief Umere said, "Go safely, child."

The blue seadragon had breathed his last. When Hanalei entered the cavern, the first thing she saw was a frill, limp and black. Catamara had grabbed a fistful in both hands. His head was bowed. Another prayer, another dragon lost.

Her sorrow was tempered by the sight of Sam, who leaned against a wall beside Moa, over by the tail. With them was a boy, about twelve. The chief's grandson. He was safe, but his safety had come at a price. Both dragonfruit had hatched. The only sign of the young seadragons was a slimy trail that led from the broken eggshells to the water.

Hanalei guided her marking past Captain Bragadin's ship. Only a small portion of the hull remained above the surface. The dragon stopped at the water's edge. Her body lay parallel to the dead seadragon; she turned her head to watch him, making no sound beyond a lone, distressed call. Hanalei stroked her frill and murmured comforting words. She jumped down onto the ledge, where Sam was waiting for her.

"You're not hurt?" He buried his face in her hair. Sam smelled of salt and seaweed, just as she did. "Catamara said Bragadin fired a cannon at you—"

"He missed. I'm not hurt. Are you?"

"I'm fine." Sam stepped back. They inspected one another to make sure. "Tane hit his head and fell into the water. Lucky for him, he fell face up." He looked at her marking and smiled. "I've never seen such a beautiful dragon." At that, her marking's ears perked up, standing tall over her frill.

Sam wasn't fine. She could see it on his face, behind the smiles and flattery. Fetu was lost. The eggs were gone. He was very close to cracking. "I'm so sorry, Sam."

Sam looked away. "They'd already hatched when we climbed out of the hull. There was no sign of them." He stepped away from her. "We have to get back. They'll be worried."

He called Tane over. There was a lump on his forehead, and he was as tired and damp as everyone else. The boy eyed the pink seadragon, and said, "With respect, Lady, I think I'll wait for a canoe." It took some coaxing, but they managed to get him on the seadragon. Moa joined them, subdued. But Catamara would not come.

"I will stay," the animal keeper said. "Send someone tomorrow."

"It *is* tomorrow, Cata," Sam said.

Catamara waved them off. "Later."

Nothing Sam said would change his mind. They left Catamara there, and the journey back to the shore was completed in near total silence. Hanalei handed Viti to Sam. He returned the pouch to his belt. A smaller crowd greeted them. Most had taken their children home to bed, but Tane's family had waited anxiously. His parents, grandparents, aunts, uncles, and cousins. Their reunion lifted Hanalei's spirits. Sam and Moa had gone off to speak, leaving Hanalei in the shallows with her seadragon.

Hanalei slid off her back, then went around and kissed her on the nose. "Thank you, my dear." A long, wet tongue flopped out and licked her. The seadragon vanished, reappearing as a marking on Hanalei's hand. Hanalei waded out in time to hear Sam tell Moa, "Go, before I change my mind." Sam went to speak to the chief.

Moa waited for Hanalei. "You didn't tell them, that I was the one who sunk Prince Augustus's ship."

"Someone will tell them." The dragoners bitten by Viti would eventually be able to speak again. They would be desperate to shift the blame. "They'll come looking for you. And your family."

"They won't find us," Moa said. "Why are you helping me?"

A life for a life. He had not meant to, but Moa had saved her, sending her on a path back to Tamarind. Bringing her home. She said, "Remember me to your mother and sisters. I wish them well."

Moa was quiet. Finally, he nodded, accepting his question would not be answered. He glanced over at Sam and lowered his voice. "I didn't want to say anything back at the cave. Those eggs, Hanalei. They didn't hatch on their own."

"What do you mean?"

"The old man, he cracked them open while your prince was down in the hull. I saw."

Her whole body went tight. "Are you certain?"

"Yeah. He took the dragons out of their shells and put them on the sand, pointing them to the water."

"If you're lying to me, Moa . . ."

"Why would I lie? Who is he, anyway?"

Hanalei looked toward the Sleeping Lady. Something was very wrong here. "Catamara works in the menagerie. He's been there for years."

"What did he do before the menagerie?"

Hanalei tried to remember what Sam had told her. She shook her head. She didn't know.

"Huh" was all Moa said.

Hanalei had nearly forgotten. "Moa, what did Captain Bragadin do with the other egg?"

"What other egg?"

"There were three," she told him. "We found eggshells near the lagoon at Tamarind City. The dragon was missing. What did you do with it?"

"Never saw it," he said. Then, "I'm not lying! We

harpooned the green seadragon in deep water, but didn't kill it. We could tell by the frill that it had laid its eggs. But we couldn't follow it back to its nest. There were too many guards near the city."

"Then who . . . ?"

"Wasn't us. I'm going to go," Moa added, eyeing Sam, who was looking over the chief's head, eyeing Moa in return. "Before your prince changes his mind. I don't like that spider."

Hanalei didn't know why she said it. The words just came out. "Do you need squid?"

Moa's brows shot up. "Gold?"

Hanalei nodded. "If you need it. Thank you for watching over him."

Moa took one step back and then another. "Keep your squid. I can make my own way. Be careful, sister." He turned and walked off down the beach until the night swallowed him up.

32

ROSAMIE WAITED FOR THEM BACK AT THE VILLAGE. She sat on the steps of the chief's pavilion, a small wrapped bundle in her arms. Sam stopped in his tracks when he saw it. Beside him, Hanalei's breath hitched.

"I kept him for you," Rosamie said, rising. "It didn't feel right to just . . ."

"Thank you, Lady." Sam took the bundle in his arms, a piece of his heart wrapped in linen. There was no weight to it. Carrying Fetu felt like carrying air.

Rosamie kissed Hanalei on the cheek and left them.

Hanalei touched the linen with her fingertips. "Will you take him home?"

"No." Sam could not bear to. "I'll say goodbye here."

"By the water? Fetu always liked the water."

"By the water then."

The village was quiet. So too was the beach. There was no longer a need for so many guards to patrol the waters. Bragadin was dead, the seadragon with him. Sam built a pyre while Hanalei sat on the sand and held Fetu close, tears falling. A part of him was glad she wept, because he could not. He could only pile log upon log, branch upon branch, and think *I am sorry, my dear. Sorry, sorry, sorry.*

When the pyre was large enough, Sam took Fetu from Hanalei and placed him at the very center, then used a blazing torch to set it all alight. His arm came around Hanalei's shoulders, pulling her close, and they stood there in the dark, by the water, until the fire burned itself out.

Sam had been offered his own chamber in the chief's pavilion. Sleep was hard to come by, and it didn't last. It felt like he had just dropped off when he woke abruptly and heard, "It's me, Sam. Don't scream."

"Jejomar?" Sam sat up, blinking in the lantern light. His cousin huddled in a corner, forehead on knees. "What's wrong?"

Jejomar lifted his head, saying miserably, "It's only me."

Sam took one look, yelped, and scrambled to his feet so fast he knocked over a vase on a table. It crashed to the floor and shattered. He grabbed his knife.

Before him was someone with his own face and Jejomar's voice. Not someone who looked like him. It was his face exactly. It was his clothing. The same tunic he had given Jejomar earlier, he realized. Sam pointed his knife, his heart pounding.

The door crashed open, and Hanalei burst into the chamber. Behind her came Liko, Bayani, Rosamie, William, the chief, Lady Umere, everyone. Half the village was in his chamber, in their nightclothes, gaping as they looked from one face to the next.

Hanalei was the first to recover. "Put the knife down, Sam. It's Jejomar." She looked at the version of Sam standing with his back pressed up against the wall, terrified. "Jejomar?" she asked, uncertainly.

He nodded, and Hanalei said, "I think . . . he took the first dragonfruit. Back at the lagoon. Did you?"

Jejomar nodded again.

Sam's flesh threatened to creep right off his bones. He lowered the knife. "What is happening here?"

With everyone looking on, Jejomar stammered out an explanation. When the green seadragon had attacked them by the lagoon, he had fled. That part Sam had witnessed himself. But then Jejomar had spotted the blue dragon leaving the cave and slipping into the water with two pink eggs in its pouch. Naturally, Jejomar had wondered about the third egg. In the old tales, there were always three. He had gone into the cave and found the solitary dragonfruit left behind. He had broken it open, killed the seadragon, ate parts of it, and made a wish. The rest he carried home. Which had not been difficult, it was like holding a small child. His mother had been horrified, frightened that the queen would learn what Jejomar had done: stolen an egg meant for Princess Oliana. She had sent the servants away so they would not see when she burned what remained of the dragon.

Sam's mind reeled. He thought of his aunt Chesa standing by an open fire. *What were you burning, Auntie?*

It was Hanalei who asked his cousin, "What did you wish for?"

Jejomar could not look at anyone, least of all Sam. "I didn't want to be me anymore," he said in a low voice. "A nobody. Never doing anything right. I wanted to be . . . like Samahti. I wanted to be just like him."

Sam said, "You watched me try to find it. *For ten years.* And when you have the chance to help, you take it for yourself? Jejomar. My mother is dying."

Jejomar slid to the floor. William stepped forward, then stopped, looking distressed and helpless as Jejomar wept into his hands. It was the only sound in the chamber, until Chief Umere stepped forward. "Prince Samahti, what do you wish to do here? This is clearly a family matter—"

"It is not." Sam turned to Bayani. "Take him back to Tamarind. At first light. It's not a family matter. This is the queen's business."

"Yes, Prince Samahti."

"No!" Jejomar's head snapped up. "Please, Sam. The queen means Lord Isko. You have to help me—"

"Stop." Sam still held his knife. Very carefully, he set it on a table and stepped away. He headed for the door without looking at his cousin. "We're not boys anymore, Jejomar. Help yourself."

Sam stayed on the beach until morning. He could not afford to wallow. Despair would not help his mother. But it tempted him. How vast the Nominomi was. How easy it would be to walk into her waters and swim and swim and never stop.

Viti bit his hand.

He snatched it away, hissing. The spider went tumbling through the air; when she landed on the sand, she was the size of a small dog.

They glowered at one another, and Sam felt his heart crack. One marking left. "You're not safe with me," he said.

Viti bared her fangs, and Sam stepped back quickly. Her bites hurt.

"I don't know what to do, Vitimahana," he confessed, using her given name, one he had not spoken aloud since he was a small boy. "I am not wise enough. The dragonfruit was our last chance, and I'm not even certain it would have helped us in the end."

The spider crawled around him, placing herself between Sam and the sea.

"I wasn't going to . . ." He trailed off, listening to the waves rolling in, the birds singing, the village behind him rising from its sleep. Life marched on, even with a broken heart. "Let's walk" he decided.

He could feel others watching as he paced along the beach, a dog-sized Viti by his side. No one approached. Except, eventually, Hanalei.

She was dressed for travel. Hat on her head. Boots on her feet. A tiny seadragon inked along her chin. Her eyes were red from weeping. It wasn't his heart alone that had broken.

Sam stopped pacing. He brushed a hand along her cheek. "Did you sleep?"

"As much as you."

No sleep for either of them. Sam looked past her. "Did he leave?"

"Yes. William went with him."

Unsurprising. The friendship between Jejomar and the Esperanzan had grown quickly. "Do you think I was too harsh?"

"No," Hanalei said, but only after a long pause.

Sam stepped away and flung himself onto the sand. "Your *no* means *yes*."

"What Jejomar did was bad." Hanalei settled beside him. "But, Sam, he'll pay for it the rest of his life. With his guilt. And with his face. He'll never be himself again."

"Don't ask me to feel sorry for him, Hanalei. *Every wish demands a—*"

Hanalei, who had coaxed a smaller Viti onto her hand,

looked up at his silence. "Why are you looking at me like that?"

"*Every wish demands a price,*" Sam said slowly. "How does the rest of it go? I only ever remember the last part."

He had her attention. Hanalei said, "*In the old tales, it is written that the egg of a seadragon, dragonfruit, holds within it the power to undo a person's greatest sorrow. An unwanted marriage, a painful illness, an unpaid debt . . . gone. But as with all things that promise the moon and the stars and offer hope when hope has gone, the tale comes with a warning. Every wish demands a price.*"

"Every Nominomi child knows about dragonfruit," Sam said. "We've always known it. Why would the gods give us that knowledge, and then punish us for using it?"

Hanalei tilted her head. So did the small dragon on her chin. They were thinking. "What if they didn't give it to us?" Hanalei posed a question of her own. "*In the old tales . . .* It could have been written by anyone."

"You're saying we were never supposed to know about it in the first place?"

"It makes a strange sort of sense." Hanalei placed Viti on his knee and dusted the sand from her fingers. "Penina told me once that when we take something from the seadragon god, he takes something in return. He gets angry when we steal from him. So he punishes us. He would not have been the one to go around telling everyone about magic dragonfruit. Perhaps someone, a long time ago, spilled his secrets."

Sam's heart pounded. His belly was in knots. "What if there is no theft?"

"What do you mean?"

"Hanalei, what if the egg itself is safe? Or what's in the egg?"

They looked at one another.

"A new seadragon," Hanalei said.

"Yes."

Hanalei held out her arm. Her marking had moved on from her chin. They watched her wind herself around Hanalei's arm, from shoulder to wrist. Sam had not appreciated the beauty of this animal last night, when the world had felt like it was ending. Hanalei said, "I have a new seadragon. We share the same blood."

33

"YOU WILL HURT HER," SAM'S GRANDMOTHER SAID. "You will hurt yourself."

Hanalei stood at the foot of Princess Oliana's bed, beside Sam. They were both weary, covered in travel dust. It would have been swifter for them to return home on Hanalei's seadragon, but they had worried about the city guards. They would need to be warned first, about Hanalei's rare, extraordinary marking, in case they shot first and asked questions later. Instead, Sam and Hanalei had raced their kandayos back to Tamarind City at a punishing speed. The others had been left behind.

"Your Grace," Hanalei said, "the last thing your daughter did was try to protect me. I would like to help if I can." She showed the queen her hands, covered in dragonscale scars. "To me, a cut is nothing. Truly. Please let me try."

His grandmother took up her usual chair beside the bed. She wore a dress of emerald green, a yellow plumeria in her hair. Viti sat upon her shoulder. Ringed fingers drummed along the bedside table, then stopped. "Isko? What do you think?"

Lord Isko hobbled over with his walking stick. The wound to his leg was healing far too slowly for his liking. "First, whatever we decide, we cannot speak of it outside this chamber. Ever. Otherwise, Hanalei will be in danger for the remainder of her life. A target for kidnappers, for anyone who thinks her blood might be of use to them."

"Agreed," Sam said.

His grandmother dipped her head. "Agreed."

"Thank you, Lord Isko," Hanalei said.

His uncle regarded her for a long moment, but the cutting comment Sam half expected never came. His uncle bowed his head. "You are welcome, Lady." He turned away from Hanalei's startled expression and addressed the queen. "Second, Your Grace. Why do you worry about a cut to her hand? It would also be nothing to her."

"And if it does not heal?" his grandmother countered. "If it continues to bleed away? It is not a normal sickness. There is no physician to tell us what is safe to do and what is not." She allowed her words to settle. "Samahtitamah, what is your opinion?"

"I defer to you, Mai Mai."

"No, grandson, in this I defer to you." Her expression

softened. "You are not a boy anymore. She is your mother."

And she had been asleep for far too long. Sam did not hesitate. "She would hate this limbo. We have to try."

Sam did it himself. He cut Hanalei's palm first, and then his mother's. Hanalei held her hand over his mother's cut, watching as blood dripped and mingled. The blood of a new seadragon. Not stolen. Given freely. He wrapped Hanalei's hand in fresh bandaging as Lord Isko tended to his mother.

And then they waited.

From morning until noon, into the darkest night. Hanalei fell asleep at the foot of the bed. His grandmother dozed in her chair. Lord Isko snored in his. Only Sam stayed awake, keeping vigil, and so it happened that he was the only one who saw when his mother's eyes opened at last, near dawn.

34

THE ANIMAL KEEPER, CATAMARA, WAS NEVER SEEN again. A boat was sent into the Sleeping Lady to bring him back to the village. But there was no sign of him there, and there was no sign of the dead seadragon. No one could explain what had happened. But many months later, as Princess Oliana, Sam, and Hanalei strolled through the gardens, the princess asked Hanalei if she recalled the last meal they had shared together, all those years ago. She had been testing young Hanalei's knowledge of the various gods. Like the trickster goddess, Kalama, and Olifat, the father of all the sea gods. Like his son, Taga, god of seadragons. Over the last thousand years, Taga had been known by many other names. Sometimes Hehu, sometimes Satawal, and sometimes, though very rarely . . .

"Catamara," Hanalei said, stopping in the middle of the pathway.

"Yes," Princess Oliana answered. A shoulder lifted. "A coincidence perhaps."

Sam and Hanalei looked at one another. *Do you think the gods still listen to us, Hanalei?* he had asked.

Sometimes they do.

Mostly they don't. I'm coming to realize.

Sam had been wrong. Ten years of waiting. But they did listen.

Not all of Captain Bragadin's dragoners perished in the Sleeping Lady. The ones at Chief Umere's supper had survived. Viti's bite had not killed them, though they did suffer painful episodes for the rest of their lives, however long or short those lives were. They never faced judgment on Tamarind. Which meant they did not have to answer for the kidnapping of thirty village children or the murder of a beloved royal marking. Instead, Queen Maga'lahi honored a request by the Esperanzan king through his ambassador. She turned the dragoners over to him. They would be shipped to Esperanza to answer for different crimes: the deaths of the king's mother and youngest son. A harsh decision, perhaps, on her part. To punish the crew for a dead captain's crimes. Queen Maga'lahi cared little. She washed her hands of the *Anemone* and everyone on it.

Sam found Jejomar in the pavilion of history and song, where the memories were kept.

The building sat on the far edge of the palace complex,

separated from other offices by a copse of flame trees. The kingfishers were abundant today; they flitted from branch to branch, singing and chirping, delighting in the sunlight that broke through the tree cover. He climbed the front steps and went inside. A memory keeper worked at a front table, surrounded by great stacks of parchment and sound-catchers. Mara was one of the newer archivists, having taken over from her grandfather. She glanced up when Sam entered, her expression puzzled.

"Where did you go? I didn't even see you leave." Sam did not answer, and Mara's eyes widened. She looked behind her, where an identical figure sat at the very back table. He had set his work aside the moment Sam walked in.

The memory keeper scrambled to her feet and bowed. "Prince Samahti, apologies . . ."

"No need. It's strange for all of us. How is your grand-father?"

"Bored," Mara replied promptly, with a laugh. "And try-ing to steal this position back from me. He's not used to all the free hours."

Her grandfather had been one of his tutors. Sam had spent much of his boyhood in this pavilion. "Tell him I'll stop by to see him tomorrow. We'll see what we can do with some of those hours."

Mara's smile grew. "I'll tell him. Thank you. Grandfather will be pleased." Another glance behind her. "Um. It's my turn to feed the birds. Excuse me." Another bow. She took a small bowl off a shelf and left.

Sam walked past rows of parchment-covered tables to the back of the pavilion. Jejomar got to his feet. He wore a sand-colored robe without sleeves, a belt made of coconut thread looped around his middle. He wore Sam's face.

Jejomar spoke first. "How do you do that?"

"What?"

"She laughed." Jejomar gestured behind Sam, to the door. "All she does is scowl at me."

"I'm nice. It's simple."

Jejomar snorted. He flopped back onto his chair. "What are you doing here?"

Sam took the chair opposite his cousin. Jejomar was copying text from limp, stuck-together parchment onto fresh, dry sheets. It was the nature of record keeping in the Nominomi. The entire collection had to be copied every few years or risk succumbing to the heat and damp.

"So this is where Lord Isko put you," Sam said. "Do you hate it?"

"No," Jejomar said, surprising him. "I thought I would, but this place . . . Here, look at this." Beside the desk was a chest, about six feet long. Jejomar opened the lid, revealing hundreds of soundcatchers in every condition: polished, scratched, carved, plain. The wood appeared very old. Jejomar reached for one and blew into it, a single quick breath. He placed it on the table. A girl's voice emerged. *My name is Maga'lahienelei of the Kingdom of Tamarind. On this day, my tenth naming day, I do pay homage to my mother and queen, Samahtinatamahenele . . .* Smiling a little, Sam listened to his grandmother's younger self. He had forgotten about this particular soundcatcher. At the end of her pledge, it fell silent.

Jejomar said, "I didn't know you were named for your great-grandmother. There are a lot of things I didn't know." He returned the soundcatcher to the trunk. "Anyway, there are worse places to be, considering."

Sam had not known what to expect, coming here. He had not seen Jejomar in months. *Unpleasant* was too mild a word to describe their last meeting. Jejomar weeping, Jejomar wearing his face. "Do you ever leave here?"

Jejomar shrugged. "Sometimes. At night. I tried during the day, but it's . . . strange."

"Where do you sleep?"

"There's a pavilion out back." Jejomar straightened some parchment, not meeting his eye. "How is your mother?"

"Weak," Sam said. "Confused sometimes. Which is how I would be if I were in her place. But it's hard to watch."

"That isn't what I heard," Jejomar said, troubled. "Everyone is saying she's doing well. Almost back to her old self."

"We've kept it in the family, mostly. She needs quiet, for a little while longer."

"Sam . . . I'm sorry." Jejomar looked down. "I'm glad you still consider me family."

"We don't get to choose, Jejomar."

"No. I know."

From outside came the sound of Mara's laughter, and birdsong.

Sam said, "Your mother left the city yesterday. She went back to the mountains."

Hurt flashed across Jejomar's eyes. "She didn't tell me."

"When did you last see her?"

"A few months ago. She took one look and screamed. Told me to get out. She said I humiliated her, cost her friends and the queen's favor."

Aunt Chesa had never had the queen's favor, but there was no need to say so. Jejomar knew.

Sam stood. "I want to show you something. Let's go."

"Where?" Jejomar asked, rising.

"It's easier to show you. I want to test a theory."

"You sound like Hanalei."

Sam smiled. "It's her theory." He twirled a finger at Jejomar's robes. "This won't work. We're going to the beach."

They rode through the heart of the city, twin princes on their kandayos, garnering stares and double stares along the way. One man dropped a basket full of mangoes. They rolled on down the street, fruit everywhere. Jejomar had offered to wear a hood, but Sam had refused. His cousin could not hide beneath a hood forever. They would have to find a way to live with it.

From the city, they entered the jungle pathway, shadowy but brief, and emerged on an isolated beach. High above was the cliff where he had first spotted Hanalei on the deck of the *Anemone*. She was waiting for them at the water's edge. And she wasn't alone.

"Whooooaaa . . ." Jejomar breathed, and Sam laughed. His cousin would have heard of Hanalei's marking. Everyone had. Seeing her was something else entirely.

The seadragon stretched along the shallows, her tail slapping at the waves. Her scales were the palest pink, and they shimmered in the afternoon sun. Hanalei stood by the dragon's white frill. She wore a green dress, her hair loose in the wind. Sam smiled at the sight of her.

"Hello, Jejomar," Hanalei said. "She won't hurt you, don't worry."

Jejomar kept Sam between the dragon and himself. "Hello, Hanalei. Are you sure? Whooaa," he said again as Hanalei leaned against the seadragon. While the dragon remained as a fully formed animal, tattooed scales moved along Hanalei's skin, over her face and down her neck, along one arm. "Your marking is the best marking."

The seadragon's ears perked up, and Hanalei laughed. "Thank you. The only thing she loves more than food is flattery."

"What's her name?"

"Nomi," Sam said. The seadragon shook her frill in acknowledgment. "Climb on up. Mind her scales, though. They're sharp."

"Climb? No." Jejomar backed away, kicking up sand. "I'm fine where I am."

"Jejomar, she's why we're here. We're going for a ride." Sam went up to Hanalei, and said close to her ear, "Do you really think this will work?"

"I hope it will, for his sake."

Jejomar said, "Going where? And why? And what is this theory you're talking about?"

Sam heard the suspicion in his cousin's voice. So did Hanalei, who said crisply, "Follow me up. Sam isn't going to take you to the deep and push you in. I know that's what you're thinking."

"It isn't," Jejomar muttered as he walked past Sam and followed Hanalei up onto the seadragon, stepping lightly along tail and body until they reached her frill.

Sam followed. He saw Hanalei studying Jejomar's face closely. "You even have the same scar on your neck," she marveled. "Your teeth are the same."

Jejomar ducked his head. He slapped a hand over the

scar. "It's disturbing, I know."

"A little," Hanalei admitted. "I'll get used to it." She turned back to the dragon, instructing Jejomar: "Sit here. You can hold on to her frill, but don't yank. You'll only upset her."

Jejomar straddled the dragon and held the frill gingerly in his hands. "What happens if she gets upset?"

"Just don't yank." Hanalei retraced her steps, took the hand Sam offered, and hopped barefoot onto the sand. She waved a cheery goodbye.

Nomi moved carefully, entering the shallows fully and then flicking her tail up on a single splash. Sam remained standing. He raised a hand in farewell to Hanalei, then turned his attention fully to his cousin.

Jejomar began the journey with his knees pressed into dragonscale and his eyes clenched shut. Nomi swam so that her upper half remained above the surface. With the exception of his sandals and feet, Jejomar remained dry. Gradually, his knees relaxed. His eyes opened a little, and then all the way. The water was changing beneath them. Clear at the shallows, now a pale blue, now a deep green. When the sea turned midnight and they drew up to a large rock that protruded from the sea, Sam asked Nomi to stop. Jejomar rose, arms outward for balance, and turned to face Sam.

Who saw at once that Hanalei's theory was correct.

"What?" Jejomar said, seeing his expression. "*What?*"

Sam said, "When we were children, I gave Hanalei a soundcatcher. She never took it off, not even when she left Tamarind. It was useless off island, but when she came home, it worked perfectly." Jejomar was listening, trying to understand. "The egg you took, Jejomar, was laid here on Tamarind. Which made it a part of this island, subject to its rules."

Jejomar looked around. "This is the boundary rock."

"It is. Look at your reflection, cousin."

Jejomar peered over Nomi's side, into the water. He gasped. Arms flailing, he would have fallen in if Sam had not grabbed the back of his tunic and held on. Sam looked over the side as well.

Their reflections gazed back at them. Two very different faces. Their own.

"Magic doesn't work off island," Sam said. "That is the rule."

Jejomar clutched his face, his hair. He stared wide-eyed at Sam, and then he turned, looking over the other side. Two identical faces peered back. Jejomar lowered himself onto Nomi's back. "I never thought I'd see me again."

Sam crouched beside him. "I brought you here to see if . . ." He waved at the water, the boundary rock. "And to offer a chance, if you wish it."

"What chance?"

"The ambassador of Raka has sent an invitation. He would like you to accompany his brother, William, who is determined to visit every island in the Nominomi. The ambassador doesn't have the time to do it himself. He has his employment and his sister to look after. But he also doesn't wish to have William travel alone. You know how William is."

Jejomar looked worried. "He gets distracted easily. And he doesn't prepare. He'll get lost, or kidnapped. Or he'll die of sunstroke."

"My fears too."

"So, what are you saying? I would be a companion? His servant?"

"No," Sam said firmly. "William asked for you specifically. You would go as his friend. But you will also go as a representative of this island, and of this family. And you will be compensated for it."

Sam saw the moment excitement turned into something else.

"You're trying to get rid of me," Jejomar said.

"Jejomar, I'm not."

"Then why would you make this offer?" Jejomar asked bitterly. "After what I did? Why would you want me to represent your family?" Jejomar lowered his head to his chin, but Sam still saw the tears. Nomi turned her head slightly, distressed. Her frill fluttered about, wrapping around

Jejomar, like a hug. He held on to it. Lightly, though. He did not yank.

Sam said, "I hope that the foolish things we do when we're sixteen, seventeen, twenty, whenever—I hope they don't define who we are forever." He swallowed past the lump in his throat. "I hope that many years from now, you'll still want to be just like me. I'm not trying to get rid of you, cousin. This is a chance. What you do with it is your decision alone."

It was quiet there, for a time. Until Jejomar said, "If I go, will I be able to come home?"

Sam was startled. It had never occurred to him that Jejomar would feel otherwise. That he would have to ask. And then he remembered Hanalei, returning home and feeling that she had no right to be there.

Sam said, "I've moved back into the pavilion. You know where it is. You have a key. There will always be a home for you there."

"No matter what I look like?"

"No matter."

Jejomar wiped his tears away. He patted the frill and got to his feet. Carefully looking over one side, and then the other. He smiled. "I want to go."

Fifty captive seadragons. How did one go about releasing them? Very carefully, it turned out, and not all at once.

Hanalei and Sam set them free in groups of threes and twos. It was a small enough number for Nomi to guide them to the boundary rock and for them to make their way into the wider sea.

Only one dragon refused to go. She was older, and purple, and once, years ago, Hanalei's father had stolen away with her dragonfruit. Hanalei kept her in the menagerie, visited often by Nomi, for many years until the seadragon breathed her last.

35

SAM WALKED ARM IN ARM WITH HIS MOTHER along Tamarind's shore. Their walks were frequent, because she wished to regain her strength, but of short duration, for she tired easily. Today, they needed only to reach a small pavilion beneath the coconut trees where his grandmother waited for them.

His mother wore a red dress and a leafy crown, which relieved Sam immensely. For years it had been nothing but nightgowns. All day, all night. Clothing for the sick. The only jewelry she wore was a gold ring carved with the image of a fruit bat. "You are thinking sad thoughts again, Samahti. I can tell."

He was. "I'm sorry I couldn't keep him safe for you." He still woke in the mornings and looked at his arms, expecting to see fur and wings. There was never anything there, except, for him, sorrow and loss.

"You have said so many times. You must stop, my darling." She squeezed his arm. "Fetu first came to me when I was sixteen years old. The same day I received my first kiss, from your father. Did I ever tell you?"

Sam smiled. "I didn't know about the kiss."

"He interrupted our kiss. Terrified both of us, to tell the truth," his mother remembered with a laugh. "I miss my friend. I miss your father. I will miss you."

Sam stopped. "What do you mean? Where are you going?"

"Not I, Samahti. You."

They had reached the pavilion, open on all sides. Liko and Bayani stood guard by the steps. Servants busied themselves around tables laden with food and drink. His grandmother was there with Uncle Isko and Hanalei, admiring an enormous map that had been placed on the floor. At least eight feet in length, its corners held down by large seashells. A lavishly painted map, not only of the Nominomi, but of the far-reaching world. Tamarind in the far west, Langland and Esperanza in the east. Hundreds of kingdoms and colonies in between. Hanalei knelt opposite Uncle Isko, placing carved wooden canoes on the map, each the length of a hand. She looked over at Sam and smiled. She wore a long green skirt and white blouse, her shoulders bare. A cheerful lei hung from her neck, yellow and white plumeria. Instead of a bracelet, a tattooed seadragon coiled around her slender wrist.

"I forgot all about this map, Uncle." Sam led his mother

to a floor pillow, then went around to kneel beside Hanalei. "When was it commissioned? A year ago?"

"Nearly," Uncle Isko said. "And well worth the wait." His gaze flicked to Sam's mother. "You look peaked."

"I feel fine."

"Nevertheless, perhaps you should not walk so far. You are not—"

"An invalid, Isko," Sam's mother finished, a snap to her voice. It was a tone she only ever used with him. Never Sam or Hanalei and never the queen. "Stop treating me like one. I'm not made of glass."

"Sea glass, maybe." Uncle Isko held up a hand and sighed. "Choose, Olli. Do I watch every word or speak as I always have? It's difficult to do both."

Sam and Hanalei exchanged a look. They edged closer to one another, away from the crossfire.

His mother's ire faded. "As always. Sorry, Isko."

"Don't be, love. It will take time."

Sam shot another glance at Hanalei, whose eyes had grown round. *Love?* she mouthed.

"Isko, Olli," his grandmother said mildly, "you are making the children uncomfortable. Tell me about this map."

"Yes, Your Grace." Uncle Isko rose with ease. His leg had healed completely. Sam had been with him when he had flung his walking stick into the fire. "We're altering our route slightly to accommodate three additional ports." He pointed. "There, there, and there."

"Three," his grandmother said, pleased. "Excellent. When will the ships depart?"

"Two months from now," Uncle Isko said. "That should give Samahti time to prepare."

Sam had been watching Hanalei's marking. Instead of staying put, Nomi had begun to coil around Hanalei's wrist playfully. Which usually meant she wished to go out onto the water. His head came up when he heard his name. "Prepare? For what?"

Hanalei had been leaning over to place another canoe on the map. She stopped. "Is Sam going somewhere?"

Uncle turned to Sam's mother, who said, apologetically, "I meant to tell him. I simply forgot."

It was not just her physical strength that needed to grow stronger. She drifted off frequently, lost in thought, often in the middle of a conversation. The healers had said to give her time. But it worried Sam. And he knew it worried his grandmother.

His grandmother reached out and brushed his mother's cheek. "Our spice ships depart in two months' time," she said. "Every Tamarindi prince and princess has accompanied our fleet at least once. Before you were born, your mother traveled every year. It is an opportunity to see the rest of the world, and to maintain the alliances that benefit Tamarind. Every prince has gone, Samahtitamah, except you."

Sam said, "I was needed here."

"You were indeed, child," his grandmother said. "You still are. You have been a comfort and a joy to me, these last ten years in particular. And if perhaps I have kept you a little too long by my side, well"—she brushed at her skirts—"I don't regret it, and I would never admit it if I did."

His mother said, "You'll be seeing to the distribution of our spices at markets around the Nominomi, Langland, and Esperanza. Two months will give you time to consult with our spice masters and the harbormasters. With any master that needs consulting, really."

Anticipation filled him, along with dreams long buried. Sam looked at the map again. "It's a six-month journey. Eight, I think, with the added ports." He looked to Uncle Isko for confirmation.

"More like nine," his uncle said.

Sam looked at Hanalei, who smiled gamely, and said, "Where is that list of yours, Sam? You will have to dust it off."

Sam's excitement dimmed. Nine months. "It's a long time away, Hana." From her.

His mother reached over and squeezed Hanalei's hand. "Hana has asked to return to Rakakala, for a time. You will escort her there, and we will arrange for her passage home when the time comes."

Sam felt his stomach drop. Hana had not mentioned

going away. "What's in Raka?"

"My father," Hanalei said. "He was buried in an unmarked grave, but I know where it is. I know the exact spot. I need to bring him home. The ambassador has promised to help. Rosamie has too. She's there visiting." Here, she hesitated. "My old teachers have also sent me a letter. They have asked if I would return to help with the school. Not for forever. Just until they can find others to take over. I'll be home before you, most likely."

"It's good you're making these friends," Uncle Isko commented. "They may be useful one day."

"That isn't why we made them, Uncle," Hanalei said.

"Nevertheless."

Sam was beginning to understand how Jejomar must have felt. "Are you trying to get rid of us?"

"How did you guess?" His mother smiled. She reached for a canoe and placed it in the middle of the Nominomi. She spun it with a finger. When the boat stopped, it pointed north. "There's a saying my mother shared with me long ago, before my first voyage. Do you remember, Mama?"

His grandmother patted Viti, who had settled on her shoulder. "To the adored child, send them on journeys. I remember."

"You are adored, the both of you," his mother said, looking first at Sam, then Hanalei. "When you return, Tamarind will be waiting."

"You're afraid I won't come back." Hanalei sat before him on her seadragon, her back pressed against his chest, against his beating heart. It was just the two of them now, and Nomi, who carried them along calm waters. A hibiscus moon settled high among the stars. Beneath the surface of the water, a pale blue glow drifted upward from the sand and coral. There was light all around them.

Sam tightened his arms around her. He was terrified she would not return. "I'm not afraid," he said.

Hanalei turned to look up at him.

"Maybe a little," he conceded.

"Why?"

Because she had gone before. "How long did it take you to come home last time?"

"Ten years. And that was different, Sam."

"You didn't ask for an answer that made sense. Just an answer."

Hanalei rose and twisted around to sit cross-legged before him. Sam studied her beautiful face, one he would not see for nine long months.

"I'm scared you won't come back too," she said, surprising him.

"Why wouldn't I?"

"Many reasons." Hanalei raised a hand and ticked off her fingers as she spoke. "A shipwreck. A shark attack. A kidnapping. You could be hit on the head and forget who you are . . ."

Sam's lips curved. "You think I'll get amnesia?"

"Don't laugh. It's happened to others." She ticked off another finger. "Malaria."

"Please not that." Sam took her fingers and kissed them. "Are you trying to frighten me into staying?"

"No." Hanalei's expression turned serious. "I want you to go. You deserve to go. But I'll worry, and I'll miss you." She tilted her head, studying him curiously. "Why are *you* afraid?"

Sam raised a hand, ticked off his own list. "A shipwreck. A shark attack. A handsome seadragon scholar—"

Hanalei dissolved into laughter. Nomi lifted her tail and slapped it into the water, spraying them.

Sam swiped seawater from his face. "You're going back to that school. It's possible."

"There are no handsome seadragon scholars on Raka, believe me." Hanalei covered his hand with hers. "I need to bring my father home, but the reason I agreed to return to the school, for a little while at least, is because I'd like to start one of my own."

Sam should not have been surprised. "On Tamarind?"

"Where else? This is my home."

"How does one start a school of that sort?"

"I don't have the slightest idea," she confessed. "I'm going to find out. Uncle Isko has promised to help. Your mother too. It will be good for her."

"Do you think my mother . . . ?" He trailed off, not wishing to put his fears into real words, spoken aloud.

He did not have to. Hanalei understood. "She's the strongest woman I know, and she has defied every odd. And you are the one person who believed in her these last ten years. You should not stop believing."

Sam was quiet. Sometimes it hurt him to look at her and know how closely they had come to missing one another. He should not have been on the cliff that night. She should not have been anywhere near this island. He said, "Tell me about this school of yours."

"Since you asked." Hanalei rubbed her hands together in the manner of an old tutor. "We live right here in the Nominomi, and there's still so much we don't know. Not just about seadragons, but about everything. The other sea animals. The caves and trenches. The ruins we sometimes see beneath the water. I have sailed over entire cities. Think of the possibilities, Sam. It is . . ."

"A lifetime's work. I'll help."

Hanalei smiled. She would have kissed him, and he would have let her, but Nomi spotted a bird. Laughing, they held on tight, to the seadragon, to one another, as she raced across open sea.

ACKNOWLEDGMENTS

When I was ten, I opened my auntie's freezer one day and found a frozen fruit bat propped up on a shelf. I was startled, but only for a moment. I knew it was meant for a soup pot at an upcoming fiesta. Nothing too unusual. I didn't give it another thought until I sat with my pencil and notebook decades later, trying to build a world around my fifth book. So first and foremost, I would like to thank that poor bat for helping me dream up Fetu. Inspiration really does come from everywhere.

Dragonfruit is the first book I wrote post-pandemic, and it took some time before I could understand what the story was really about. Thank you so much to my editors, Amy Cloud and Elizabeth Agyemang, for their wisdom, guidance, and patience (so much patience!). Hanalei's story has come a long way from that first draft, and I could not have done it without you.

My book cover is glorious, and for that I would like to extend my heartfelt thanks to illustrator Tran Nguyen and designer Molly Fehr. Thank you also to everyone working behind the scenes at Clarion Books/HarperCollins Publishers, especially Erika West, Ana Deboo, Susan Bishansky, Lisa Calcasola, Danielle McClelland, and Sammy Brown.

In her wonderful article "How We 'Island' Our Writing: A Deep Dive into Pacific Islander SFF" (*Apex Magazine*), Manuia Heinrich Sue advises writers to "cultivate the little things that feel like 'home' in your stories; embrace the oral myth that reminds you of your childhood and let it flow through your writing; let your characters and places have names that are familiar and matter to you; keep the words in your language that translating would weaken; find the balance between marketability and culture, and make room for your Oceanic roots." I have tried to do that with *Dragonfruit*. Tamarind is the name of a favorite childhood candy. I was born in the village of Garapan. Many of the character names come from across the Pacific Ocean. And, as mentioned earlier, I am no stranger to fruit bats in soup pots. Thank you to Manuia for her lovely words and insights, and for her steadfast support of Pacific Islander writers.

And finally, much appreciation and gratitude to my family, Chris and Mia, whose encouragement I can always count on. Love you lots.